LONG DANCE HOME

JULIE MAYERSON BROWN

Publishers note: This is a work of fiction. Names, characters, places, and incidents are products of author's imagination. Any similarity to real persons, living or dead, is coincidental.

Edited by Angela Houle

Cover by Katie Garland, Howard Marketing

For Mom and Dad,
my first fans

1

*C*ece studied the painting clipped to the wooden easel in front of her, as if waiting for a sign from above. She touched her brush to the red paint and dragged a watery streak of color through her subject's cascading, dark hair. Then, with her finest brush, she added a few jet-black lashes to the edges of the eyes. She dropped her chin and groaned.

Patty leaned over her shoulder. "You know what they say. The enemy of good is better."

Cece eyed her best friend. "I know. I just can't seem to let it be finished." She stood and walked behind the counter of The Art Stop, the trendy Venice Beach gallery where she and Patty worked, to wash her hands. "I keep needing to make it better, but I know if I mess with it too much, I'll ruin it."

Patty handed Cece a paper towel, then boosted herself onto a stool. "Ah yes, the perfectionist predicament. Why do you think all artists are depressed?"

"I'm not depressed. And I'm not really an artist." Cece wound her brown curls into a bun and secured it with a pencil.

"Not true," said Patty. "You're a fabulous painter."

Cece rubbed a spot of paint off her thumb. "I'm a good painter, but that doesn't make me an artist."

"The problem is you don't believe in yourself. Too many years of ballet lessons and that Russian taskmaster telling you you're not good enough. It damaged your self-esteem."

"My self-esteem is perfectly intact," said Cece. "And Ilana never told me I wasn't good enough. She just told me I could be better."

Patty laughed. "Sounds like the same thing to me."

Cece scoffed at her roommate. The two had met in an art history class at UCLA when Cece was a junior and Patty a freshman. They functioned like big and little sister from the start. Bonding over a shared frustration with their living arrangements, they found a tiny one-bedroom apartment off campus where they lived for the next four years. Their friends dubbed them "The Odd Couple." Tall, graceful, and proper, Cece was the polar opposite of Patty, a petite tomboy with short, spiky red hair and little-girl hands, usually covered in wood stain and dry glue.

"Don't you have artwork to frame?" Cece asked.

"Yeah." Patty returned to her workbench. "Hey, don't forget! I'm taking you to lunch for your birthday."

"How could I forget that? Where are we going?"

"Taco stand on the beach," Patty said. "That's about all I can afford. Besides, I don't know where Doug's taking you for dinner, but I'm pretty sure it won't be out for tacos."

Cece smiled. Doug had a special night planned. "He has been mysterious about where we are going, which makes me a little nervous. I like to know what to expect."

Patty picked up a piece of molding. "Yes, you do. And that's why you're so antsy. It's all about 'the plan'."

The plan. Cece's roadmap for her life.

"Well," Cece said, tapping a pen on the desk. "You're right about that."

2

Patty sanded the wood. "Just be warned: when you do get married, I'm not wearing any hideous bridesmaid's dress."

Engaged, married, babies. For Cece, there was always a plan, and at this point in her life, that plan revolved around Doug. She shook off the anxiety percolating in her stomach. "Don't say that. You'll look adorable in a frilly, pink gown. Now, give me ten minutes to organize this paperwork, and then we'll go eat."

Cece picked up a stack of folders and pushed all thoughts of Doug to the back of her mind. She opened a folder and thumbed through the bills, most stamped 'past due' in red ink. A worried frown darkened her face.

Barbara, the owner of the gallery, had an incredible eye for art but no head for finances, so she relied on Cece's meticulous attention to money and numbers. Cece had approved payment on those bills weeks ago. The overdue notices were an unpleasant surprise. Between Doug's mysterious dinner plan and the unpaid bills, Cece couldn't concentrate.

She stood and went back to her painting. It was an eight-inch square watercolor of a face she had seen only once in her life. Her subject was a young woman with long black hair, dark eyes, and flawless ivory skin. She had a straight, narrow nose, pink lips, and a thin, sculpted neck. Her eyes crinkled around the edges, revealing the smile that her mouth did not.

For Cece's ninth birthday, her dance instructor, Ilana Lurensky, had taken her to San Francisco to see *The Nutcracker*. They were invited backstage after the performance. Cece froze when she saw the ballerina, still in costume, who had danced the part of the Sugar Plum Fairy.

The ballerina looked down and placed a graceful hand on Cece's shoulder. "Are you a ballerina, too?" she asked, her voice soft and musical.

Cece nodded, unable to speak.

"Will you show me?"

Cece nodded again. She removed her shoes and performed her best *pas de chat*, leaping high into the air.

The ballerina's eyes sparkled. She took Cece's hands in both of hers. "You are a magnificent dancer," she whispered. "Work hard, and one day you will dance the Sugar Plum Fairy." The corners of her mouth turned up almost imperceptibly, her cheeks were flushed pink, and her eyes were fringed with thick lashes. It was the most beautiful face Cece had ever seen. And the most thrilling words she'd ever heard.

"Hey, you ready?" Patty said, interrupting Cece's daydream. "I'm starving."

Cece stretched and pulled the pencil out of her hair. "Yeah, I'm ready. Let's go."

A crisp, clear November day greeted them. They walked past a vintage clothing shop, a used-book store, and a homeopathic pharmacy. Cece's cell phone rang.

"Who is it?" Patty asked.

"*Unknown number.* Again." She declined the call, disappointed it wasn't Doug calling to wish her a happy birthday.

"Another unknown? I think you have a stalker," Patty teased.

Cece laughed. "Yeah, right. Maybe next time I'll answer if Doug doesn't come through tonight."

On the boardwalk, they jumped out of the way of a group of skateboarders. Beachgoers dotted the sand, vendors sold everything from toys to churros, and mimes twisted skinny balloons into silly hats and animals.

They got in line at the taco stand. Cece inhaled the smell of sizzling homemade tortillas and put an arm around her friend. "Thanks for taking me to lunch, Patty. I'm sure lucky to have you."

Her friend snuggled against her. "We're both lucky."

After wolfing down two tacos each and a basket of chips, they returned to work.

~

It was late afternoon when the bells on the door jingled. Cece looked up, bleary-eyed after hours of crunching numbers, and was delighted to see Mae Adamu, a jewelry designer and Venice boardwalk icon. The ageless Nigerian hippy with smooth, brown skin and beaded cornrows in her hair wore Birkenstock sandals, a jean jacket, and a bright yellow, flowing skirt.

"Hi, girls!" Mae closed the door. She had her tabby cat, Goldie, on a leash and held a brown grocery bag. "I brought some new designs for you to look at. And some leftover tofu lasagna."

"Oh yum," said Patty, who was sitting on the floor sanding the edges of a wood frame. "But you know what? I'm allergic to tofu."

"Nobody's allergic to tofu, Patty," Cece said. She gave Mae a hug. "I'll have some."

"Wonderful. It's so delicious." Mae unhooked the cat's leash. "There you are Goldie. Be good."

The golden orange cat went straight for Cece, slinking around her ankles. Cece nudged Goldie with the back of her hand. "Go on, scoot."

"Goldie knows you don't like her," Mae said. "She can sense it. That's why she pesters you."

"It's not just Goldie. I don't like any cats."

"I don't know why," Mae said, unwrapping her casserole. "You love dogs and monkeys."

"Dogs listen, and monkeys are adorable and intelligent. Cats are ornery and unpredictable." Cece stepped aside, but Goldie followed her. "And I hate it when she winds herself around my legs like this."

"She's releasing her pheromones on you," Mae said. "Marking her territory."

"See? That's just creepy." Cece handed a stack of paper plates to Mae.

Goldie jumped into a chair as Mae scooped up large portions of lasagna. Cece sat, avoiding Goldie's suspicious glare, and took a bite. The tofu squished in her mouth.

"Good, huh?" Mae said, finger-feeding Goldie bits off her plate.

"Mmmm." Cece forced herself to swallow. She didn't know which was worse, eating tofu lasagna or watching the cat eat it.

"Patty, come try it."

"Sorry, Mae, tofu gives me that closed-up throat thing. And besides, I had two steak tacos and almost the entire basket of chips for lunch." Patty turned over the frame and continued sanding.

Mae tsk-tsked and turned her attention back to Cece. "Let me show you my new pieces." She took a wooden box out of her bag and opened it. Each piece of Mae's jewelry was one-of-a-kind, made of sterling silver, crystals, beads, and semi-precious stones.

Cece picked up a necklace—a small butterfly of sapphire-blue crystals hanging on a sterling chain. "This is stunning."

"Let me see it on you," Mae said.

Cece fastened it around her neck. The butterfly landed just below the soft spot between her collarbones.

"Ahhh, fabulous." Mae leaned in for a closer look.

Cece reached for a hand mirror. With her wide-set blue eyes, fair skin and long, brown hair, the butterfly was striking on her.

"It's such a pretty piece. And I love the crystals." She reached back to unclasp it, but Mae stopped her.

"Happy birthday, dear."

"Oh Mae, I couldn't."

"You most certainly can." It was an order, not a request.

"Really?" Cece hugged her friend. "Thank you. I love it."

"Cece's gonna get another piece of jewelry tonight," Patty blurted from her seat on the floor. "A diamond."

Mae gasped. "From Doug? An engagement ring?"

Cece's heart quickened, and her anxiety returned. "I don't know, maybe. We haven't specifically talked about marriage, but he's been acting kind of weird, like he's planning something special." Cece toyed with the butterfly. "We've been together three years, I'm turning twenty-nine, and we're in love. It's time. It's part of the plan."

Mae patted Cece's hand. "Ah, yes, the plan."

Cece sensed amusement in Mae's voice. Nobody understood her need for structure and certainty. She rubbed her forehead. "We have to stop talking about Doug. I don't want to jinx it."

"I agree," Mae said. "So, let's get down to business. What pieces do you want me to leave with you?"

Cece picked up a dangly silver earring. "I hate to tell you this, but the jewelry's not selling. It's discounted already, and we'll probably cut prices again after Thanksgiving."

Mae shrugged. "The money's not important, Cece. You know that. An artist just wants her work to matter, especially to the person who is lucky enough to possess it." She nodded in the direction of Cece's watercolor.

Cece felt her throat constrict. Mae was right. She didn't paint for money. She painted because she loved painting. In the end, she just wanted her art to belong to someone who would cherish it as much as she cherished the memory that inspired it.

Mae closed the box on her creations. "I'll take these to the boardwalk tomorrow. We'll decide after the holiday weekend." She stood and clipped Goldie to her leash.

Cece pushed away from the table. "Sounds good."

Mae gave Cece a quick hug, then stepped back and admired the butterfly. "My goodness, those sapphire crystals practically match your eyes." She gave her a sly smile. "I'd swear someone made that butterfly just for you."

7

2

*T*he restaurant hung out over the Pacific in Malibu, and the moon cut a silvery streak of light through the water. Cece and Doug sat at a table by the window, candles casting soft shadows across their faces. Doug picked up Cece's hand and clasped his fingers through hers.

"You look great tonight, Ceece," Doug said, using her nickname.

"Thanks." Cece's right leg bounced nervously, and she felt hot. She had on a white blouse with long sleeves and a draped neckline. Her hair fell in loose curls over her shoulders.

"Pretty necklace." Doug's eyes drifted down. "Matches your eyes." He lifted the jeweled butterfly, his hand brushing against her skin.

"A birthday gift from Mae." Cece toyed with her necklace. Dinner was over, and the uncertainty of what might, or might not, happen next made Cece queasy.

"That was nice of her." Doug reached under the table and squeezed Cece's leg. At almost thirty, he could have passed for a college kid. But in his crisp blue dress shirt and khaki slacks, he looked handsome and sophisticated. His hair, brown that tended toward dark blond in the summer, curled around his shirt collar.

"Dinner was delicious," Cece said. "And this spot is beautiful. What a view! I didn't even know this restaurant existed." Cece rambled, waiting for the moment she had been anticipating ever since she was a starry-eyed little girl. There was no doubt in her mind that Doug Whitman was her dream come true.

They had met three years ago when The Art Stop needed photographs for a new postcard. The owner of a nearby camera store gave Cece Doug's card. When she called, a woman answered.

"I'm calling for Doug Whitman," Cece had said.

"Doug doesn't live here anymore. This is his mother. I could take a message for you."

Cece couldn't help smiling. His mother, how cute. "Thank you. I'm looking for a photographer."

"Wonderful. Is it for a wedding or bar mitzvah or something?"

"Not an event," Cece said. "I just need photographs taken of an art gallery in Venice Beach."

"Oh, you're in Los Angeles. Doug lives in San Diego now, but I'll give him your number. If he has time, maybe he'll drive up."

Within one hour Doug Whitman called, and Cece hired him over the phone.

Two days later, on a warm Saturday morning, Doug walked into The Art Stop. He was tall with broad shoulders accentuated by a tight blue T-shirt. He had on faded Levi's and slip-on tennis shoes. His hair was a mass of light brown curls.

They worked together for several hours, Cece arranging art pieces, adjusting the lighting and asking casual questions. They took a break and walked down to the boardwalk for lunch. By the time they finished hotdogs and lemonade, Cece was beyond infatuated with her photographer.

Late in the afternoon, as Doug packed up his equipment, Cece watched him, trying to work up the nerve to invite him to dinner.

"I'll go through the photos tonight," Doug said, "and have a file to you by tomorrow."

"Great. Tomorrow's great. Or the next day. Whenever."

"Do you want to get some dinner?" Doug asked.

Cece caught her breath. She tucked her hair behind her ears. "Oh, um, tonight?"

He nodded. "It's okay if you're busy, I just thought…"

"I'd love to."

From then on, they were together every weekend. Within a month Doug introduced her to his family, and a month after that, he moved up to LA.

Doug lifted his champagne flute. "Happy Birthday." They tapped the tall glasses. To Cece's surprise, Doug drank his down in one gulp. *This is it!* she thought. There had been no sign of a gift, but a ring was small and easily hidden—in a pocket or a wallet or a…

"Chocolate soufflé!" The waiter put the dessert in front of them in the middle of the table, placing two spoons beside it.

"Oh!" Cece said. "Did we order one?"

"I did. I know how much you love chocolate. And this one is special. Now, make a wish."

Cece closed her eyes and wished the obvious. She blew the candle out, plucked it from the soufflé, and licked the bottom. "Yum."

Doug picked up a spoon and broke through the top. Liquid chocolate oozed up through the middle and mixed with the whipped cream. He scooped the first bite and held it out to her. She opened her mouth, welcoming the spoon filled with rich chocolate and a special surprise.

"Mmmm," she said, rolling the dessert around in her mouth, her tongue searching.

Doug smiled, a glint in his dark brown eyes. "Good?"

Cece nodded, her mouth still busy. "Best I've ever had." That much was true, with or without the buried treasure.

Doug put the spoon in and helped himself to a substantial bite. He licked a bit of whipped cream from the corner of his mouth. "I knew you'd love it."

Cece forced a smile. She gave up her search and swallowed her disappointment along with most of the soufflé.

"Do you want me to get another one?" Doug asked. "I should order it now—they take like twenty minutes."

Cece put her spoon down. He had to be the sweetest boyfriend in the world. "I'm sorry, I'm being a pig. Here." She pushed the dish toward him. "You finish it. We don't need another one."

"Just one more bite," Doug said. "Then the rest is yours."

Two cappuccinos arrived, and Cece scraped the last remnants of chocolate off the bottom and sides of the ramekin.

"I have a present for you," Doug said.

And just like that, hope was renewed. Cece pulled the spoon out of her mouth. "You do?"

"Of course I do." Doug reached under his chair and pulled out a colorful gift bag. He put his hand in, and Cece's heart lurched as she caught a glimpse of turquoise.

It was flat, rectangular, the size of a book. Her heart sank, but as she untied the white ribbon, it occurred to her that the shape of the box might be a ploy. Her emotions were like jumping beans.

Cece lifted the top, separated layers of tissue paper and pulled out a flannel Tiffany bag. It contained a sterling silver picture frame with a beautiful photo of Cece and Doug sitting on the beach. She had her knees drawn up to her chest as she leaned against Doug, his legs on either side of her hips and his arms wrapped around her. The lens caught her profile as she looked toward the ocean, her hair swept up in a gentle breeze and Doug's face nestled over her shoulder.

Cece recalled the day. They'd gone wine tasting with friends near Pismo a few months back. After a picnic on the beach, Doug and Cece slipped away to a secluded cove. They spread a blanket on the sand and made love to the sound of waves crashing into the rocks and washing up onto the shore.

Afterwards, they walked through the surf, their feet leaving deep footprints in the wet sand. Then they sat and watched the sun drop into the horizon. "You're the one," Doug had said, "the one for me."

"Wasn't that a great day?" Doug's voice pulled Cece away from her memory. "I don't even know who took the picture. Somebody must have grabbed my camera."

"It's beautiful," Cece said.

"*You're* beautiful." He pointed to a spot on the photo. "See the way the light touches your hair and you're smiling only with your eyes? Like it's telling a story."

Cece blinked back tears and ran her fingertips over the edges of the frame. "I love it, the photo and the frame."

"I knew you would." Doug refilled their champagne glasses. "Oops, I almost forgot, one more little present."

Cece's stomach flip-flopped. Would it happen now? Would her plan finally fall into place?

Doug handed her a long, narrow gift box wrapped in little kid birthday paper. It was surprisingly heavy.

"Cute wrapping." Cece tore off the paper, her pulse pounding.

Doug leaned forward on his elbows as Cece lifted the lid. Inside the box was a wooden case. Cece unlatched the delicate brass hook, holding her breath. Her mouth dropped open. A paintbrush, the Da Vinci Kolinsky fine point sable, the brush she had coveted for years but could never justify buying. After all, no starving artist spends over two hundred dollars on a paintbrush. She looked up at Doug. "How did you know I wanted this?"

"I saw your catalog," he said. "You'd circled this in red and written 'someday' beside it. So babe, today is someday."

"Doug, wow, thank you." Cece touched the smooth, hardwood handle. It wasn't a ring, but it was something special.

"You're welcome." Doug touched her hand. "What do you say we get out of here?"

Cece nodded. Doug dropped more than enough money on the table and pulled Cece to her feet. "Let's go."

They ran across the parking lot through a light drizzle and jumped into Doug's truck. Cece's teeth chattered. "I'm freezing."

Doug started the motor and turned on the heater. "Come here. I'll warm you up."

Cece leaned against his strong chest. She loved him so much. And the night wasn't over. Not yet.

"I'm crazy about you," Doug said. He kissed her, lightly at first, then his lips parted, his smooth tongue slipped around hers, and his fingers caressed the back of her neck. Cece responded the way she always did, melting into him as if she were still a teenager.

"Can't wait to get home," Doug whispered.

Traffic was light, and as they approached Santa Monica, Doug put a hand on Cece's leg. "How about I build a fire in the fireplace?"

"Sounds good."

Doug stopped short at a red light, and Cece's packages tumbled from the bag. The sight of the Tiffany blue box reminded her of her disappointment.

Doug brought Cece's hand up to his lips and kissed it. "You okay? You seem a little quiet."

Cece looked out the car window. Crowds of people were milling about the street, going in and out of restaurants and bars.

"I'm fine, a little stressed about work. Sales are slow. Barbara comes back tomorrow, and..." Cece's voice trailed off.

"You're upset about something," Doug said. "I can tell."

"I'm not," Cece said, forcing herself to sound cheerful.

The light changed, and Doug let go of her hand. They drove the rest of the way without talking. Doug turned into the narrow driveway and parked his truck. "Cece, tell me what's wrong."

Cece leaned down to get her purse and the bag containing her presents. "Nothing's wrong, Doug."

"Is it the paintbrush? Is it the wrong one?"

Cece felt awful. "No, no. It's the exact one I wanted. You put so much thought into everything." She looked at him, his eyes wide and adoring like a puppy's. "Now let's go inside."

They walked up the driveway holding hands. Cece unlocked the front door of the house, a Spanish bungalow with arched windows and red tile roof.

In the dim light of a single lamp, Cece could see Doug's preoccupied expression. Doug took off his jacket and threw it over the back of the couch. The white, slipcovered sofa stood in the center of the small living room across from a brick fireplace. The coffee table in front of it was an old leather trunk Patty had picked up at a flea market.

"Want tea?" Cece asked. "Or something stronger?"

"Tea's good," he said. "Where are the matches?"

"On the mantle where they always are," Cece said.

Doug shook his head. "No, they're not."

"Yes they—oh wait, sorry. I put them in the trunk yesterday." Cece lifted the lid on the coffee table and retrieved the fireplace matches. She handed them to Doug. "I'll make tea."

"Cece, stop. This is ridiculous. There's something you're not telling me."

"I'm fine," Cece said impatiently. "Now please stop asking."

"Wow." Doug rubbed the stubble on his face. "You're really not yourself."

Cece turned around. "I'm sorry. I didn't mean to snap at you." She went to him, reached up, wrapped her arms over his shoulders, and wound her fingers into his curls.

Doug leaned into her, nuzzling and kissing her neck and shoulders. "I love you, babe." His lips brushed over her ear. "And all I want is to make you happy."

His words echoed. How simple it would be for him to make Cece happy. One little question.

"I thought you were going to propose!" The words fell out before she had time to stop them.

"What?" Doug's mouth hung open.

"Oh my God! I didn't mean to blurt it out like that, but you're right, I am upset." Cece wrung her hands. "I feel like such a fool now, but I did expect, or at least I was hoping. I even thought you might have hidden a ring in the chocolate soufflé."

Cece burst into tears, feeling exposed and humiliated.

"I...I don't know what to say." Doug looked at her in disbelief. "I had no idea."

Cece sniffled. "No idea what?"

"That you were expecting me to...to propose." A nervous laugh escaped his throat.

"No idea? Really?" Cece said, suddenly feeling less foolish and more practical. She wiped her face with her hand.

Doug's stunned expression irritated her, but she tried to hide her annoyance.

"We've been together three years, Doug, and we're not getting any younger."

"Wait." Doug's eyes widened. "You're not pregnant, are you?"

"No, I'm not pregnant. But I'd like to be sometime before my grade A eggs turn into grade C."

Doug swallowed. "Oh. You mean the biological clock thing."

"It's not 'the biological clock thing,' " Cece said. The wooden clock on the mantel chimed, as if to weigh in on the matter. "Wow. I can't believe we're not on the same page about our relationship."

"But we are." Doug pushed his hair back with both hands. "At least, I think we are. Could I have that drink now? A shot of tequila would be good."

"Seriously?" Cece said. "I say I want to marry you, and you ask for tequila? How insensitive are you?"

"Now I'm insensitive?" Doug circled the room, shaking his head. "This is not the way I thought tonight would go."

Cece's legs trembled so much she had to sit. She was mortified. "Me neither."

Doug picked up his jacket. He looked like something had hit him in the head. "Listen, I'm gonna go. We'll talk tomorrow, okay?" He gave her light kiss on the cheek and left.

Cece stood in the open doorway and watched Doug disappear into the dark night. A prickle of fear burned inside. Her plan was veering off track.

3

*P*atty's jaw hung open. "And then he just left?" She poured coffee into two mugs and sat down across from Cece at the breakfast table.

Cece nodded. She rubbed her eyes.

"On the one hand I feel awful, and on the other I feel like, you know, is he a complete idiot? I mean, how could he not think that I'd want to get married? I don't know of any woman who'd date a guy for three years and not expect to marry him."

Patty raised her eyebrows. "Maybe it's ultimatum time."

Cece groaned. "I don't want to be that girl. What a cliché I've become."

Her cell vibrated.

"Doug?" Patty asked.

Cece nodded. She picked up her cell and went into her room.

The conversation started with Doug's apology. "I was just caught off guard, babe. It's not that I don't want to, um, you know, get, well, get…"

"Married. That's the word you're struggling with."

Doug laughed. "Right. Married. I can say it. I just, you know, well…"

"It's okay, I get it." Cece said. Hearing him stumble over the words annoyed her, but she had decided there would be no emotional outbursts. And definitely no ultimatum. At least not yet.

"You do?" Doug sounded relieved.

"I do. Let's just forget it ever happened."

"Are you sure?"

"I'm sure." Cece said.

She wanted to push the whole event out of her mind. She had ruined her own birthday and felt terrible. The topic of marriage would be put on hold, at least for the time being. Cece ended the call before she said anything to undo what she'd just fixed.

~

Barbara leaned against the counter beside the espresso machine, twisting her short, dirty-blond ponytail around her fingers. "I hate to cut hours right before the holidays, but I promise it's only temporary. Sales will pick up after Thanksgiving, I'm sure, and then we'll be good."

Cece looked at her boss with a skeptical eye. "I worked on bills yesterday, Barbara. The account was low, but it wasn't that bad."

"I know that, dear." Barbara pulled at a loose thread on her oversized red sweater. "But my sister manages the payroll account, and, um, well, evidently that one is running short. But don't worry, she's going to be here all weekend. She'll sort everything out." Barbara smiled. "You both will be back at work Monday after Thanksgiving."

Patty put a hand on Barbara's shoulder. "No problem, Barb. We'll be fine."

Cece pinched Patty on the arm to shut her up. "So, you want Patty and me to take off all next week without pay, including Black Friday, and come back to work on Monday, right?"

Barbara nodded. "Exactly. And once my sister gets me organized, I'll be able to pay you for the week including vacation time and holidays." She gave them a hopeful smile. "Sound good?"

"Does to me," Patty said.

"I guess." Cece sighed.

"Now, you girls have a wonderful time up north with the family. Everything will be straightened out in no time."

"Phil's going to be so excited," Patty said, referring to Cece's father. "He adores me."

Cece rolled her eyes and tried to ignite a flicker of enthusiasm. The original plan was to spend only two nights, but now they might as well make it a longer stay. And Cece knew her father would be thrilled to have them a few extra days.

Ever since she had moved away at eighteen, her father constantly asked, "Aren't you ready to move back home?" A firm "No" was always the answer. But it wasn't her home she wanted to avoid—it was her hometown, where everybody knew everybody's business, the word 'privacy' had been erased from the city charter, and too many people remembered an extraordinary young ballerina named Cecilia Rose.

Later that night as Cece packed, Doug sat on her bed eating pizza and drinking a beer. "My mom said to tell you to have a good trip, and that she's very disappointed you won't be at our Thanksgiving dinner."

"Very?"

"That's what she said. *Very.*"

"That's sweet."

Doug wiped his mouth with a paper napkin. "Maybe my parents can take us to the club next weekend. We haven't done that in a while."

"Sounds good," Cece said without meaning it. She wasn't a country club kind of girl. Too many fancy ladies who spent more on a pair of shoes than she spent on rent.

She stuffed a sweatshirt into her suitcase. "I just wish I were more excited about going up north."

Doug took another slice of pizza from the box. "You'll have a good time. At least your family is normal. And way more fun than mine."

"I know." Cece tucked socks into the side pockets. She adored her father and her step-mother, Julia. They'd been married only two years, but Julia had been a family friend forever. When Cece's mother left, Julia stepped in to help Phil deal with his mortified daughter and his traumatized son. "I just hate going into town. And now that we'll be there all week, I don't know how I'll avoid it."

"When are you coming home?"

Cece groaned. "Probably Saturday. I'll call you when I get close. Maybe we can catch a movie or something."

"I'm working Saturday."

"You are?" Cece asked.

"Yeah, I told you the other day. Some spoiled girl's sweet sixteen in Beverly Hills on Saturday night and a wedding Sunday afternoon."

Doug had never said a word about either, but she didn't want to make it an issue. And just hearing him say the word "wedding" set her on edge. "If you did tell me, I...never mind, it doesn't matter." Cece rubbed her eyes. "Sorry for being grumpy. It's just between work and this trip, I'm so..."

Doug pulled her onto the bed next to him. "You worry too much."

Cece tried to smile. She looked into Doug's eyes, fringed with long lashes that most girls would envy. She lifted her lips toward his and initiated a deep, delicious kiss. Cece felt his hands slide under her shirt and up her back.

The front door slammed. "Stop whatever you're doing in there," Patty called from the living room.

"Quick, lock the door," Doug said.

But it was too late. Patty waltzed in as if she had been invited. "Hi, guys." She plopped herself onto the bed. "What's happening?"

Doug laughed and adjusted his crotch. "Nothing now."

"Don't let me stop you," Patty said. "Carry on. I'll just watch."

"Jesus, Patty." Cece threw a pair of rolled up socks at her. "Get out of here and go pack. We're leaving early. I promised Dad we'd be there by dinner time."

Patty jumped on the bed like a little girl. "I can't wait to see Phil and Julia!"

Cece shook her head and looked at Doug. "Get rid of her, would you?"

"With pleasure." Doug lifted Patty and threw her over his shoulder.

As Doug carried her out, Patty lifted her head, grinned, and blew a kiss in Cece's direction.

4

The mountains shimmered in the morning sun, as Cece drove into the San Fernando Valley. Patty dozed in the passenger seat. Cece yawned. She hadn't slept well. Doug seemed to have forgotten all about her embarrassing outburst the night of her birthday, which was a both a relief and an annoyance. For the millionth time, Cece wished she had kept her mouth shut. But now that the subject of marriage had been brought up, there was no undoing it. It weighed on her, and so did her job. Despite Barbara's reassurances, Cece knew everything would not be fine. The numbers proved it.

Patty stirred and stretched. "Want me to drive?"

"Not yet." Cece sipped her coffee from a travel mug and looked at the fuel gage on her old BMW. "We'll stop in Ventura to get gas. We can switch then."

Patty leaned her head back and looked at Cece. "You do know he's in love with you. Give him time. He'll come around."

Cece looked in her side view mirror and changed lanes. "That's just it though, Patty. I have this horrible feeling I'm running out of time."

"It's only because of your birthday," Patty said.

"Maybe. But if I feel that way, and if I'm ready to get married and Doug's not, then—"

"Stop right there." Patty put a hand on Cece's shoulder. "You two are gonna be fine."

Cece gave Patty an appreciative squeeze. "I hope so."

~

The ocean was dark blue, almost black, as they drove through Santa Barbara, the waves tall and clean. Two surfers in wetsuits carried their boards into the water, reminding Cece of Doug and how much he loved to surf.

"Are you listening?" Patty asked, breaking for slow traffic up ahead. "I said let's play *first kiss*."

"Okay," said Cece. "You first."

"Fine." Patty shimmied her shoulders. "I forget his name, but I was in third grade."

"Third grade?" Cece asked, somewhat appalled. "You kissed a boy when you were eight years old?"

"Yup," Patty said. "On the lips but no tongue. I waited for him to fall from the monkey bars and just did it. Then he ran."

"Can't say I blame him," Cece said with a laugh.

"Your turn. Let me hear it."

"Okay, good story. Sixth grade, my first boy-girl party. We were playing seven minutes in heaven, and Ross Tucker picked me."

"Oh wow. I like it already." Patty made kissing noises.

"Yeah, so, I could barely contain myself, because he was a year older, and I'd had a crush on him for ages." Cece sighed at the long-forgotten memory. "He closed the closet door, and there was just enough light coming in for me to see his face. He was so cute, and I was so nervous. Then Ross asked me if I'd ever kissed a boy before, and when I said no, he said to me, 'Your first kiss should be special, so if you don't want to, it's okay. I won't tell.' " Cece paused for effect. "Then I said, 'Kissing you would be special.' And he leaned down and put the softest kiss on my lips. It was…it was good."

"Wow," Patty said. "No wonder you're such a hopeless romantic."

"Yep. I blame everything on Ross Tucker." Cece looked dreamily at the highway stretched out in front of her. Maybe she *was* hopeless.

They stopped in Pismo Beach, a seaside town halfway between LA and San Francisco, and sat on a bench looking out over the water where gray clouds were gathering. Cece unpacked the sandwiches she had made that morning and handed one to Patty.

"I would rather have grabbed a burger somewhere."

"We're unemployed," Cece said. "Remember?"

"We're not unemployed, Ceece, we're on a temporary hiatus from work. You need to chill out a little."

Cece licked her thumb. "You're right. Sometimes I wish I could relax and be more like you."

"Believe me, so do I." Patty nudged Cece with her shoulder. "But then we'd probably kill each other."

Cece's cell buzzed, and she glanced at the screen: *Unknown number.*

Patty raised her eyebrows. "Told you you've got a stalker."

"Silly girl," Cece said. "If anyone should have a stalker, it's you. Come on. Let's go before it starts to rain."

Traffic crawled on the Golden Gate Bridge as Cece drove from San Francisco into Marin County. A blanket of fog covered the city, but the sparkling lights still glimmered in the distance.

"Feeling better?" Cece asked. They had stopped in Gilroy for garlic ice cream.

"No." Patty moaned. "I might throw up."

"I knew you'd regret that second scoop."

Patty rolled onto her side and pulled the seatbelt under her arm. "Just one more thing to add to the list."

"The list?" Cece asked.

"My list of regrets," Patty said. "Don't you have one?"

"No." Cece thought for a moment. "Well, not a list anyway."

"I have a list, and it's long."

"What's on it?" Cece asked.

"That second scoop of garlic ice cream for starters."

Cece laughed. "That's a fleeting regret. A real regret is something you wish you had done differently because of how it impacted your life. I want to hear about one of those."

Patty rubbed her belly. "I have to think. You go first."

"That's easy," Cece said. "I regret telling Doug I thought he was going to propose."

Patty cracked open her window and pulled on her sweatshirt. "Yeah, I get that," she said through the fabric. Her head popped out. "What else?"

Cece brushed some hair off her face. "Well...I must admit, I do regret quitting ballet."

"Big deal. Everyone quits eventually."

Cece pictured her painting and the ballerina who inspired it. "Not everyone."

Cece could see Patty looking at her with curiosity. Although Cece had shared bits and pieces of her teen years with her, she'd left out critical details.

"I loved dancing more than anything in the world. And," she paused and took a deep breath, "I had just auditioned for the San Francisco Ballet."

"What?" Patty interrupted her. "I never knew you were *that* good."

"I was that good."

"Then why'd you quit?"

It was a Pandora's box of reasons. Once Cece opened the lid, the story would fly out like butterflies escaping a net. She had spent years pushing it out of her mind, but here it was front and center, and Patty deserved more than vague generalizations. The memory of what her mother had done came rushing back, and she braced herself for the grief that came with it.

"I quit to punish my mother for ruining our family." Cece tried to sound detached.

"Because your parents got a divorce?" said Patty. "Jesus, when I was kid almost everyone I knew had divorced parents. My family was the odd-ball."

"It was more complicated than that," Cece said. "My mom had an affair in a small town, and it was…it was mortifying. The boys at school teased me about my mother's sex life. And poor Tommy. He was only twelve, but he understood what they were talking about. So first she humiliated us, and then she left us."

"Wow," said Patty. "But I still don't get the quitting ballet thing."

Cece didn't like thinking, let alone talking, about her mother and the disintegration of her family, but the long drive toward home under a sky thick with gray clouds brought it back, and telling Patty actually felt cathartic.

"My mom," Cece said, sighing, "was the most over-the-top stage mother ever, and she believed my success reflected on her. It was like it belonged to her as much as to me. But even more than that, I think she was desperate for me to achieve what she couldn't."

"She was a dancer too?"

"A great dancer, but not quite great enough." Cece tapped a nail on the steering wheel. Revisiting the worst time in her life made her anxious, sad, and ashamed all over again, even in front of Patty.

"Anyway," Cece said, "my life fell apart because of what she'd done. And the thing she cared the most about in the world was me becoming a prima ballerina. So, I stole her dream away, and there was nothing she could do about it." Cece remembered the day she told her mother she had quit. She still could see the hurt and anger in her mother's eyes and feel the intoxicating power.

"Jeez," said Patty. "Why'd you never tell me all this?"

"Not something I like to think about. And now, thirteen years after the fact, I'm not proud of what I did. Ballet might have been my mother's dream, but it was my dream too."

Cece felt the familiar squeeze inside her chest, like a hand reaching in and gripping her heart. She'd intentionally tried not to think about ballet over the years because the loss was too great. And yet, the yearning never really went away. She missed all of it—the sensation of her body moving, the sound of the music pounding, the thrill of her mother's approval and admiration.

"What about the audition? Did you mess up on purpose?" asked Patty.

A smiled played on Cece's lips. The audition. It had been... perfect. "No, I was good, great actually, but I didn't get in."

The memory of those days blurred like a child's finger-painting. Her father's hurt, her brother's bewilderment, and her own rage. They had all converged at once, suffocating Cece under the weight of so much emotion.

She choked, and for a moment, she couldn't breathe.

"Are you okay?" Patty touched her arm.

Cece shook off the memory, forcing it back into her subconscious. "I'm fine," she said, taking a deep breath. "Hey, that was another life, right?"

She refocused on the road ahead, and the squeeze in her chest disappeared.

5

*C*ece grew up in Clearwater, a small town on the eastern edge of Sonoma County. It consisted of a long main street with a village square in the middle and family owned businesses on both sides.

Named for a sparkling blue lake on the outskirts of town, Clearwater was surrounded by farms, wineries, orchards, and peaceful neighborhoods.

Cece pulled into the driveway of her childhood home, gravel crunching beneath the tires. She parked in front of the house, a traditional craftsman that sat on an acre of land. It had broad eaves with exposed rafters, dormer windows, and a wide front porch.

"Finally!" Patty said. "I feel like a pretzel."

They got out of the car just as Cece's father threw open the front door. "You made it!" He ran down the front steps and hugged them both.

Over six feet tall with broad shoulders, excellent posture, and thick, mostly gray hair, Phil looked like a rugged, old Marlboro man. Cece pushed her nose into his flannel shirt and breathed in the familiar scent, a mixture of sawdust, autumn leaves, and musky cologne. It made her feel young and safe and loved.

"Hi, Daddy." Cece kissed his cheek.

"Hi, Phil." Patty kissed his other cheek.

"My girls are home. I'm a happy man. Come on in, dinner's almost ready."

The warm kitchen smelled of hot, spicy chili and melted cheddar cheese, and Cece felt the familiar comfort of home.

"I can't wait for your enchiladas, Daddy," Cece said. "Where's Julia?"

"Just ran to the store. Should be back any minute."

"Okay if I go take a quick shower?" Patty mimed to Cece that her stomach still hurt.

"Sure," Phil said. "Julia put fresh towels out."

As Patty headed upstairs, Cece gave her father another hug. She relished a few minutes alone with him.

"How's my girl?" Phil asked.

"Good," said Cece. "A little tired. Where's the dog?"

As if in answer to her question, Boomer, her father's sweet, old boxer, flew through the doggie door.

"There you are," Cece said, sitting on the floor. Boomer licked her face and wagged his stubby tail while she petted his huge head.

A car door slammed, and Cece heard Julia's familiar quick steps approach. She got up and opened the door. "Julia!"

"Cece!" Julia dropped her grocery bags on the table. She threw off her down jacket and gave Cece a tight hug. "I'm so glad you made it in time for dinner, what with the traffic and rain and—"

"Slow down there, sweetheart," Phil said. "Where's my kiss?"

Julia looked at Phil with an adoring smile. She lifted her face to his, and Cece watched as they kissed, their lips puckering in matching fashion. It made her happy to see her father with a woman like Julia. After Cece's mother left, Cece thought her happy-go-lucky dad would never be himself again. But now, with Julia, he was happier and more content than Cece could have hoped.

"Where's Patty?" Julia asked.

"In the shower," Cece said, unpacking Julia's canvas bag. "Is Tommy coming?"

Phil looked out the window. "Just drove up."

Cece's younger brother blew in. "Hey, Sis!" Tom wrapped his sister inside his long arms. He was built just like his father, only bigger. A football star in high school, he was strong and handsome, if a bit disheveled, with the same blue eyes and curly brown hair as Cece. "Been a long time since you were here."

"I know." Cece ruffled her brother's curls. They had always been close, especially after their mother left them. "I've missed you. You should visit me more."

"Oh no," Tom said. "I can only take so much city life, especially LA."

He let go of Cece and turned his attention to Boomer, rubbing the dog's face with both hands. "Who's a good boy? Who's the best boy?" After roughing up Boomer, Tom kissed Julia on the cheek. Then he went to his father. The two men embraced. "Hey, Pop."

"Hello, Son." Phil put his hands on Tom's shoulders and squeezed them, as if Tom were still a teenage boy. Cece smiled at the obvious affection between her father and brother. After his wife moved out, Phil had dedicated every possible moment to his children, and especially to Tom, who never could comprehend why his mother had left him.

Patty appeared, her hair wet from the shower, dressed in gray sweat pants, a large navy sweater that draped off one shoulder, and fuzzy yellow slippers. "Hi, Tommy!"

Cece watched her brother's expression. He'd always had a thing for Patty.

"Hey, you!" He scooped Patty up as if she weighed nothing.

"You're squeezing me to death." Patty giggled like a little girl.

"Okay, everyone," Julia said. "Dinner time."

They sat at the long farm table that separated the kitchen from the family room. Tom filled everyone's wine glasses, and loud conversation interrupted by spurts of laughter and raucous teasing filled the room.

"Where's Ryan?" Cece asked, referring to Julia's sixteen-year-old son.

"Dinner with his father," Julia said. "He'll be back in an hour or so."

"I can't wait to see him." Although they had never lived in the house together, Cece considered Ryan her little brother. She had known him since he was a toddler.

Cece bit into a piece of buttered cornbread. "This is delicious."

Phil poured hot sauce on his food. "So, how was your birthday?"

Cece pushed her fork into an enchilada. "Oh, um, good, really nice."

"Are you kidding?" Patty said.

"Patty…" Cece warned.

"What?" asked Phil.

"Cece thought Doug was going to propose, and he didn't." Patty took a large bite of food and looked at Cece. "Right, ooooh, dat hot."

"You have the biggest mouth I've ever seen," Cece said.

Tom reached for a second serving. "Sounds awkward. What happened?" He glanced at Patty and winked.

"Now hold on," Julia said. "If Cece would like to keep it private, that's up to her." She patted Cece's hand.

"If my baby girl was upset," Phil said, "I'd like to know."

"Daddy, it's fine," Cece said. "I just, well, I got a little ahead of myself. Caught Doug off guard."

Tom's jaw dropped. "You mean you told him?"

"I didn't do anything wrong. I just mentioned that I thought he might've gotten a...a certain gift that..." Cece stopped talking. She drank down half a glass of wine. It all sounded so awful.

Tom leaned his elbows on the table. "Had you guys even talked about getting married?"

Cece frowned at her brother. "Maybe not in those exact words, but he tells me I'm 'the one' all the time. Says he's crazy about me." Cece cringed. She sounded like a foolish teenager.

"You gotta be kidding," said Tom. "All guys say stuff like that. It's how we get—"

"Stop right there, Son," Phil interrupted. "Now Cece, you know I like Doug very much. But if he doesn't think my little girl is good enough for—"

"Phil!" Julia almost jumped from her chair. "Nobody has suggested that. Cece, honey, don't you worry. You may have surprised him with your, um, suggestion," she said, wiping her mouth with a napkin, "but give him time to digest the idea. He'll come around."

"I hope so." Patty picked up her wine glass. "Cece is almost thirty."

"Jesus, Patty, I just turned twenty-nine!"

"So thirty's right around the corner," Tom said. "Now I get it. The biological clock thing, right?"

Cece pushed her plate away. "Why do all men think that? Why can't it be that he's the man I love and want to spend the rest of my life with? Yes, I'll be thirty in one year, thank you Patty, and I want to know. A woman likes to have a plan. We don't like to be left hanging."

"And *we* don't like to be blindsided," said Tom.

The room fell quiet, and Cece's head spun in the awkward vacuum of silence.

Phil cleared his throat. "Well, now that that's settled, what's for dessert?"

6

*C*ece pushed and squeezed the pillow underneath her head, trying to get comfortable.

Patty groaned from the trundle alongside Cece's bed. "Can we switch tomorrow? This cot is too small."

"No. If it's small for you, it'll be way too small for me. Besides, I'm mad at you."

"I know," said Patty. "You'll get over it though."

"And by the way," Cece said, "Ryan's room is right down the hall, so no running around in your underwear."

"He's sixteen and a total hottie. You think he's never seen a naked girl before?"

Cece kicked Patty's leg. "I have no idea, but he's my little brother, and I don't want him traumatized."

Patty sat upright. "Me naked would traumatize him? He'd probably love it."

"Patty, could we just go to sleep?"

"Fine." Patty flipped herself over. "G'night, fussy."

"G'night." Cece turned onto her back. A sliver of moonlight illuminated her childhood bedroom, and she could see the comforter her mother had picked out for her fifteenth birthday, flowers and butterflies in pale pastel colors. Cece had wanted turquoise and purple, but her mother insisted that would be impractical. Neutral, soothing colors would stand the test of time. Maybe her mother had been right. After all, the bedding was still there, even though her mother wasn't.

Cece drifted in and out of sleep. Tom's suggestion that she'd blindsided Doug had renewed her worries, and she wondered how, or if, she ever could make everything go back to the way it was.

∾

The house was quiet when Cece awoke, and Patty's bed was empty. She stretched her long legs, crawled over the trundle, and went to the closet for her old bathrobe. It was hanging on a hook on the back of the door—purple chenille—the one her father bought her the year her mother left. "To hell with practical," Phil had said, "you pick any crazy color you want." She slipped into the robe. It smelled fresh, like spring rain laundry detergent.

Cece pulled on a pair of socks and padded down the stairs. "Patty? Are you here?"

"In the kitchen," Patty called out.

Cece found Patty standing in front of the stove. "Do I smell bacon?" Cece asked. "And coffee?"

"You do. I got up early and had breakfast with Phil and Tommy before they left for work."

Phil and Tom were partners in Camden Electric, a company Phil had started when Cece and Tom were kids.

Patty handed Cece her coffee. "How do you want your eggs?"

"Are you doing this so I won't be mad at you anymore?"

"Yes," Patty said, a piece of crispy bacon hanging out of her mouth.

"Well, it's working. Scrambled with cheese, please, Missy."

"Comin' right up. How'd you sleep?" Patty asked.

Cece nibbled on a piece of toast. "Awful. You?"

"Like a baby."

~

For the next few days, they cleaned and prepped, shopped and baked. To Phil Camden, Thanksgiving weekend was the kick-off of a two-month celebration that lasted all the way until Super Bowl Sunday.

The serious cooking began Wednesday afternoon.

"Oh no!" Julia threw a kitchen towel over her shoulder. "I forgot celery. Patty, see if there's any in the crisper."

Patty pulled open the drawer. "Nope. Want us to run to the market?"

"Would you? That would save the day."

Cece looked up from chopping onions, her eyes teary. The last thing she wanted to do was venture into town. She ran a paper towel under cold water and wiped her face. "Ugh. I'll go get my keys."

At the market, Cece parked the car and looked at herself in the rearview mirror. She wiped black smudges from her eyes with a finger. "I look like crap."

"Who cares?" said Patty, not contradicting her.

Cece scowled at her roommate. "You don't understand small towns. Let's just get in and out fast. You have the list?"

Patty shook the piece of paper as they got out of the car. "Right here. That one bunch of celery turned into fifteen things."

They scurried through the aisles with Julia's list, filling the cart. "Okay," Cece said. "Did we forget anything?"

Patty ran her finger down the list. "Ummm, box of cornstarch."

As Cece rounded the corner and passed a display of Thanksgiving decorations, she halted. "Oh my God," she said under her

36

breath. She started to back up, trying to decide if she should turn and run or stay and face the one person she should never have lost touch with.

"What's wrong?" Patty asked.

Cece ignored Patty's question, too stunned to reply. She steadied her breathing and moved toward a tall, slim woman with dark hair and golden-green eyes. "Natalie."

The woman's eyes widened. Her hand went to her throat. "Cece? My God, I haven't seen you in ages."

"It's been a while," Cece said, her hands shaking. "I...I moved to LA."

Natalie nodded, her eyes glassy. "I remember."

Cece found herself unable to do anything but stare at the woman who had been her best friend throughout childhood. When Cece quit dance, she had also abandoned the friendship. Another regret. Natalie had been like a sister to her.

Patty stepped between them, breaking the tension. "Hello. I'm Patty," she said with rare maturity.

"Oh, sorry." Cece put a hand on Patty's shoulder. "Natalie's an old friend of mine from ballet."

"Old friend," Natalie said, as if she were testing the value of the words.

An awkward silence weighed heavily. Natalie had been by Cece's side when her life unraveled. She would have done anything for her, but Cece had been too damaged and embarrassed by her family's crisis to accept help.

"So," Natalie said, her voice lighter. "Here for Thanksgiving?"

Cece nodded. "Yes. You know my dad, he's all about the holidays."

"That he is." Natalie laughed and her expression softened. "I can't believe you're standing in front of me. I've missed you."

Cece pulled on a curl and twirled it. "How's your mom? Still running the studio with an iron fist?"

Natalie's smile faded. "Actually, she's not doing so well."

The news surprised Cece. Her former teacher and mentor, Ilana Lurensky, had been a force of nature when Cece knew her, and Cece could not imagine her weakened.

"I'm so sorry."

"Anyway," Natalie continued, "she's not teaching anymore. It's…it's been hard."

"I understand." Cece had loved Natalie's mother more than her own. "Be sure to tell her hello for me."

"Of course," Natalie said. Her chest rose as she inhaled. "How long are you in town? Maybe you could come by the studio. My mom would love to see you."

Cece blanched at the idea of seeing Ilana. "I wish I could, but we leave early Friday morning." The lie came out more easily than expected. "I'm sorry."

"No, I understand." Natalie extended a slender hand to Patty. "So nice to meet you. And Cece, wow, can't believe we just bumped into each other after all this time. Give your family my best, okay?"

"I will," Cece said. A sense of longing gripped her. How could she deny Natalie's request? Visiting Ilana would be a small gesture that would mean so much. "You know, we could leave later. Will ten on Friday work?"

"Ten's perfect." Natalie's face lit up. "We'll meet in front of the studio, just like we used to. My mother will be so happy to see you."

"Okay. I'll see you then."

They exchanged numbers, and Natalie pulled Cece into a tight hug. "You have no idea how much this means to me."

Cece hugged her old friend, ashamed and sorry she had pushed her away so many years ago. Natalie's hug was tight and unrestrained, and Cece felt that something had been forgiven.

7

The sound of clattering dishes woke Cece Thanksgiving morning. She leaned over the side of her bed and pulled her cell phone from the charger. It was too early to call Doug, so she texted: *Hi call me when you're up xoxo.*

They'd missed each other's calls on Wednesday, but Cece was not concerned. Maybe a few days apart would end up being a good thing, a break from the tension she had created.

She climbed over a sleeping Patty and went downstairs. The kitchen already smelled delicious.

"Good morning," said Julia. "You're up early."

"There's work to be done." Cece filled a mug with coffee and watched Julia smear butter over the turkey's pale skin. "I'm so happy you married my dad." She kissed Julia's cheek.

Julia looked over her shoulder at Cece and smiled. "So am I, honey."

Cece took a sip of coffee. "That is an enormous turkey."

"We'll have lots of leftovers for the weekend. You're staying, aren't you? You know how your dad likes to start putting up Christmas decorations right away."

"Oh, I know. We'll probably leave early Sunday. Doug's working all weekend, and I don't have to be at the gallery until Monday, so there's no rush to get back."

Julia turned on the oven. "Good. Your dad will be thrilled. He misses you a lot."

"I know."

Julia washed a bunch of herbs and patted them with a paper towel. "By the way, Patty mentioned you're going to the studio to see Ilana."

"Yep. Tomorrow morning at ten."

"I think it's very sweet of you to visit her."

"I didn't know she was sick, did you?"

"No." Julia looked concerned. "I did hear she wasn't working as much lately, but that was all. It can't be serious or the whole town would be talking about it."

"I guess," Cece said. "But she's one tough lady. Nobody can suffer in silence better than she can. Anyway, put me to work."

The house phone rang.

"Grab that for starters," Julia said.

Cece put her coffee down and picked up the receiver on the old yellow wall phone with the long, curly cord. "Hello?"

"Hey there, it's me.

"Doug, hi!" She warmed at the sound of his voice. "You got my text."

"Sure did. You didn't answer your cell."

"It's upstairs. How are you?"

"Lonely."

Cece glanced at Julia who was busy chopping. "Me too." She stretched the telephone cord around the wall into the hallway and sat on the floor, her knees bent. "I wish you were here."

"So do I. But you got Patty."

"Not the same." Cece scratched her ankle.

"I hope not," said Doug. "I miss you."

"I miss you too. A lot."

"Hey, I was thinking you should come with me to that party on Saturday. It'll be fun, well, maybe not fun, but entertaining."

"But I'm not driving back until Sunday."

"Oh. I thought you were coming home sooner."

Cece wrapped the cord around her foot. "I...I was, but there's so much going on here, and my dad likes me to be around to start the Christmas decorating."

"Okay."

Cece could hear disappointment in his voice. "I'm really sorry."

"No big deal," Doug said.

"I would've come home earlier, but you said you were working all weekend."

"Yeah, I know." Doug's voice dropped. "I should have thought of it sooner."

Cece played with the phone cord. They had just gotten through a rough couple of days, and she wanted to avoid any more tension. "I'll tell you what, let me talk to my dad. He'll understand if—"

"No, don't do that," Doug said, his voice apologetic. "You probably won't be back up there for a while, so you should stay."

"Are you sure?" Cece asked, feeling a surge of love for him.

"Yeah. I just really miss you, babe."

"Me too," said Cece. "I can't wait to get home and have everything, you know, just go back to normal."

"Same here."

Cece sighed. "By the time you see me on Sunday, you'll want me even more."

"I don't think that's possible. And don't get me thinking about it either. I'm at my parents' house."

Cece laughed. "Say hi to your family for me, okay?"

"You too."

"And I'll call you after dinner. Love you." Cece hung up with an uneasy feeling in her chest.

~

The farm table looked like a Norman Rockwell painting with the huge turkey browned to perfection, white tablecloth, gold napkins, antique china, and a centerpiece of orange daisies, yellow mums, and red lilies.

Julia lit the candles and blew out the match.

"Okay family," Phil called, filling wine glasses. "Time for dinner!"

They took their seats: Julia and Phil at either end of the table, Ryan next to Tom on one side, Patty and Cece across from them.

Cece squeezed Patty's hand. "Thanks for being here."

"Are you kidding? I love your family, probably more than my own."

Ryan, a shy boy with a slight build and straight blond hair that covered one eye, looked at Patty. "Where's your family?"

"Dallas, but my parents practically live in their RV." Patty shook out her napkin and spread it over her legs. "They just drive from state to state visiting my siblings who are scattered across the country."

"So Patty belongs to us this Thanksgiving," Julia said. "And we are delighted to have her."

"Thanks, Julia," Patty said, blowing her a kiss.

Phil went and stood beside his wife. He put an arm around her and placed a soft kiss on her head. "This is the most magnificent turkey I've ever seen." He picked off a strip of crispy skin.

Julia slapped his hand playfully.

"Make a toast, Pop," said Tom.

"Okay, but I'm not very good at this."

"Yes you are, Daddy," Cece said. "You're the best."

"Thank you darlin'. Well," Phil said, lifting his glass, "to this wonderful family. All of you, everyone at my table, is my family." He winked at Patty. "And to the start of the holidays, my favorite time of year—gift giving and non-stop football—doesn't get better than that. Cheers everyone. Now let's eat!"

~

It was after midnight when Cece took her cell into the living room and sat on the couch. She had meant to call Doug earlier. Dinner had been wild and full of laughter, and it was not until they finished cleaning up that Cece realized how late it was.

She listened to the rings, surprised he didn't answer.

"You've reached Doug Whitman Photography. Leave a message. Thanks, and have a great day."

"Hi, sweetie. Thought you'd still be up. Maybe you are…um, just wanted to say g'night and, well, sorry about this weekend. Call you tomorrow. Love you."

She pressed 'end call' and put down her phone. *I need to get home*, she thought.

8

*F*or the second morning in a row, Cece was awakened by noise. It sounded like Santa was clomping around on the roof. A loud boom shook the walls.

Patty bolted upright. "What the hell is that?"

"My father putting up Christmas decorations."

"Oh. Okay." Patty put the pillow over her head and went back to sleep.

Cece lay on her back and stared at the ceiling. Today she would see Ilana Lurensky for the first time in more than ten years. "It's going to be an interesting day," she said to herself. She got out of bed and went downstairs to the kitchen.

The sight of Tom, bent over with his head in the refrigerator, welcomed her.

"Don't you have your own apartment?"

Tom turned. "Good morning to you too."

"Sorry, but what are you doing here so early?"

"I told Dad I'd come help him with the lights. And besides, I have no food at my place, so for breakfast I'm making a Thanksgiving leftovers omelet. Want one?"

"Yuck, no. Any coffee left?"

"Sorry, just took the last of it. Hey, did you see those light-up reindeer things Dad bought? I think he's getting a little whacked."

"He is not. He just loves Christmas. Where's Julia?"

"Driving Ryan to soccer or something."

Cece reached out. "Gimme your coffee, Tommy."

Tom handed his mug to her. "You won't like—"

Cece took a big gulp before he could finish. "Yuck. Did you dump in the entire sugar bowl?" Cece handed the mug back to Tom.

"You want me to make another pot?"

"That's okay," Cece said. "I'll get some at the bakery before I see Natalie."

"Natalie Lurensky…she still so hot?"

"Hotter than ever. Exceptional actually, in that exotic Russian model sort of way." Cece leaned on the kitchen sink. "But there's something different about her, I don't know, more sentimental than I remember." Cece wondered if it had something to do with Ilana's illness, but she didn't mention it to her brother.

Tom scooped yams, stuffing, and turkey into a frying pan and poured eggs over his concoction.

"That looks completely disgusting," said Cece.

"That's okay, because I'm not giving you any."

Cece punched his arm. "That's okay, 'cause I don't want any."

Tom smiled at Cece. "It's good to have you home, Sis, it really is."

A chilly breeze blew against Cece's face as she stepped outside. She buttoned her black peacoat and wrapped a red muffler around her neck. The cashmere scarf had been a gift from Doug their first Christmas together. Putting it on reminded Cece that they hadn't spoken since yesterday morning. She would call him as soon as she finished visiting with Natalie and Ilana, unless he called her first.

As she walked down the steps, she looked up to see her father at the top of a ladder holding a long string of lights. Boomer was barking and jumping around in circles underneath his master.

Cece patted the dog. "Daddy!" she called out.

Phil turned. "Hey there, baby girl. Where're you going?"

"Into town to see Natalie and her mom. I won't be gone long."

Phil waved. "All right, have a good visit. When you get back I'll let you help me set up my new reindeer. Patty too."

"Oh boy," Cece said with a smile. "See you in a bit."

Cece got into her car and rubbed her hands together. She backed her car down the driveway and into the street. A huge canopy of oak tree branches hung over the road.

In less than five minutes, Cece was driving into her past. She saw the shoe repair, beauty salon, and candy shop, businesses that had been in Clearwater for as long as Cece could remember. She pulled into a parking space and took a few coins out of the ashtray before remembering there were no meters. She laughed at herself. "At least this town still has free parking."

In front of Nutmeg's Bakery, a few people were sitting at tables clustered under the heaters. Cece pushed open the glass door and stepped inside, inhaling the sweet, familiar smell. Memories flooded in.

The bakery had been the teen hangout. A few years after Cece left for UCLA, the owner's daughter, fresh out of Stanford with a business degree, decided they needed to do something to keep Starbucks out of Clearwater. She transformed the little bakery into a trendy coffee bar, with state-of-the-art espresso machines, wooden tables, and intimate seating areas in the corners. Historical photos lined the walls. Of the few things Cece missed about her hometown, Nutmeg's was one of them.

"Help you?" a teenage boy asked. He had short, bleached hair, a gold hoop earring in one ear, and a thin goatee. Over his T-shirt he wore the requisite brown apron with "NUTMEG'S" embroidered on the front in orange lettering.

"Large black coffee, please."

"For here or to go?" the boy asked.

"To go." Cece's stomach rumbled. "And do you have any pecan sticky buns left?"

"Lemme take a look."

He disappeared for a moment and came back with a giant square pastry covered in chopped nuts and buttery, brown sugar icing.

"You're in luck. Last one."

Cece clapped her hands together. "Oh, I haven't had one in ages." While she waited for her order, Cece checked her cell. Nothing from Doug—no text, no missed calls. Disappointed, she dropped the phone into her purse.

"That'll be $7.40"

Cece looked at the teenager. "Wow. Guess prices aren't what they used to be." She gave him a ten-dollar bill.

The boy looked at Cece as if she were from another century and handed back the change. Cece tucked a dollar bill into the tip jar. "Thank you," she said, taking her coffee and sticky bun.

There were no seats available inside, so Cece headed outside, anticipating her first bite of sticky bun. Hopefully, it would be as delicious as she remembered.

As she was about to sit, the person in the chair behind her scooted backwards, knocking her arm.

"Oh no!" Cece's coffee spilled and her pastry tumbled out of the bag onto the ground.

"I'm so sorry! I didn't even see you."

Cece turned. A tall man stood beside her chair. He looked down where Cece's coffee was flowing toward the sidewalk.

"Don't move. I'll be right back." He disappeared into the bakery.

Cece sighed. As she picked up her cup and plastic lid, a dog came by and sat down beside the sticky bun. He looked up at Cece. "Go ahead, take it," Cece said. The dog wagged his tail, grabbed it, and ran off.

Cece wiped up the mess with a handful of napkins, questioning her decision to visit Ilana. The day was not off to a good start. She thought about Doug and felt a yearning to get home. She looked at her watch and calculated. After a quick visit at the studio, she could run back to the house, pack up, and be on the road by mid-afternoon. Cece relaxed, having made the decision. She'd be home by tonight, and everything would work out perfectly.

"I'm so sorry about your breakfast," the man said, placing a large mug in front of her. He appeared to be in his thirties with neatly trimmed dark hair and a beard that was several days old. He looked guilty. "And more bad news," he said. "No more of those gigantic pecan roll things."

Cece cleared her throat. "I know. I got the last one." She picked up the mug and was about to say she wanted a to-go cup. Instead she took a sip. The coffee was hot and smooth, and a real mug made it taste even better. She smiled at the man. "So, what are you going to do about my sticky bun?"

The corners of his mouth turned up, and his eyes narrowed. He pointed one finger in her direction. "Stay here." He took two steps toward the doorway then turned back. "Please," he added with a polite nod of his head.

Cece sensed a stirring in her chest. Had she just flirted? She peered through the window to see the man talking to the teenage boy. He shook his head, leaned to the side, and pointed to something behind the glass. Cece sat up straight. "I'm being ridiculous," she whispered to herself. A minute later the man appeared carrying a large plate with what looked like a giant square of pecan pie.

"You've got to be kidding," Cece said.

"What? I saw that huge sweet roll you were about to eat."

"I was only going to have a few bites. The rest I was taking home."

"I'll bet you were," he said, holding out a paper napkin with a fork resting on top. She took it from him.

"Thank you." Cece pressed the side of the fork through the pecans, gooey filling, and dense crust. She tasted it. "Oh really, really good," she said, her mouth full.

The man looked like a schoolboy showing a good grade to his mother.

Cece licked a crumb off her lip. "There is no way I can eat all this."

"Then I'll help you." The man sat and pulled a fork and knife out of his pocket.

Cece laughed, surprised by the bold move. "Are those weapons, or do you always walk around with silverware?"

"I didn't want to seem presumptuous." He sliced off a thin piece.

"No, no, you have to do better than that." Cece picked up the knife and cut the pastry in half. "Does that look even?"

The man took a bite. "Like you measured it with a ruler," he said chewing slowly. "Mmm, that is good."

The teenage boy appeared with a carafe of hot coffee. "Refill?"

Cece wiped her mouth with a napkin. "Yes, please."

"Would you like a cup of coffee, sir?"

The man glanced at Cece then at the teenager. "Please."

The boy filled another mug and placed it on the table.

The man picked it up, and steam rose in front of his face. "Best coffee in town. Have you had it before?"

"Only about a thousand times," Cece said. "High school hangout."

"Really? You live here?"

"Not anymore," said Cece. "Just home for Thanksgiving. I live in LA."

"Ahhh, City of Angels. I love that town. I used to live in Manhattan Beach," the man said.

Cece looked up. "I live in Santa Monica."

"Nice. And what do you do in Santa Monica?"

"I manage an art gallery in Venice Beach," Cece said, taking another bite. "What do you do?"

"Lawyer."

That was all he said. Cece eyed him over the edge of her coffee cup. "Small town lawyer, huh? Come to think of it, you do look a little like Atticus Finch."

The man threw his head back and laughed. "If only! I do have an office here, but I'm in the city most of the time."

A truck pulled up, and two men with fresh pine wreaths got out. They each picked up a half dozen or so and started hanging them on every lamppost.

"Can't believe the holidays are already here," the man said.

"I know. Clearwater sure loves Christmas. Main Street will be twinkling in no time."

"It will." The man watched as one of the workers attached a wreath to a lamppost. "Maybe I'll decorate my house this year."

They continued their small talk and finished off the pecan square. Cece licked one finger and picked the remaining crumbs up from the plate. "So good." She put her finger in her mouth. The man seemed amused.

"Oh wow," Cece said, chagrined. "That was completely uncouth of me."

"Not at all. I thought it was…adorable."

A layer of clouds moved across the sky and blocked the sun,

darkening the patio where they sat. Cece looked at her watch. "I'd better be going."

The man nodded. "All right. Well, again, sorry I knocked over your coffee and ruined your sticky bun." He rubbed the stubble on his cheeks. "Do you think I could make it up to you with, say, dinner tonight?"

Cece nearly choked. This handsome, somewhat older man was asking her out. "Oh, I...I'm sorry but no, I can't tonight." She felt her face grow warm.

"When are you heading back to LA? Maybe another night would work."

Cece shifted in her chair. She felt clumsy and inept. "You're so nice, but I'm, um, I'm in a..."

"Ah, you're in a relationship," the man said. He smiled and ran a hand through his hair. "I should have guessed. I hope I didn't embarrass you. It's just that, well, you're very attractive... and funny. I thought that maybe bumping into you was somehow meant to be."

Cece cast her eyes downward. She couldn't speak, and for a few seconds she let herself imagine what a date with this man might be like. He stood and extended his hand. She reached up and felt his strong grip.

"It was a pleasure having breakfast with you," he said.

She let go of his hand. "I enjoyed it too." Cece rose and scooted her chair back, tipping it to the side. She caught it and pushed it into place. "Thank you for the coffee and the, uh, delicious pecan thing."

The man smiled, and a dimple appeared near the corner of his mouth. "You're welcome. Have a safe drive home."

Cece buttoned her coat and willed herself to stop behaving like a silly teenager. "Goodbye," she said, wrapping her scarf around her neck. As she walked to her car, she glanced back. The man was still looking at her. Embarrassed, Cece turned away and quickened her steps.

9

The old Mayfair Hotel was on the corner, across the street from the town square. The two-story, Southern style inn with white wood siding, black shutters, and a wide front porch no longer accommodated guests, but from the outside it looked the same as it did when it was built in 1925.

Cece parked her car, realizing she had intended to walk. But her strange encounter with the man at Nutmeg's had distracted her. Gazing at the hotel, the place where she had spent more time growing up than at her own house, Cece felt wistful and a little anxious.

She took a deep breath and got out of her car.

Natalie was standing on the porch in front of the entrance to the Lurensky Dance Academy. She raised her hand and smiled. Cece did the same. On the steps, Natalie hugged her. "I'm so glad you're here."

"Me too," Cece said, keeping her tone light.

There were three sets of French doors across the front of the building, and the middle one was ajar. Natalie put her hand on the doorknob then stopped. "I told my mother last night that you'd be coming to see her, but she's a little off this morning. She didn't remember."

"Okay." Cece still did not know what was wrong with her former instructor.

"And she's, um, a bit confused lately. Might not recognize you right away."

"That's understandable," Cece said. "She hasn't seen me since I was a teenager."

Natalie pursed her lips. "Well, it's a little more than that."

Cece hesitated. "I don't want to upset her."

"I don't think that'll happen. If anything gets weird, I'll take care of it." Natalie put a hand on Cece's arm. "Don't worry."

Of course, with that warning, Cece worried even more.

They stepped inside. Nothing had changed in the past thirteen years. The high, dark wood ceiling, crystal chandeliers, and carved moldings that Cece had loved as a little girl were still polished and gleaming. Spotless mirrors covered the walls, and ballet barres of differing heights cut horizontal lines across them.

Cece followed Natalie through a doorway into a long hall.

"This is amazing," Cece said. "Same bathrooms, same cubbies, same smells." She loved the scent of the old wood and cool plaster walls.

"Remember how my mom made us polish the moulding around the cubbies if she didn't think we'd worked hard enough?"

"Of course I do," Cece said, thinking about how much they'd giggled as they worked.

At the end of the hall was an open door. Classical music played.

"We're rehearsing *The Nutcracker*," Natalie said. "Every Christmas, same show. You'd think this town would get tired of it, but they don't."

"Hey, it's tradition." Cece felt warm and nervous. She

slipped off her coat, folded it over her arm, and entered the office of Madam Lurensky.

Ilana sat behind an antique French desk in front of a large window. On either side of the window, panels of beige drapery reached the floor. A crystal chandelier, similar to those in the studio, hung from the middle of the ceiling, and framed photos of ballerinas lined the walls.

Natalie held Cece's hand. "Mamma, look who's come to see you."

Miss Ilana looked up. Her face hadn't changed. A few wrinkles around her eyes, smile lines deeper, but that was all. Her dark hair was streaked with gray and pulled into a tight bun at the nape of her neck. She wore the same uniform Cece remembered—long, black ballet skirt with leotard and tights. Cece felt intimidated just being near her again.

Ilana looked at her daughter and then at Cece. She seemed confused, her lips pursed. Then she glanced at the wall clock and frowned.

"You are late." Her strong Russian accent resonated through the room.

Cece smiled and raised her eyebrows. "It's just a little after ten."

"I tell you a thousand times, lesson begins on zee hour." Ilana clapped her hands twice. "Go dress. Quickly. Vee rehearse all day today."

Cece gulped. Ilana thought she and Natalie were children.

"Mamma." Natalie took her mother by the shoulders. "Cece is here for a visit. She's all grown up now, just like me. You know that."

Ilana's harsh expression softened. She focused on her daughter's face. As reality dawned, her eyes cleared. "Of course I know," she said. "Who has come to visit?"

"It's Cece. You remember Cecilia Rose, don't you?"

Cece took a few steps forward and touched Ilana's hand. "It's wonderful to see you, Miss Ilana."

Ilana smiled at her, but still without recognition.

"Come on, Mamma," Natalie said, her voice impatient. "It's Cece, my best friend my whole life." She walked across the room and opened the doors of a large armoire. The shelves were lined with black leather albums. She ran a shaky finger over the spines of the books until she found what she was looking for.

Natalie placed the album on the desk in front of her mother and opened it. The first photo was Cece at twelve years old. She was dressed in a crimson and gold costume, and standing on pointe with her left leg extended behind her. Her brown curls were wound into a tight bun on top of her head.

Natalie tapped on the photo with one finger. "Remember this, Mamma? We were doing *Don Quixote*, and Cece was Dulcinea. Look at how well she did her arabesque."

Ilana's eyes grew watery. "Ah, Cecilia Rose, to see her dance…"

"Mamma, she's right here in front of you!"

Ilana looked at Cece. She stood and put her hands on Cece's cheeks as recognition dawned. "Cecilia? I think I never see you again. Vat a beautiful girl you become."

Cece felt her eyes fill with tears as she hugged Ilana. The woman was smaller than Cece remembered.

"Come. Vee sit down." Ilana pulled Cece's arm.

They sat at the desk and continued looking through the album.

"I have book for my best dancers. In zurty years, I make maybe eight book." Ilana smiled at Cece and patted the open album. "Zis dancer here, my best ever."

Cece trembled as she turned the pages slowly, and long forgotten memories of her days as a ballerina unfolded. She smiled at a snapshot showing a line of girls, only four or five years old, in pink tights and tutus. It was Cece and Natalie's first recital. The two little girls stood side-by-side holding hands.

She turned the page. "Look at this one," Cece said, pointing at another picture. "That's me with Jenna. I idolized her. Didn't she go to London?"

Natalie nodded. "She did. Still dancing, I think. She sends a card every Christmas."

Suddenly Cece wished she had kept in touch. "I'm sorry I never came back to see you in all these years, Ilana."

"Ah," Ilana waved her hand, dismissing the apology. "I understand. It vas difficult time for you."

The scrapbook captivated Cece. Photos, newspaper articles, recital programs—all recognizing Cecilia Rose Camden as the ballerina to watch.

"I can't believe these pictures," Cece said, turning through the last few pages. A piece of stationery fell out of the back of the album and fluttered to the floor. Cece leaned over to get it, but Natalie got it first and tried to slip it back into the book.

"What's that?" Cece asked.

"Just an old letter. It's nothing."

But Cece had caught a glimpse of the header on the stationery. It was from the San Francisco Ballet. "Please," she said, extending her hand with palm up.

Natalie reluctantly handed Cece the letter.

Dear Ilana,

So disappointed to learn that Cecilia has stopped dancing. The committee had just accepted her when I got your message. At this point we have filled our openings, but if she changes her mind in the next week or so, I will see if I can pull some strings. I haven't come across a ballerina like her in ages. She is the kind of dancer we dream of, and I truly believe that she has what it takes. Do what you can to get her to rethink it and if...

. . .

Cece stopped reading and looked up. "I made the company?" It had been a lifetime ago, but the news made her hands shake. She had a vague memory of Ilana trying to reach her after she'd stopped showing up for her lessons, but Cece had refused to return her calls. Her life was in chaos, her dancing days over. There was nothing Ilana, or anyone else, could have done to change her mind.

Cece put the letter on the desk and went to the window. A light rain was falling, and moisture dripped from the leaves on the trees behind Ilana's office. Cece stared outside.

"You okay?" Natalie asked.

Cece nodded. "I need to use the restroom." She hurried down the hall, her heels clicking on the wood floor. Inside the bathroom, she leaned on the sink and pressed her palms on the cold porcelain. She took deep, even breaths.

Following her audition, she had waited and waited, checking the mailbox every afternoon for a letter from the ballet. But before any letter arrived, her mother dropped the bomb that she wanted a divorce. Cece's world unraveled and ballet no longer mattered. If there had been a letter, she would have thrown it out.

Cece looked in the mirror and wiped her eyes. "You had every reason in the world to quit," she said to herself.

She returned to Ilana's office.

"Cece," Natalie said. "I'm sorry. I didn't even know the letter was in there."

"It's fine. Ancient history now." Cece glanced at Ilana. She was going through the album again. The clock on the wall ticked rhythmically. She felt out of place. "I need to go."

"Okay." Natalie touched her mother's shoulder. "Mamma, Cece's leaving."

Ilana continued looking at the book as if she hadn't heard her daughter speak.

"Wait just a sec, I'll walk you out." Natalie stood behind her mother and coaxed her out of the chair. "I think you should have a little nap, Mamma, before rehearsal starts."

Ilana stood. "Did I have tea?"

"Not yet, Mamma. I'll get it for you after your nap. Say goodbye to Cece."

Cece hugged her teacher. "It was good to see you, Miss Ilana."

"And you, my dear." Ilana put her hands on Cece's shoulders and studied her face. "Like second daughter to me, Cecilia Rose." She kissed her on both cheeks.

Natalie walked her mother to the couch against the wall. "I'll be back in a little bit, Mamma."

"Thank you, Natalia." Ilana curled her legs up and put her head on a cushion. Natalie covered her with a thin blanket.

Cece followed Natalie through the studio and out the French doors. The rain had stopped, but water dripped from the balcony onto the porch.

"Oh, Cece," Natalie said, "I am so, so sorry."

Cece shook her head. "Don't worry. Probably one of those 'all for the best' things." She crossed her arms against the cold breeze. The clouds were clearing, and the air smelled of fresh pine from all the Christmas wreaths on the lampposts.

"Listen, what you're dealing with is way more important," Cece said. "When you said your mom wasn't well, I was thinking arthritis or something."

"I wish," said Natalie.

Cece put her hands in her pockets. "What does her doctor say?"

"Some kind of dementia." Natalie leaned against the railing. "Maybe Alzheimer's. We're going back after the holidays for a more thorough evaluation. At this point, I have no idea what's ahead of me."

"You really have your hands full, don't you?"

Natalie took a breath. "I guess. Life does get messy."

Don't I know it? Cece thought.

They stepped off the porch. A teenage girl in a gray jacket, ripped jeans, and clunky boots walked toward them.

"Hey, Dawn," Natalie said putting on a cheerful face. She removed the girl's earbuds. "How was your Thanksgiving?"

"Fine."

"This is Cece, an old friend of mine."

The girl had wisps of blond hair sticking out of a black knit cap. "Hi," she said with a vague smile.

"Dawn is our Sugar Plum Fairy this year," said Natalie.

"Congratulations," Cece said. "That's a tough part."

Dawn raised one shoulder. "I guess."

"Go on in," Natalie said. "I'll be there in a few minutes."

"Nice to meet you, Dawn," Cece said. "Good luck."

"Thanks." Dawn's flat expression didn't change as she went into the studio.

"Geez, were we like that?" Cece said.

"Who can remember? Teenagers are so cranky these days. I suppose they always were, just seems worse now that we're the old ones."

A large, silver Lexus pulled up and four little girls in pink tutus jumped out. "Miss Natalie!" The girls swarmed and wrapped their arms around her waist and hips, giggling and pushing on each other like puppies trying to get attention.

"Run inside," Natalie said. "Lots to do today. Hurry, hurry."

The little pink girls scurried away like mice, and Cece's heart swelled at their adorableness.

The woman driving the Lexus honked and waved Natalie over.

Natalie groaned as she approached the car. "Hi, Teresa. What's up?"

The woman leaned toward the open passenger window. She

had short black hair and wore a blue flannel shirt. "Where on earth is your mother? I've been trying to reach her."

"Just a busy time of year," said Natalie. "Can I help you with something?"

"Well, it's your new instructor—I don't like her."

"Kendall? Why's that?"

"I watched the lesson the other day, and she practically ignored Brianna. Now you know I'm not one of those mothers who thinks her daughter is better than everyone else, but let's face it, Brianna is."

Cece squirmed. The woman sounded just like her mother had so many years ago.

"I'll talk to Kendall," said Natalie. "Don't worry. Brianna will get all the attention she needs."

Teresa's frown vanished. "Thank you, Natalie. Oh, by the way, I got a great referral for the costumes. Tell you about it later." She waved and took off down Main Street.

Natalie stepped back from the curb.

"Between the mothers and the teenagers, I don't know how you do it," Cece said.

"It's hard sometimes, but the little ones always cheer me up."

"They are adorable. And still all pink, just like us."

They started walking toward Cece's car.

"That mom, Teresa, she drives me crazy," Natalie said. "But she's right. The new instructor is, well, just too young and inexperienced. I wish you lived here—I'd offer you the job."

"Yeah, right, like I could teach ballet."

"Are you kidding me? You'd be amazing." Natalie bumped her with her shoulder. "The pay's pretty good. Can I tempt you?"

Cece laughed. "Me leave LA? Not a chance. I'm a So-Cal girl now. And small-town life is not for me. Not anymore."

Natalie stretched her shoulders. "I don't blame you. What I wouldn't do for some big city anonymity right now."

Cece brightened at the thought of being home and with Doug in a matter of hours.

"It was great seeing you, Natalie. And I'm really glad I saw your mom."

Natalie reached for Cece's hand and squeezed it. "Thank you for coming. And again, sorry about that letter."

"Listen, I changed my life a long time ago. I might have a few regrets, but who doesn't?"

"Very philosophical." Natalie hugged her with strong arms. "Please stay in touch. Let's not let another decade slip by before we see each other again."

"It's a deal." Cece opened the door to her car. "I really hope things work out for you."

"Oh, you know me. I always land on my toes." Natalie's smile did not sparkle like it used to.

Cece watched her friend walk back into the studio. Her list of regrets was growing.

10

*C*ece slammed the front door, marching into the house with a purpose. "Patty! Where are you?"

"In the kitchen. Want a turkey and cranberry sandwich?"

After the overly sweet breakfast, real food sounded good. At the kitchen counter, Patty and Phil looked like short-order cooks. "Wrap two up. We're going home," Cece announced as she entered the kitchen.

Phil stopped slicing meat. "What? I thought you were staying through the weekend. I'm getting the tree tomorrow."

"I'm sorry, Daddy, but I just have to get home. We've been here five days already."

"I know baby, but what's another day or two? And you haven't even said if you'll be back for Christmas."

"I'll try to come up for a few days," Cece said. "Maybe, if Doug can come." There was no way she would leave him behind again.

Patty pulled off a long piece of foil. She pouted. "I don't want to go home."

Cece's father hugged Patty. "You can come back any time you want."

Boomer jumped up and stole a slice of turkey from the platter.

"Hey!" Phil hollered at the dog. "Bad boy!"

Boomer flew through the dog door into the backyard, turkey hanging out of his mouth.

After making sandwiches, the girls packed up in thirty minutes, and Ryan carried their suitcases to the car. Everyone gathered in front of the house where strings of lights were stretched out in every direction.

"The Grapevine might be foggy," Phil said. "Which route are you taking?"

"We'll take the coast, Dad." Cece squeezed her father's hand. "Don't worry."

"And it's going to rain, so drive slowly. And be sure to call me when you get home. I don't care how late."

"I will." She hugged her father and then Julia. "Take good care of him, okay?"

"You know I will, honey." Julia kissed Cece's cheek. "See you soon, I hope."

Tom came down from his ladder. "Bye, Sis."

Cece wrapped her arms around her brother. She looked up at him. "Don't be such a Northern California snob, Tommy. Come visit us."

"Maybe." He released Cece and hugged Patty, lifting her off her feet.

"Bye, Tommy. I'll miss you." Patty planted a big kiss on his cheek. Then she hugged Julia and Phil. "Thanks again for having me."

"Anytime," they said in unison.

Cece kissed Ryan, making him squirm. "And you can visit too. We'll go to Disneyland or something."

"Sweet," said Ryan. "Can I bring a friend?"

"Of course." Cece pulled Patty's arm. "Let's go, Missy."

They got into the car, and Cece rolled her window down. "Be

careful stringing the lights, Dad. I don't want to hear about you breaking any bones."

"He'll be fine; he's got me," Tom said, putting his arm over Phil's shoulder.

The four of them stood together.

Patty leaned forward. "God, they're perfect." She picked up Cece's cell phone and snapped a picture.

"They really are." Cece's eyes stung. It hurt to leave them.

~

They were passing Palo Alto by the time Cece finished telling Patty about Ilana, the letter that fell from the album, and her encounter with the man at the bakery.

"You must be exhausted after all that," Patty said.

Cece stretched her neck. "I'm definitely running on adrenaline."

"And I can't believe you made the ballet company. You'd always thought they didn't want you, but they did. That's kind of tragic, isn't it?"

Cece shook her head. Knowing the truth highlighted even more what a mistake she had made by quitting, but a tragedy? "It's sad, I'll give you that, but I wouldn't call it tragic." What was tragic was Ilana's heartbreaking decline.

"Okay," said Patty. "Let's go back to the man at the bakery. How handsome was he?"

Cece pinched Patty's leg. "I've told you twice already. Very handsome."

"I love it that he replaced your sticky bun after the dog took it. That was really nice. So what was his name?"

Cece thought for a moment. "You know what? I don't think we ever introduced ourselves."

"Seriously?"

"Doesn't matter. It's not like I'm going to cyber-stalk him."

"Well *I* could. You already have a boyfriend. Maybe a cute redhead is just Mr. Sticky-bun's type."

"Mr. Sticky-buns—that's terrible." Cece laughed and pushed the accelerator. She could not wait to get home.

They had been on the road over two hours when the rain let up. A ray of sun peeked through the clouds.

"I'm surprised I haven't heard from Doug," Cece said. "Check to see if I have any missed calls."

Patty picked up Cece's cell. "Does he know we're on our way home?"

"No. I just left a message for him to call me back."

Patty held up the phone. "There's a voicemail."

"There is?" Cece reached for her cell, but Patty slapped her hand away.

"Keep driving. I'll put it on speaker."

Cece smiled at the sound of Doug's voice.

"Hey babe, got your message. What's up? Call me back. Miss you. Can't wait 'til Sunday."

"That's a nice message," Patty said.

"Yes it is. He's going to be so happy I'm home early." Cece imagined their reunion tonight and the feel of his arms around her.

A little over halfway home, they took a quick break. Cece was standing in line waiting for the bathroom in a McDonald's when her cell vibrated. She grabbed it.

"Hi!"

"Hey, babe," Doug said. "I got your messages. You've been hard to reach."

"I know. Service is terrible."

"How's everything going? Your dad put up the Christmas tree yet?"

Cece grinned. "Good news," she said, ignoring the question. "I'm on my way home." She squeezed the phone anticipating an enthusiastic response.

"You're kidding, right?" He didn't sound happy.

Cece's heart dropped. "No. We're on our way. I left early."

"But I'm not home," Doug said.

"What do you mean?" Cece said, more confused than upset. "Where are you?"

"I'm in Coronado with my brother. The waves are phenomenal, so we decided to go surfing."

"But I thought you were working this weekend."

"I gave the jobs to Mike. He really needs the money. And I just couldn't pass up these waves."

Cece's feet felt like they'd been glued to the floor. She didn't want to be mad, but she was.

"I'm sorry, Ceece. I didn't think you'd be back until Sunday."

"Well," she said, trying to keep her voice in check, "I assumed you'd be home because you had to work, so I...never mind."

"I'm really sorry," Doug said. "Tell you what. I'll only stay one night. I can surf tomorrow morning and leave in the afternoon. I'll be home in time to go to dinner. Sound good?"

"I guess." Cece tried to muster some enthusiasm. "Sure."

"I'll call you when I'm on my way."

"All right," Cece said. The restroom door opened. "Bathroom's free. I've got to go."

"Okay. See you tomorrow, babe."

She ended the call without saying goodbye, which only made her feel worse. After all, she was the one who had changed the plan.

11

*C*ece stood in her bedroom wrapped in a towel, water dripping on the carpet. It was Saturday afternoon, and she was waiting for Doug's call. She dried off, threw on some sweats, and looked at her phone, willing it to ring. Then it did.

"Doug?"

"Hi. I'm at a gas sta—" static interrupted him.

"You're where?"

"Encinitas," Doug said. "Truck broke down. Looks like I need a new radiator hose. I'm getting towed to the nearest garage, and I'll call you from there."

"Okay. When do you think you'll be back on the road?"

"Depends on the garage. If they have the hose, probably in a few hours. I'm really sorry."

"Don't worry," Cece said, hiding her frustration. "Just drive safe and let me know."

"Thanks for understanding, babe," said Doug. "We'll go to a late dinner or something."

Water dripped from Cece's hair onto the phone. "Sounds good," she said, infusing her voice with cheerful patience.

Cece pushed 'end call' and threw the phone onto her bed. It

bounced off, fell to the floor, and slid under her dresser. "Aaaaaaaargh!"

Three hours later, Doug called again.

"The mechanic didn't have the right hose, so he tried to patch the old one, but it—"

"Did they fix it or not?" Cece's patience was running dry.

"Not."

Cece took a deep breath. "Okay, so…"

"So I won't get home until tomorrow."

What was left of her restraint evaporated. "I rushed home just to be with you, Doug."

"Don't be mad, Cece, crap happens. You know that."

"If you'd stayed in LA and worked like you said you were going to, it wouldn't have." The minute she said the words, she knew it was a mistake.

Doug didn't respond.

"Guess I'll see you tomorrow," Cece said. "If you make it back by then."

"I said I'm sorry like ten times."

"I know you did," Cece said.

"I'm really—"

Cece hung up before he could apologize again.

∾

It was late Sunday night when Cece heard a knock on the front door. She and Patty were sitting on the couch in their pajamas watching *It's a Wonderful Life.*

"That's Doug," Cece said.

"Want me to get it?" Patty asked.

"Sure."

Patty paused the movie on Jimmy Stewart's face, got up, and opened the front door. "Hey, Doug."

"Hey, Patty."

Cece didn't turn around. She heard Doug walking toward the couch where she sat.

"Hi," he said.

Cece looked at him through the corner of her eye. He looked tired and guilty and as adorable as ever. "Hi."

"What're you doing?" Doug asked.

Cece didn't answer.

"Looks like you're watching TV and eating Christmas cookies."

Cece put a whole butter cookie into her mouth. "That's right." Crumbs blew off her lips.

Doug started to laugh. "Can I have one?"

Cece tried not to smile, but she couldn't help it. "I guess."

Patty came around the front of the couch and picked up the plate. "Here," she said, offering the last cookie to Doug. "I'll get more while you two make up. But be quick about it. I want to get back to my movie."

"Do you have any with the red and green sprinkles?" Doug asked. "Those are my favorite." He sat down on the couch.

"Yes, we do," said Patty. "And would you kiddies like hot chocolate with that?"

"Sounds great," Doug said, popping the cookie into his mouth.

"Thanks, Patty," Cece said. "You're the best."

Patty disappeared into the kitchen, and Doug picked up Cece's hand. He kissed it. "Look at that, you have red frosting on your knuckles."

Cece twisted her hand to see, but Doug pulled it back toward his mouth. He licked the frosting with his soft tongue.

"If you think kissing my hand's going to make everything fine, you are mistaken."

"Then how about this?" Doug leaned in and kissed her mouth gently, his lips soft and parted. Cece tasted the cookie he'd just eaten.

"Better," she said.

Doug wrapped Cece into a tight hug. "I'm sorry, babe, you were right. I should've stayed here. The waves weren't even that great."

Cece sighed. "And I'm sorry I was so hard on you. It wasn't your fault. I just really missed you."

"I missed you more." Doug leaned into Cece's damp hair. "You smell so good."

"It's my shampoo."

"I don't think so. You always smell like, I don't know, like a rain forest."

Cece laughed. "How do you know? You've never been."

"I just know." Doug took the clip out of her hair, and it fell in soft waves over her shoulders. "Someday I'll get there though, and I'll bring you back a monkey."

"Promise?"

"Promise." He nuzzled Cece's neck, and she felt his lips and tongue against her skin. Then he took a little nip.

"Wait a minute, Mister, none of that yet," Cece said.

"Sorry, I lost my head. Your intoxicating scent overwhelmed me."

Cece gave him a shove. "You know, I still have to punish you for messing up the weekend, don't you?"

"Of course. What's it gonna be, Boss?"

"You have to sit right here between Patty and me and watch the rest of our sappy movie with us."

"You're making me sit through a movie before I can get you into bed?"

"Yes, and that's not all." Cece touched the tip of his nose. "When it's over, you have to explain why it's a happy ending."

"Geez, you're killin' me."

"And if you get it right," Cece said, kissing his ear with wet lips, "then we can go to bed."

"You two are disgusting," Patty said, putting a tray of hot chocolate and cookies on the coffee table.

Cece picked up a mug and took a sip. "Mmmm, hot cocoa with Kahlua. I love it."

"It's the best." Patty snuggled in on the other side of Doug, picked up the remote, and un-paused Jimmy Stewart's face.

An hour later, Cece was wiping her eyes, and Patty was sobbing.

"Tissues," Cece said through her tears.

Doug leaned forward, pulled a bunch out of the box, and held them to either side.

Cece and Patty sniffled and sang "Auld Lang Syne" with the movie, their faces as red as the poinsettia plant sitting by the fireplace.

"You two look really, uh…sad." Doug pushed the blanket to the side and stood up. "Please just tell me I don't have to explain it."

"Sorry." Cece straightened her back and curled her legs under her. "You still have to explain it." She looked at Patty. "That's the last part of his punishment."

Patty scooted next to Cece and spread the blanket over them. "We're ready."

"Okay, it's a happy ending because George's friends bring him the money, and that solves all his problems."

Cece looked at Patty, her head shaking. "Close, but that's not the answer we're looking for."

"Is this a test?" Doug asked.

"Sort of," Patty said. "Come on, try again."

"Um, it's a happy ending because George didn't really jump off the bridge, and his wife didn't become a librarian."

"No!" Cece and Patty said together.

"Jesus, gimme a hint then."

"Okay," Cece said. "Ting-a-ling-a-ling-a-ling." She shook her hand as if ringing a bell.

"Oh! It's a happy ending because Clarence got his wings!" Patty and Cece cheered.

"Finally," Patty said.

"You figured it out," Cece said. "Now we can go to bed."

"About time." Doug tossed the blanket over Patty's head. "G'night little one."

"Just keep it down in there, you guys," Patty said, her voice muffled by the blanket. "I need my beauty rest."

12

"Good morning." Cece kissed Doug's cheek.

Doug stirred and stretched. "G'morning." He rolled over and pinned Cece with his arm. "Let's stay in bed all day."

Cece wiggled out from under him. "Wish I could, but I have to get ready for work." She stood and put on her white, terrycloth robe. "God only knows what I'll be walking into."

Doug reached for Cece's hand and pulled. "Sit down a sec. I want to ask you something."

Cece sat. "What?"

"I was thinking, you know, about the thing last week."

"I told you, just forget it." Cece had no desire to revisit her birthday. She still felt humiliated by her outburst.

"No really, listen, Ceece. What would you think if I moved in?"

Cece wasn't sure she had heard him correctly. "Moved in? With me and Patty?"

Doug raised his eyebrows. "Uh...yeah."

"In this house? The three of us?"

Doug gave her a hopeful smile. "Yeah. I stay here half the

time anyway, and well, I can leave some stuff at my parents' house, so I wouldn't need much room in the closet. There's plenty of parking out front, just need to move my truck on street cleaning day—"

She cut him off. "You've really thought this out, haven't you?"

"It's a good idea, babe. We'd be moving in the right direction, you and me. And Patty's great. She'd love the idea."

Cece stood. "I don't think she would."

He pushed the blankets off his legs. "Well I do, and besides, think of the money we'd save, all of us."

Cece tightened the sash on her robe. "Don't even mention money, Doug. If that was your concern, you wouldn't have given up work to go surfing."

Doug paused. "I thought we were past that."

"So did I, but you're the one who mentioned money."

"Just forget it then." He ran his hands through his hair. "It's obviously not what you want."

"That's right, it's not. And I don't think it's what you want, either. I think you're just trying to appease me so that I quit..." Cece stopped herself.

"Quit what? Tell me."

"It's just—no, never mind. I have a roommate, Doug, and I don't need another one."

Cece left the room, slamming the door, and went to make coffee. She stewed. What was he thinking? That moving in could somehow appease her?

A few minutes later, Doug appeared, dressed and ready to leave.

He leaned against the door jamb. "I hate fighting with you, Ceece. I thought you'd like the idea of my moving in."

"Well, I don't."

"Yeah, I got that. Do you want me to call you later?"

Cece glanced up. Doug looked more sad than mad. "Yes. Call."

"Okay. Sorry I upset you." Doug kissed her cheek. "I seem to be good at that lately."

He left, and Cece went back to washing dishes. Almost all their conversations seemed to be ending with apologies.

Patty came into the kitchen looking like a sleepy child. Her hair stuck out in all directions, and she had on a red nightshirt with a picture of Santa Claus on the front. "Coffee ready?"

"Yeah." Cece poured two cups. "Guess what?" she said, handing Patty a blue mug. "Doug wants to move in with us."

Patty laughed. "Really?"

"Uh-uh."

"Fine with me. We could use some testosterone around here, not to mention a live-in handyman."

"It's not going to happen. I don't want to live together. It's not part of my plan."

Patty wrapped her hands around her mug. "Your plan, huh? You're pretty rigid with that plan of yours."

"Statistically speaking," Cece said, "couples that live together before marriage have a higher divorce rate. That's just a fact."

"Is that so?" Patty raised her eyebrows.

"Yes." Cece cleared her throat. "It is so."

"Okay, fine. So why are you upset? Did Doug get mad?"

"He didn't. I did." Cece covered her eyes.

"Again?"

"Yeah." Cece sighed. "Again."

"Listen, I know I'm not an expert when it comes to relationships, but I think you need to loosen up a little. Doug's great, and you're kinda being a pain in the ass."

Cece looked at Patty. She was right.

~

The sidewalk in front of the gallery was wet from the late-night rain. Cece unlocked the door and pushed it open, ringing the hanging bells.

"Angel got his wings," Patty said.

"Yep." Cece closed the door and flipped on the heat.

"Cece!" Patty stood behind her workbench. "Look at this." Patty held up a poster:

"GOING OUT OF BUSINESS SALE" A second one said: "EVERYTHING MUST GO," and another: "CLEARANCE— 75% OFF."

"Oh my God," said Cece. "I knew we shouldn't have left town."

Patty put the posters down. "What are we going to do now?"

"I have no idea." Cece was so angry she wanted to tear the signs up. "I should have seen this coming."

The bells tinkled again, and Barbara walked in. She had dark circles under eyes, disheveled hair, and no makeup. "Oh girls, hi. I'm glad you're here. Sorry you had to come home to such bad news."

Cece pounced on her. "Barbara, what is this? Going out of business, seventy-five percent off... what on earth happened?"

"I know. I can't believe it either. I never should have opened this business."

"What are you talking about?" Cece asked.

"It's a failure." Barbara's voice cracked. "I'm a failure."

"That's not true." Cece argued. "You had a vision, and look what you created: the gallery, the coffee bar, all the handmade jewelry and beautiful artwork. It's fabulous."

Barbara took a few steps toward the girls. "Yes, I'm brilliantly creative. But I'm an idiot with finances."

"Cece is crazy smart when it comes to math. She can help you, right Ceece?"

Cece nodded. She thought that was what she had been doing.

Barbara picked up Cece's hand. "It's too late. I quit paying the bills months ago."

Cece pulled her hand away. "You what?"

Barbara started to cry. "I just buried my head in the sand. At first I only put off the minor ones. I thought if I got organized and the holiday shoppers boosted sales, well, then I'd get everything sorted out. But it just got worse."

"Wait a minute," Cece said. She checked the heater and the lights. Nothing. "They shut off our electricity?"

Barbara swallowed. "And the gas. We still have water though. Landlord pays that one."

Cece's legs went weak. "Barbara, what were you thinking?"

"That's just it, I wasn't thinking."

"What about your sister?" Cece said.

"She's the one who told me to liquidate. I've borrowed a lot of money from her the past couple of years. She wants to kill me."

"Can you blame her?" Patty said out of the side of her mouth.

Barbara toyed with a Kleenex. "I'm so sorry. I really am."

Cece wanted to scream. If she heard 'I'm sorry' one more time, she would scream.

A knock on the door startled them. Mae Adamu, cupping her hands around her eyes, was peering through the glass.

Cece opened the door, and Mae blew inside with Goldie tucked underneath her yellow slicker. She pushed the hood back, and her beaded cornrows fell around her shoulders.

"Oh Mae, thank you for coming," Barbara said, giving her friend a hug, "I've made such a mess of things."

Hearing Barbara's lament irritated Cece. She pulled a hand-knitted blanket out of a basket and wrapped it around her shoulders.

Mae took off her slicker and put the cat on the floor. "So your sister wants you to close up shop?"

Barbara nodded. "Looks that way."

Mae raised her eyebrows. "Is that what you want to do then? Throw in the towel?"

"Of course not, but I don't think I have a choice."

"Then let's see what we can do." Mae pulled a laptop out of her satchel. "In a prior life, I studied business."

Cece's head snapped up. "Seriously?"

"Seriously. You know the creative brain works in mysterious ways. Barbara, before you jump ship, let's run some numbers."

Cece wound her hair through her fingers, trying to remain calm. If The Art Stop closed, she and Patty would end up in the unemployment line.

The situation seemed hopeless. A week ago, she had a plan— a plan for work and Doug and her future. Now all of it was crumbling.

Mae set herself up at the table, and everyone went to work.

For the next few hours, they studied statements, sales receipts, and inventory lists. They shuffled and reorganized and cleaned. A few customers wandered in and purchased from the clearance table. The prices were ridiculously low, leaving almost no profit and adding to the growing sense of doom.

It was mid-afternoon when Cece checked her phone. She had two missed calls from Doug. "I'm taking a break," she said, walking out the door.

It rang four times before he picked up.

"Hey, babe."

Cece almost cried, hearing his gentle voice. "I'm sorry I was such a bitch this morning."

"It's okay. I'm sorry too."

"No." Her voice quivered. "You didn't do anything wrong."

"I kinda did. I should've known moving in was a stupid idea."

"Let's just forget it, okay?"

"Good idea," said Doug. "What's going on at work?"

Cece walked down the sidewalk to keep warm. "Complete disaster." She told him the whole story.

"You think things will get straightened out?"

"We'll see," Cece said, although she knew there was little hope of that. "What are you doing tonight?"

"Basketball with the guys. Want me to come over after?"

"Yes," she said. "I really do. I can't believe what a mess I'm in. If Patty and I lose our jobs, I don't know what we're going to do."

"It'll work out, babe. Things always do."

"Okay," Cece said. "See you tonight." She hung up. Doug was wrong. Things didn't always work out. And Cece was pretty sure The Art Stop would be one of those things.

The gallery was almost dark, illuminated only with candles. Cece put a box on the floor beside a basket of wool yarn imported from Australia. Goldie was nestled on top of the cushy mound, pushing her paws into the yarn, but Cece didn't care. She was too exhausted and depressed.

Barbara had been on the phone all day with artists telling them to come pick up their pieces. At six-thirty she locked the door. Cece looked at her boss. She felt sorry for her.

Barbara lit more candles, eyeing Mae. They were all anxious to know what the artist/accountant thought. Finally, she lifted her head. "Well…it is a mess."

Goldie stretched and meowed, then tucked her face back into the yarn.

"You're not very good at billing, are you?" Mae said.

Barbara chewed her fingernails. "I guess not."

"I went through a bunch of receipts," Cece said. "You forgot to take your percentage on a lot of the pieces we sold."

"I kind of did that on purpose," Barbara said. "The artists needed the money more than I did."

"That was sweet of you," Patty said.

Cece wanted to say, *No, that was stupid of you,* but she controlled herself.

"This is business," said Mae, "not charity work."

"Okay," Barbara said, straightening her back. "So what should I do?"

"I can help you reorganize, but I think it's smart to close at least temporarily. With some smart changes, there's a good chance you can reopen after the first of the year."

Cece's stomach dropped. She was officially unemployed. At least for a month.

Mae looked at Cece and Patty. "I'm sorry girls."

Cece couldn't respond. It was as if she'd been watching and waiting for a mountain to fall, and it finally did.

"Barbara," Mae said, "why don't you help the girls out with their Christmas shopping?"

"Oh, that's a good idea," said Barbara.

Patty sniffled. "Can I keep this blanket?"

"Take all of them." Barbara handed Patty the entire basket. "They were cheap."

"Cheap?" Cece said. "They sell for a hundred bucks."

"Huge mark-up on blankets, girls. Remember that." Barbara played Santa Claus. She gave them each a box of hand-painted ornaments, bunches of colorful bangle bracelets made of silk threads, an armload of scarves, and all the candles that were left.

Cece felt uneasy accepting the gifts, but they weren't really gifts, she reasoned. Barbara owed her over a thousand dollars, and who knew if she'd ever see a penny of it?

"Go on now," said Barbara. "Get out of here before I start crying."

It was no use. The four of them wept together for another half hour before Cece and Patty could tear themselves away. As they said their goodbyes, Mae pulled Cece to the corner and pointed to the ballerina painting.

"Oh my God," Cece said. "I forgot it was there."

Mae put it in her hands. "It's finished, my dear. And it is magnificent."

"Thank you," Cece whispered.

"Remember what I told you," Mae said, her voice soft. "It's not about the money. We just want our work to matter."

Cece nodded, blinking back tears. "I know."

She packed up all the gifts and followed Patty out into the chilly, moonless night. As she closed the door, the bells jingled, as if they were saying goodbye too.

13

*P*atty picked up the knife and sliced herself a piece of cake. They were sitting at the table in the breakfast nook with their checkbooks, calculators, and a holiday fruitcake Patty's aunt had sent for Christmas. Cece yawned. She'd had enough of numbers for one day.

Patty got up. "I'm getting some milk."

"Okay," Cece said. Her cell vibrated and flashed Doug's cute face.

"Hey," she said, her voice flat.

"How's it going?" Doug asked.

"Pretty grim." Cece heard raucous laughter in the background. "Basketball over?"

"Just finished. I'm gonna run home for a shower before I come over."

"You know what?" Cece said. "It's almost ten, and I can't keep my eyes open." As much as she wanted to see Doug, she was exhausted.

"Are you sure? I'll bring cookies."

"I would love to see you, but I'm a mess." She picked a pecan off the top of the fruitcake and ate it.

"All right. I'll call you in the morning on my way to work. I've got a photo shoot downtown."

"Really? Where?" Cece perked up. At least one of them still had a job.

"Office building. A decorator just finished some huge project in a law firm, and they want me to photograph the space."

"Oh, that's cool," Cece said. "Come over after you finish, okay?"

"Sure. You making dinner?"

"I can. Macaroni and cheese from a box most likely."

"One of my favorites," Doug said. "See you tomorrow, babe. Love you."

"Me too. 'Night."

Patty came back empty handed.

"Where's your milk?" Cece asked.

"We're out of milk."

"That's terrible," Cece said. "Let's call it a night before anything else goes wrong."

She put an arm around Patty as they headed to bed. "Maybe we'll come up with something brilliant in our dreams."

Cece slept hard for two hours, then tossed and turned the rest of the night, unable to pull herself out of a disturbing dream in which she was dressed in her Sugar Plum Fairy costume dancing around her father's living room. She had not rehearsed, and she kept making mistakes as Ilana reprimanded her for not being as good as she could be.

Cece bolted upright, shaking off the dream. She tried to go back to sleep, but there was something that kept poking at her, as if the dream were delivering a message.

And that's when the idea struck. She replayed her last conversation with Natalie over and over in her mind. Had

Natalie been serious when she offered her a job? The question buzzed around her brain like an annoying fly.

As the first ray of light peeked through the window, Cece gave up on getting any more sleep. She got out of bed and made a pot of coffee, still wrestling with the idea. The mere thought of calling Natalie made her sweat. But going up north for a few weeks was not a big deal. She could help Natalie get the show ready, make some money, and be back in time to spend New Year's Eve with Doug. She mulled over the plan and waited for Patty to get up.

Around nine, Patty emerged. Cece was on her third cup of coffee and jittery as a mouse. She told Patty what she was thinking.

"I hate it. It's a terrible idea." Patty said. "I knew that gorgeous old best friend of yours wanted you back."

"You're being ridiculous, Patty, and a little immature too."

Patty pushed out her lower lip. "I don't care."

Cece put her arms around Patty. She loved her like the little sister she never had. "Listen, you are my best friend in the whole world. Nothing's ever going to change that."

"No matter what?"

"No matter what." Cece smoothed Patty's messy hair. "The truth is, I can't even remember exactly what Natalie said the other day. And if she did say something about hiring me, she probably didn't even mean it."

"But what if she did mean it?"

"Well," Cece said, "then I go up north for a few weeks, make some money, and come home. Hopefully, Mae and Barbara will get things figured out, and in another month, everything will go back to normal."

Patty took a deep breath and exhaled loudly. "Okay. It's not like we have a ton of options."

"Yeah? Really?" Cece was relieved.

"Really." Patty got up. "What about Doug?"

"I'm calling him first, don't worry."

"Okay then," Patty said. "Do what you gotta do. I'm going to shower."

Cece watched Patty trudge off to the bathroom. She sat at the table in the breakfast nook and called Doug. No answer. She almost left a message but changed her mind. She went into her room and made her bed, picked up her dirty clothes, put them in her laundry basket. She called again. Still no answer. Cece paced in circles, wavering back and forth. What-if questions whirled in her mind. Cece fell onto her bed and groaned. "You're being ridiculous," she told herself.

Chances were nothing would come of it, so why bring Doug into the equation before calling Natalie? That made no sense at all.

Relieved he hadn't answered, Cece searched her cell phone for Natalie's number. Her hands were clammy as she pressed 'call.' She readied herself to leave a message, but Natalie picked up after the third ring. "Cece, what a nice surprise."

"Natalie, hi. Um, how's your mom doing?"

"Not bad," Natalie said. "Actually, she was good yesterday, but today's not going so well."

"You must be really busy." Cece knew she was beating around the bush, but she couldn't help it.

"Like you can't imagine. Hold on a sec. Robby! I told you those don't go there. Put them in the back, and make sure you cover them." Natalie returned. "Sorry about that."

"If it's a bad time, I can call back later."

"No, I'm just working on *The Nutcracker* and screaming at everyone. What's up?"

Cece cleared her throat. "Well, um, here's the thing. I came home to LA, you know, and it's such a long story, but where I work, the business isn't...Oh shit, Natalie, were you serious about hiring me?"

"Really?"

"I just need to work for a few weeks. The gallery's going to reopen in January, so I—"

"Oh my God, Cece, you have no idea how much I need you! When can you get here?"

"Wow," Cece said, surprised by Natalie's eagerness. "When would you want me?"

"Is today too soon?" Natalie laughed.

"Yeah, well, I have to get a few things organized, but—"

"Doesn't matter," Natalie said. "Just get here as soon as you can."

"Okay." Cece stood and started pacing again. "I guess I can pack today and drive up tomorrow."

"That's great, excellent. I can't wait. Listen, it'll be intense. *The Nutcracker* opens in just over two weeks, and we are far from ready. We'll be rehearsing late almost every night."

Cece swallowed, feeling strangely exhilarated. "That's okay. I remember how crazy it gets."

"Crazy is an understatement," Natalie said. "Gotta run. See you when you get here."

"Okay. And thanks, Natalie. You're really doing me a favor."

"Don't thank me," Natalie said. "You're my Christmas angel!"

Cece ended the call. She placed her phone on the dresser. "Wow," she said aloud. "Wow."

Patty came in wrapped in a towel and sat on Cece's bed.

Cece folded her lips together and gave her friend a thin smile.

"You got the job?" Patty asked.

Cece nodded.

"Good." Patty's voice was firm. "That's good. What did Doug say?"

Cece's heart skipped a beat. Suddenly she wasn't so sure that spending a few weeks up north really was no big deal.

"I couldn't reach him. He didn't answer."

"Oh." Patty's tone shifted. "Well, he'll probably be okay with it."

"Yeah," Cece said, twirling her hair. "He'll be fine with it. I'm...I'm sure he will."

14

"Hey," Doug said as he walked in the door. He pushed over a stack of mail and put his camera bag on the table in the entry. He took Cece into his arms and kissed her. "How did your day go?"

Her stomach had been churning for hours. "Fine, good," Cece said, thinking it was anything but. "Tell me about the shoot."

"It was great. The space was amazing."

"What did it look like?" Cece asked, although she could not have cared less.

"Well, let's see, hardly any walls, the coolest furniture you've ever seen, and huge, high windows."

Cece went to the kitchen, and Doug followed her, rambling on. "Incredible view. You could see everything from Santa Monica to the mountains. And the snow level is so low. Maybe we could go skiing next weekend."

Cece felt one eye twitch. She took two beers from the refrigerator and handed them to Doug. "Are you hungry?"

"Starving," Doug said. "Worked right through lunch."

"That's great," Cece said, slipping her hands into oven mitts.

"Great?"

Cece looked at him. "I'm sorry, what?"

"I said I worked through lunch, and you said, 'That's great.'"

"Oh, I must not have heard you." Cece tried to suppress her growing anxiety.

She put a lasagna casserole on the table along with a bowl of green salad. "I made this instead of mac and cheese. I know you love it."

"I do," said Doug. "Smells delicious."

They sat. Cece served Doug a huge portion and a small one for herself. She took a bite. The food felt like paste in her throat. She stood. "I'm going to get water. Want some?"

Doug raised his eyebrows. "Are you okay?"

"Of course I am." Cece went to the kitchen. She stood at the sink and filled a tall glass with ice and water from the tap. Guilt was chewing her up. *What was I thinking? Why didn't I talk to Doug before I made my decision?*

Cece took a deep breath to steady herself and returned to Doug. "Tell me more about the photo shoot," she said as she sat. "Who was the decorator?"

"Some big name I've never heard of. Quite the talker too."

Doug's voice filled her ears, but it was merely background noise as Cece imagined the various ways she could deliver the news.

Doug put a bite of lasagna into his mouth. "And what's even crazier is that she looked a lot like you."

Cece's head snapped up. "Who looked like me?"

Doug put his fork down and leaned toward Cece. "The decorator."

Cece forced a smile. "So, she was pretty."

"Beautiful, in a sexy older woman kind of way." Doug reached for his phone. "Here, I'll show you a picture."

A rare stab of jealousy struck. "Why on earth would you

have taken a picture of her? I mean, that's totally unprofessional."

Doug raised one brow. "Because the law partner who paid me for the photo shoot asked me to." Doug's voice was low and measured.

"Oh." Cece pushed her barely touched plate of food away.

Doug drank down the rest of his beer and put the bottle on the table with a light thump. "What's going on here?"

Cece looked down at her fingernails. She hadn't bitten them in years, but in the last week she'd returned to her old nervous habit. "Nothing. I'm sorry. I'm just anxious about not working. Patty's and my finances are not in the best shape."

"Cece, don't worry. I'll help you."

His offer made her bristle. Doug came from a family with plenty of money. He never worried like she did.

"And besides," he continued, "you said the gallery will probably reopen in a month or two. So, until it does, you should just enjoy being on vacation. We can go—"

"I got a job," Cece blurted. "A temporary job."

"Oh. Well. That's good news. What's the job?"

"Not something I ever thought I would do."

"Okay..." Doug gave her one of his adorable, crooked smiles. "Pole dancer?"

"No." Cece didn't find his joke funny. "Teaching ballet."

Doug took her hand in his. "Sounds perfect for you."

"Yeah, I know."

"Then why aren't you happier about it?"

Cece looked into Doug's eyes, full of love and concern. "It's in Clearwater."

Doug blinked. "Oh, okay."

"It's only temporary. And I'll be back before Christmas. I'm pretty sure. Or New Year's... probably."

Doug nodded. He rocked his chair back and forth. "Kind of sudden. I mean, you didn't say anything about it last night."

"It just happened today," said Cece. "I was talking to Natalie and—"

"Who's Natalie?"

Cece had never mentioned her old friend to Doug. There'd been no reason to up until now. "Natalie runs the studio where I took dance lessons when I was a kid."

Doug opened the second beer and poured some into his mouth. "Got it. Natalie, old friend, dance studio."

"Right, well, we were just catching up, and I told her about the gallery and how I was temporarily unemployed. And then she said that she was looking for someone to help her with the annual Christmas show, *The Nutcracker*, which I know like the back of my hand, and, well, she offered me a job, like, totally out of the blue." Cece looked away. She had spun the story and felt horrible.

"All right." Doug rubbed his chin. "So you said yes? Just like that?"

Cece's leg quivered. "I did. I really need the money. I'm so worried about the bills and the rent here, so yeah, I said I'd do it." Cece felt herself breaking out in a sweat. "Please don't be mad."

"I'm not mad." Doug took a deep breath. "Just surprised. When do you think you'll leave?"

"I leave...tomorrow." Cece winced.

"Tomorrow." Doug repeated what she'd said as if he had to think about what the word meant. "Tomorrow?"

Cece nodded. "Tomorrow," she whispered.

Doug stood and bumped his chair. It fell over and crashed to the floor. He picked it up and shoved it back in place. "Wow."

"I know it happened fast," said Cece, "but you know I can't stand uncertainty. I hate not knowing what's next."

Cece got up and walked over to Doug. She tried to put her arms around his neck, but he caught her wrists and stopped her. She swallowed hard. She had never seen him look so hurt.

"I don't know what to say. I mean, you give me a hard time about being impulsive, and now without even talking to me, you decide to take a job out of town for a month? That's pretty impulsive, Cece."

"This is different," Cece said, guilt making her defensive. "I didn't decide to go surfing instead of working. And this may come as a surprise to you, but I *have* to work. I don't have rich parents to fall back on whenever I run short on cash." As soon as she said the words, she regretted it.

Doug turned away. He clasped his hands over his head and walked into the living room. Cece felt panic rise in her throat.

"Doug, I'm sorry."

He turned and faced her. "I don't know what's happening with us. Two weeks ago, we were the happiest couple I knew. And now, it's like every time we're together, one of us is apologizing for some stupid thing."

"That's not true," Cece said, although it was.

"I feel like I can't get it right. Whenever I see you, I do something wrong. Ever since your birthday we've been arguing." Doug leaned on the back of the couch and pushed a hand through his hair. "And your whole, I don't know, uptightness and freaking out over everything—it's not okay."

Cece's eyes burned. Yes, she was uptight and controlling, but she couldn't help it.

"Cece, we have a great relationship. Why are you messing it up?"

His words jolted her. "Why am *I* messing it up?"

"Yeah. I get it that your plan is off track, but it's not the crisis you think it is."

Cece stiffened. "How do you know? You have no idea how upset and nervous I've been."

"I'm pretty sure I do. And it feels like you're taking it out on me because I screwed up on your birthday."

"I never said that."

Doug looked lost and completely worn out. "You might as well have."

Cece started to object then stopped herself. She had expected him to propose, and when he didn't, she flipped out. Her plan *was* off track, and she couldn't handle it.

"Maybe you're right." Cece could barely get the words out. "You know what? I won't go. I'll call Natalie and tell her I changed my mind."

"This isn't about you going to Clearwater, Cece. And if you changed your mind now, you'd end up resenting me for it."

Cece felt a pain in her jaw. How long had she been clenching it? "I would never resent you, Doug."

"You already do." Doug paced back and forth. "I just want everything to go back to the way it was."

"I do too."

"Do you really?" The question was like a slap in the face.

"I...I don't know." Cece's heart pounded. At that moment, she had no idea what she wanted.

Doug put his hands on her shoulders and gave her the saddest smile she had ever seen. "I love you more than anything in the world, but..." He looked down at her, tears in his eyes. "But you're not happy with me anymore." Doug wiped his eyes with his palms. When he looked at Cece again, his anguish was palpable.

She sank into her chair. There was no denying it—resentment or disappointment or whatever it was she felt—Cece was miserable. She reached for his hand and entwined her fingers with his. "I don't know what to do. Nothing is going the way I thought it would."

A painful and familiar ache hit Cece's stomach. It was the same ache she'd felt when her mother left and her life careened in the wrong direction. Ever since then Cece had to be in control; it was the only way to make sure she wouldn't get hurt again.

"I need to figure this out," Cece said, tears rolling down her cheeks. "There's something about me that's just, I don't know, missing."

"Maybe we both need some time." Doug withdrew his hand. "Time to think."

Cece felt her stomach drop. Time to think—a euphemism for breaking up. She wanted to say 'Stop! Wait! Don't go!' But the words stuck in her throat.

Doug studied her face, as if he were waiting for Cece to object, to take control, to tell him to stay. But she didn't.

He went to the door and opened it. He stopped, but he didn't look at her. "I don't know how I'll live without you," he said. "I just don't know."

15

*C*ece cried into her pillow until it was soaked. She turned it over and cried herself to sleep. She awoke in the middle of the night to soft knocks on her bedroom door.

"Ceece?" Patty whispered.

Cece rolled over and turned on her bedside lamp.

"Oh my God," said Patty. "You look awful. What happened?"

"We…we…broke up."

A whole new set of tears started.

Patty sat beside her. "Just because you're going up north?"

"Not just that," Cece hiccupped. "It's…it's a lot of things. Everything! And it's all my fault." She threw herself onto her pillow, sobs racking her body.

Patty curled up behind her and wrapped her into a tight hug. She held her best friend and cried alongside her.

In the morning, Cece couldn't wait to leave. The house was heavy with misery from the night before.

"This is all you're taking?" Patty pointed to Cece's small bag. "You'll be there a while."

Cece was sitting on her bed. She had dumped out her purse and was repacking it. "Don't need much. I'll be wearing ballet pants and sweatshirts most of the time." She got up and looked in the mirror that hung over her dresser. She pulled her messy hair into a ponytail and tried to wipe off the remnants of yesterday's makeup, but it was hopeless. "I look like hell."

Patty didn't contradict her. "I'll go get your coffee."

Cece took one last look in her room to make sure she had everything. On her desk, propped against the wall, was her ballerina painting. The dancer looked at Cece as if she were saying, 'Take me with you.'

A sob caught in her throat. Doug had watched her paint it. On many occasions they had gone to the beach where he set up her easel for her. Then, while she painted, he took pictures of dolphins and whales. But most of the time, he took pictures of her.

Cece picked up the painting and started to pack it, but what was the point? The picture would be there when she got home. Even though Doug probably wouldn't.

She went into the kitchen. Patty handed her a travel mug. "Drink it slowly, or you'll have to pee at that yucky gas station by the freeway."

Cece tried to laugh, but it hurt her head. "You're going home for Christmas, right? See your family?"

"I don't know, maybe."

Cece took a sip of coffee, burning her tongue. "Ouch."

Patty handed her a napkin. "You have to talk to me every single day, okay?"

"Yes, I promise."

Patty nodded. "You'd better go. It's a long drive."

"Right." Cece hugged her friend.

"And no more crying," Patty said. "It's not safe to cry and drive."

"I'm pretty sure I'm all cried out."

She squeezed Patty extra tight. It would be a lonely month.

Traffic slowed as Cece drove through the Valley. She glanced at her cell phone lying on the passenger seat. She didn't expect Doug to call, but she still wondered if he would. She was in uncharted territory and had no idea what the protocol was. She turned on the radio. An old '70s song was playing. *'I would give everything I own, just to have you back again, just to hold you once again...'*

The tears rolled down her cheeks, dripped off her chin, and soaked the front of her shirt. Cece reached into the tissue box and pulled out the entire stack.

An hour later, down one box of tissues and a tank of gas, she stopped at a gas station near Santa Barbara.

"Forty dollars on seven," she said. "And two candy bars." She pushed two twenties and a five under the bulletproof glass.

The man at the register looked at her with what Cece construed as a sympathetic smile. *God, I must really look awful,* she thought. *Even this guy feels sorry for me.*

He took the money and passed her a small amount of change.

She picked up two Snickers and went to pump her gas. Then she used a bathroom that wasn't completely disgusting and got back on the road.

In the mid-afternoon Cece took a detour. She drove through Cambria, a small town on the Pacific Ocean, and turned onto a narrow street lined with art galleries, small hotels, and exclusive shops.

She parked a block from the cliffs. It was cold and windy,

and the ocean air smelled fresh. She put on her jacket and walked along the pathway toward a beach where elephant seals had been mating and giving birth for over a hundred years.

Cece leaned on the railing. Below her, sprawled all over the sand, were dozens of seals. The small ones were the size of compact cars, and several of the males looked as if they were as big as minivans. A harem formed around the dominant male as he bellowed and thrashed to intimidate the competition.

Cece watched a fight break out between two smaller males. They appeared to be vying for a gentle looking female. She lifted her huge head and watched, as if she were wondering which suitor would win her affection.

With a sigh, Cece tore open the wrapper of her second Snickers bar. She thought it must be good to be a female elephant seal. All they had to do was eat and watch the boys fight over them.

Cece shoved the rest of the chocolate bar into her mouth, went back to her car, and continued the drive up north, the same drive she'd made less than two weeks before. How did it all go so wrong so fast?

~

It was dark when Cece pulled into the gravel driveway. Her father's over-the-top Christmas decorations lit up the entire yard. As Cece got out of the car, she saw her father walking toward her, his arms open wide. Cece fell against him.

"How you doin', sweetheart?" Phil asked.

"I'm okay."

They walked toward the house. Cece admired the lights all around the roof and winding through the trees. The silly reindeer stood on the lawn next to a couple of snowmen. "House sure looks festive, Daddy. You and Tommy did a great job."

"We did, didn't we?" Phil wrapped his arm around her. "Let's get you inside; it's freezing out here. They're even talking snow, believe it or not."

Cece smiled to herself. In awkward moments, her father always brought up the weather.

Tom was standing by the door as they walked up the steps. He had on ripped jeans and an old Cal Berkeley sweatshirt. "Hey, Sis."

"Hi, Tommy."

"You look like shit."

Cece couldn't be mad at him. "I know."

They stepped inside. Julia walked toward Cece, her arms outstretched. Her hair was scrunched on top of her head, and she wore a white apron over her red maxi dress. "Hi, sweetie," Julia said, pulling Cece into her arms. "How are you?"

"Terrible."

"I know."

Cece had called Julia before she'd left and given her the 'in a nutshell' account of what had happened.

"I hope you don't mind, honey. I told the guys about you and Doug."

"It's okay," Cece said. "Better than me having to tell them."

"Want me to get your stuff?" Tom asked.

"Thanks." Cece handed him her keys. "Be sure to lock it."

"You're back in Clearwater, Ceece. We don't lock up here."

Cece followed Julia into the kitchen. She inhaled the warm smell of something delicious. It made her hungry and sick at the same time. "What are you making?"

"Roast chicken," Julia said. "Do you feel like eating?"

It was after seven, and she hadn't eaten all day except for the two candy bars. "Kind of. Not really. I'm going upstairs to wash my face."

"Okay, honey. Let me know if you—"

Cece left the kitchen without hearing the rest of Julia's sentence.

After washing up and unpacking a few things, Cece returned to the kitchen and sat at the table where Julia put a piece of chicken and a baked potato on her plate.

Cece picked at the potato without eating it. She was wearing her purple robe over her clothes. Julia, Phil, and Tom exchanged concerned looks.

"Where's Ryan?" Cece asked, staring at her plate.

"Wednesday night dinner with his dad," Julia said.

"That's right. It is Wednesday, isn't it?" Cece took a tiny bite of chicken. Only one week ago, she had been happily preparing for Thanksgiving. Now, it seemed, her life was in shambles.

"So," Phil said, "thought we'd go get the tree tomorrow. How does that sound, baby girl?"

"Fine."

"You want to go with us, honey?" Julia asked. She ran a hand over the back of Cece's hair.

"Where?"

"To get the Christmas tree," said her father. "We can hunt for the perfect one together, just like we did when you were little."

Cece gave her dad a weak smile. "Maybe. I'm not sure. I might be at the dance studio. Natalie said rehearsals are non-stop."

More silence.

Tom cleared his throat. "So, how's Patty?"

"Almost as heartbroken as me," Cece said. She looked at her brother. "Oh. That's not what you meant, is it?"

"What do you mean?" Tom asked.

Cece put her fork down. "You're such an idiot, Tommy. We all know you have a crush on her, so quit pretending you don't."

Phil and Julia eyed each other, but they didn't say a word.

"Whoa. Where did that come from?" Tom looked at his sister.

"You act like it's a big secret. And it just, I don't know, pisses me off."

"First of all, Cece, I'll let that go because of your, whatever, broken heart. And secondly, if I did like Patty, which I don't, at least not that way, it really wouldn't be any of your business. Besides," Tom grinned at his father, "she's way too little for me. I'd probably crush her."

Cece's mind wandered back to Cambria and the gigantic male elephant seals mating with the much smaller females. She shook the image of her brother on top of Patty out of her mind. "Whatever."

Tom got up. "Anyone want a beer?"

"I'll take one," Cece said.

Tom returned from the kitchen. He flipped the caps off with a bottle opener and handed one of the beers to Cece. She took a drink, and the taste reminded her of dinner with Doug the night before. She put the bottle down, dropped her head into her hands, and sobbed.

Julia rushed to her side.

"I don't know what's happened to me." Cece blew her nose into her napkin. "I never cry like this. I'm not a crier."

Phil nodded. "That's true. You were a very low-drama teenager."

Tom shifted in his chair. "Yeah, this really isn't like you."

"I know it. I'm sorry." Cece wiped her face with her bathrobe sleeve.

"You have nothing to apologize for, baby girl. We're your family," Phil said. Tom nodded in agreement.

"And, maybe," said Julia, "when you get home after being away for a few weeks, you and Doug can sort this all out."

Cece looked up at Julia. Maybe she and Doug could recover. Couples broke up and got back together all the time. But then she pictured his devastated face as he left her house. It was an image she'd never forget. How could Doug get over the hurt she had caused?

Cece got up. "I need to go to bed. I'm sorry."

"That's fine, honey," Phil said. He stood and hugged her. Cece leaned against her father's broad chest and pushed her nose into his soft flannel shirt. He stroked her hair. "A good night's sleep is what you need. You'll feel a whole lot better in the morning. I'm sure of it."

Phil released her. Cece turned and trudged up the stairs. *If sleep can solve my problems*, she thought, *then I need to sleep for a year*.

16

*C*ece slept for thirteen hours. When she woke up, she raised her head. It felt like it had been hit by a hammer on both sides. She put her head down and went back to sleep.

It was after eleven when she dragged herself out of bed. She opened her bedroom door and bumped into Julia.

"Cece," Julia said. "How are you feeling, honey?"

"I have a little headache."

Julia reached into the linen closet and pulled out a fluffy blue bath towel. "Take something. Meds are in the cabinet. And a nice hot shower will help too." She handed Cece the towel.

"Thanks." Cece went into the bathroom. She got in the shower and stood under the hot water, letting it pound on her head and neck and back.

She got out, brushed her teeth, and examined her eyes in the mirror. They were still red, but the swelling had gone down.

Back in her bedroom, Cece lifted the window shade, and bright sunlight flooded her room. "Great." She yanked the shade down. "A cheerful, sunny day. Just what I'm in the mood for."

She put her suitcase onto the bed and opened it. She caught her breath. On top of her clothes was the wooden case holding the paintbrush Doug had given her. Lying next to it was the photo in the Tiffany frame. She hadn't packed them, so Patty must have slipped them in.

Cece looked at the picture. Seeing herself leaning against Doug as they sat on the beach made her heart feel like it was about to crack. Her eyes burned and filled with tears. She wiped them away and stuck the picture in a dresser drawer.

Cece then opened the latch on the wooden case. The paintbrush rested on a bed of black velvet. She picked it up and swept the fur over the inside of her wrist. It was a remarkable brush. She put it back into the case and placed it in a box that held all her old art supplies. Her desire to paint had vanished.

Inside her closet, Cece rifled through clothes on hangers searching for a pair of dance pants. "Ah-huh," she said, "I knew I left these here." She put on the stretchy black pants that were at least fifteen years old. They were tattered, but wearable. She layered two tank tops over her workout bra and threw a gray sweatshirt on over the tanks. After one more glance in the mirror, she picked up her purse and went to start her new job.

～

The dance studio looked empty when Cece arrived. The front doors were locked, so she walked around to the back of the building and went in through the service entrance. It opened into a narrow hallway used by the staff when the Mayfair Hotel was still in operation.

"Hello? Natalie?"

"Whoa!" A young man jumped. "Who are you?" He had a mop of dark hair that hung over his eyes and wore jeans, a green flannel shirt, and tennis shoes.

"Cece Camden. Who are you?"

"Robby Martinez." He pulled a rolling garment rack jammed with costumes out of a closet.

Cece sized him up. He was too skinny to be a dancer. "I see. Do you know where Natalie is?"

"Running an errand," Robby said, his hand on the rack. "Should be back anytime."

"Okay, well, I'm meeting her here," Cece said. "I'll just wait in the office."

"I can't let you do that."

"What do you mean?" Cece looked more closely at the young man. He could have been seventeen or twenty-five; it was hard to tell.

"I'm in charge when Natalie's out. You know, head of security."

"Security?" Cece almost laughed at him.

Robby jingled the keys hooked to his belt. "Until I receive confirmation as to who you are, I cannot unlock any doors nor allow access to restricted areas." He spoke as if he had delivered that line many times before.

Natalie came down the hall from the other direction. "Cece, you're here!" She approached with outstretched arms.

"Oh. Guess she does know you," Robby said.

Cece gave Natalie a hug. "Your head of security here takes his job very seriously."

Natalie rolled her eyes. "Head of security? Robby, I told you to quit calling yourself that."

"Yeah, but it sounds better than *gofer*."

"Sorry, but that's what you do," Natalie said.

"Fine. Where do you want these costumes? The basement is damp, and I don't want them to get mildewed," Robby said.

Cece was impressed. Security and costume care. She liked Robby already.

"Put them in the girls' changing room," said Natalie. "And after you do that, run to Nutmeg's and get two large black coffees. And you can get yourself one, *one*, cookie on my account."

"Gotcha. Be right back," Robby said, pushing the costume rack down the hall.

Natalie led Cece into the office and closed the door behind them. "Please, don't ask. He's the son of some friend of somebody around here."

"What a character," Cece said. "Real cute, but a little strange."

"Ya think?" Natalie put her bag on the desk. "He's a good worker though, and meticulous with the wardrobe."

Cece looked around Ilana Lurensky's office. "Where's your mom?"

"At home. Her condition's been up and down for a few days." Natalie opened her bag and pulled out a variety of pain relievers.

"Do you have a headache?" Cece asked.

"Not yet," Natalie said, "but by this afternoon, we both will."

Cece laughed. Natalie always had a good sense of humor.

"So," said Cece, "we should get started, right? I mean, I really have no idea what I'm supposed to do."

"Well, a little bit of everything, but I need you to spend most of your time with our Sugar Plum Fairy."

"You mean the girl I met the other day? The one with the attitude?"

"That's the one. Dawn Redmond. Fifteen years old, smart as can be, dances like a dream, and a little bit, ah, bitchy. I tried having Kendall work with her, you know, my new instructor, but that wasn't a good fit."

"I see." Cece felt hesitant already.

"I think they're too close in age, and Kendall is a very young twenty-two. She's great with little ones but not the teenagers. Anyway, don't worry. You'll be fine with Dawn."

"If you say so."

"I say so."

Natalie showed Cece a list of all the dancers and their roles in *The Nutcracker*. Cece remembered the ballet well. She had danced one part or another every Christmas from the time she was five, working her way from mouse to soldier to snowflake. At nine years old, she danced Clara, and she and Natalie shared that role, among others, for the next five years. In high school however, Cece surpassed her best friend.

"Do you remember," said Natalie, "the fight we had when my mother picked you to be Sugar Plum Fairy?"

"I'll never forget it. I said something so awful to you that I still have nightmares over it."

Natalie laughed. "All I remember is that I shoved you into the wall and got grounded for two weeks."

"You had good reason," Cece told her.

"Why?" Natalie asked. "What did you say?"

Cece hesitated, but decided what the hell, it had been fifteen years. "I said, 'Your mamma loves me more than she loves you because I'm a better dancer.' It still haunts me."

"You said that?" Natalie's jaw dropped.

Cece nodded. "I did. Took me years and a few therapy sessions to understand why I said it."

Natalie looked perplexed. "And why was that?"

"Jealousy," Cece said. "My mother I did not get along, to put it mildly, and I loved your mother so much." Cece scratched her lower lip. "For years I wished I were you."

"Well, we're even then. I can't tell you how many times I wished I were you, with your sexy, wavy hair and sparkly blue eyes."

"Oh right, and you were the ugly duckling?"

"Damn right I was," said Natalie. "All nose and braces and gangly limbs. It took me forever to grow into these feet!" Natalie held out a size ten foot to accentuate the point.

"I guess that's the plight of the teenage girl...always wishing to be somebody else."

The door opened and Robby came in with the coffees. He put them on the desk. "Anything else?"

"That's it for now. I'll track you down if I need you."

"Want me to mend those tutus?"

"Oh yeah, could you?" Natalie said. "And be sure to let Brianna's mom know when they're done. She'll be moving all the costumes over to the theater next week for dress rehearsal."

"Gotcha," Robby said. "And thanks for the snack."

After he left, Cece said, "Kind of adorable, I must say."

Natalie sipped her coffee. "Sweet kid, and he follows Kendall around like a lost dog. But from what I can tell, they never talk, only text."

"Things have changed," Cece agreed.

"And the girls? If you think we saw drama in high school, these kids have it so…"

Cece had stopped listening, thinking about her own drama over the last two days. But Natalie brought her back to the present with a tap on the arm.

Are you okay?" Natalie asked. "You look like you're about to cry."

"I'm fine."

"Cece, I don't care if it has been ten years, I can tell when something's wrong."

Cece straightened her back. "It's just the talk about drama. My boyfriend and I broke up the other night. It's too hard for me even to talk about it." Somehow, she managed to keep the tears at bay.

Natalie gave her a sympathetic smile. "Hey, I get it."

"Anyway," said Cece, "being here is what I need right now. Distance and distraction cure everything, right?"

"Absolutely, and the only thing you have time to think about now is ballet," Natalie said with raised eyebrows. "Ballet and nothing else."

17

$\mathcal{B}$y two o'clock that afternoon, a dozen little girls in tights and tutus were scurrying around the studio. Kendall Pakuri, a petite cheerleader type with long black hair and captivating black eyes, clapped her hands, trying to get the girls' attention.

Cece watched, wondering if she'd made a terrible decision. What on earth made her think she had the stamina to be a dance instructor?

"They do have a lot of energy, don't they?"

Kendall nodded. "Yes they do. And gathering them up is like herding cats."

A little Asian girl with a long braid down her back, dressed in pink from head to toe, ran to Kendall and hugged her around the waist.

"Olivia," Kendall said. "Guess what? We have a new teacher, Miss Cece."

Cece leaned down toward the little girl. "Hi, Olivia."

Olivia grinned, revealing a large gap where her two front teeth used to be. "Hi, Mith Thee-thee!"

Cece was smitten. "Are you missing some teeth?"

Olivia opened her mouth wide. "Theeth two," she put her finger into the open spot. "Thanta will bring my new oneth for Chrithmath!"

"Wow, that's exciting," Cece said.

Kendall put a hand on Olivia's back. "Let's go, cutie pie. Time to get started."

Olivia raised her hand. "Bye, Mith Thee-thee."

"Bye." Cece looked at Kendall. "Are they all that cute?"

Kendall made a sour face. "Not by a long shot."

In a whirlwind of dancing bodies and Tchaikovsky music, Cece immersed herself in learning who was who, who did what, and what needed to be done by when. She even had a moment or two, brief snips of time, when she didn't think about Doug. They were fleeting, however, and whenever thoughts of him returned, she felt a painful jolt.

It was nearly three-thirty when Cece glanced at the clock on the wall and realized that Dawn was late.

Natalie shook her head. "If she's not here in ten minutes, I'll try her cell. She's usually...oops, there she is."

Dawn Redmond sauntered into the studio. She had on the same black cap that she'd been wearing the day Cece met her.

Natalie put her hands on her hips. "You're late."

Cece flinched. How many times had she heard Ilana say that over the years?

"Sorry," the teenager mumbled. She pulled her earbuds out.

"Dawn, this is Cece Camden. She's going to work with you on your solo."

Dawn shifted her dance bag to her other shoulder. "I have to go change."

Cece inhaled nervously as she watched Dawn walk away. Natalie patted her shoulder. "Don't worry. Her bark is worse than her bite."

Cece waited for Dawn in a smaller dance room connected to the main studio. It had mirrored walls all around except for the outer wall with windows. On a table in one corner was a portable CD player. Cece popped it open. Inside was an old disk labeled "Dance of the Sugar Plum Fairy."

Cece pushed 'play.' The familiar melody of her favorite dance in her favorite ballet filled the room. She closed her eyes for a moment and relived the dance. When she opened them, Dawn Redmond was standing in front of her.

"Oh good," Cece said. "You're ready."

Dawn said nothing, and Cece tried not to stare at the tiny gem on the side of one of her nostrils. *That must've hurt*, Cece thought.

Cece looked at Dawn's feet. "Where are your toe shoes?"

A shoulder went up. "I forgot them. Sorry."

Cece chewed her lip. Kids forgot their essentials all the time. She didn't want to make a big deal out of it. "Well then, we'll have to work without them."

Dawn moaned, as if she'd hoped to get the day off, but Cece ignored it. "Start from the left so I can see your entrance."

Dawn went to the side of the room, and Cece started the music.

For thirty seconds, the teenager danced, and her talent surprised and delighted Cece. Even in her ballet slippers, her pirouettes were precise and balanced, her allegro smooth and light.

Without warning, Dawn stopped. "I need to start over."

"Okay, that's fine." Cece was about to push 'play' again, when another tune interrupted them. It was coming from Dawn's bag.

Dawn jumped. "That's my cell." She ran to get it. Cece sat in a chair and looked at her watch. She tapped her ballet-slippered feet while Dawn carried on her conversation, her back turned to Cece and her hand over the mouthpiece. When she finished her call, Dawn dropped her cell on top of her bag.

"Maybe you should turn that off until we're done," Cece

said.

Dawn gave her a look that Cece interpreted as: *Are you kidding me?*

Cece let it go. "Okay, let's start over."

This time Dawn got through about a minute of the number, again startling Cece with her grace. Then she stopped. "I really can't do it without my pointes."

Cece wanted to say something snide, but she resisted. "We'll practice hands and arms then."

Dawn leaned her head back and rolled her eyes. "Fine."

The cell phone chimed again, and Dawn ran for it. Cece sighed. She sat down and waited.

Dawn finished the call, leaned over, and picked up her bag. "I have to go."

"Excuse me?"

"My boy…um, someone's waiting outside for me."

"Dawn, we have to practice."

"I usually take Thursdays off, so…"

"The show opens in two weeks," said Cece. "It's crunch time."

Dawn gave her a pleading look. "This is really important. I promise I'll be here tomorrow."

"Fine," Cece said, letting her exasperation show. "But don't forget your toe shoes."

After Dawn left, Cece spent the rest of the day helping Kendall with the younger kids. It was dark outside when she and Natalie finished up their day. They were in the office putting on their coats when Cece told Natalie what had transpired with Dawn.

"Definitely annoying," said Natalie, "but don't worry."

"But what if she doesn't rehearse enough?" Cece finally understood why Ilana pushed them so hard before shows opened.

"I'll call her parents tonight. They're pretty good about kicking her butt when she gets lazy." Natalie took out her keys, and they walked outside. "But if she doesn't come through soon, I'll have to give the role to somebody else, somebody not nearly the dancer that Dawn is."

Part of Cece wished for it. Working with a younger, less skilled dancer, but without the attitude, would be so much easier. Besides, this was just a small-town studio production. Who would even care if the Sugar Plum Fairy couldn't do a perfect *pas de bourrée?*

Natalie locked the door. "This town is very demanding, you know. Ever since you were Sugar Plum Fairy, they expect us to put on a professional level production."

That's who would care; the entire town.

"But I have to say, you did a great job with the little kids. Boy, did they love you."

Cece smiled. She enjoyed helping the mice and snowflakes with their numbers. She even worked with the two boys who were sharing the role of Fritz.

"Are you sure I'm not better suited for working with the younger kids? I mean, other than my step-brother, I don't even know any teenagers. They're real enigmas to me."

"Let's see how it goes tomorrow. This was just your first day."

They walked down the block toward their cars. "I guess you're right," said Cece, opening her car door. "Have a good night."

"You too, Cece. Oh, and by the way, in case I haven't said it enough, I'm really glad you came back."

"Thanks," Cece said. She almost added 'me too,' but that wouldn't have been completely true.

Cece got in her car and waved to Natalie as she drove away. On Main Street, Christmas lights glimmered in every direction, and the windows in all the restaurants and shops glowed with decorations. Cece shook her head. "This town sure loves Christmas."

18

*C*ece's cell buzzed next to her ear, waking her up earlier than necessary. She glanced at the screen.

It was Patty, whom she'd forgotten to call yesterday.

"H'lo?"

"You forgot about me, didn't you?"

Cece stretched. "I'm sorry, Patty. Yesterday was crazy."

"No excuse," Patty said. "You promised me."

"You're right." Cece rubbed her eyes. "I'll try not to forget again."

"You'd better not forget again," said Patty. "So, how'd it go at the studio?"

Cece propped her pillows and leaned against them. "Some good, some not so good. My project is the Sugar Plum Fairy, and believe me, she's a project." Cece told Patty about her all-too-brief rehearsal with Dawn.

"Wow, no wonder you're so tired."

"What's going on at home?" Cece asked.

"Not much…Oh! I got a temp job at The Main Frame on 3rd."

Cece perked up. "That's great. When do you start?"

"Today. They tell me I'll be framing tons of those giant family portraits. Very popular gift this year. Can you imagine all the hideous Christmas sweaters I'll have to stomach? God, I hate those perfect-looking families."

"Somebody sure is a Scrooge today."

"It's lonely here without you." Patty paused. "Speaking of lonely, how are you doing?"

"I'm not talking about him. I cried so much for two days, I think I'm dehydrated. Anyway, I've got the perfect job for avoiding the harsh realities of my life—working with a teenager. Nothing more distracting than that."

"I'll bet," Patty said. "Listen, I've gotta run. You'd better call me tonight."

"I will," Cece said. "I promise. And be a good girl at work. Follow directions and do your best."

"Don't I always?" Patty said, a grin in her voice.

"Uh, no."

"Bye-bye." Patty made kissing noises into the phone and hung up.

Cece leaned against her cushy pillows, snuggled under her comforter, and tried to go back to sleep, but all she could think about was Doug—his smile, his laugh, his smell, his touch. Cece pulled the blanket over her head. *I will never get over this,* she thought. *Never.*

～

Cece walked from snowflake to snowflake, positioning their arms correctly. "There we go," she said. "Now, make a big circle over your heads. Remember we're in second position now. Olivia, feet apart, sweetie."

"Like thith Mith Thee-thee?" Olivia spread her feet and pointed her toes outward.

"Good job!" Cece grinned. The eight sweet little girls were

great for keeping her mind off of Doug. "Now let's bend our knees into a plié, keep it smooth, straighten, and up. Good. Again, and…excellent!" Cece clapped her hands. "Nice! Okay, quick potty break, then hurry back. Lots of work to do this afternoon with Miss Kendall."

The tiny ballerinas scattered. Cece grabbed a bottle of water and went to check in with Natalie. She found her in the office studying a large chart with dozens of colored Post-it notes, each one indicating who would dance what role in which performance.

"Boy," said Cece, admiring the chart, "that's impressive. I never realized how much work went into figuring all this out."

Natalie switched some notes around. "My mom used to sit at the dining room table late into the night with charts just like this. She'd rearrange over and over."

Cece leaned on the table, trying to put faces to some of the names. She pointed to one. "Who's Gabe Martin?"

"Our best male lead, sixteen years old and fabulous."

"Good for Cavalier, huh?"

"He's just right, and it'll help with Dawn. We have a better chance of getting her to rehearsals if she's dancing the *pas de deux* with Gabe. They've been friends for years."

Cece hoped so. The dance of the Cavalier and the Sugar Plum Fairy was one of the most intense and artistic numbers in the entire ballet.

Cece looked at her watch. "Dawn should be here soon. Did you talk to her parents?"

"I did." Natalie looked up. "They're coming to see us this afternoon."

"Okay," Cece said. "Can't wait." She was not looking forward to meeting the parents of her talented, but undependable, Sugar Plum Fairy.

~

116

Cece returned to the studio to work with the two girls who were dancing the role of Clara.

Jennifer was a classic Clara—long, blond curls, sweet smile, a splash of freckles across her nose. Her friend, Brianna, was the opposite, an exotic beauty, with dark skin, green eyes, and black hair down to her waist.

Both were excellent dancers, and Cece enjoyed teaching them. They followed her every instruction, and imitated her positions and movements. Cece wished she could pass Dawn off to somebody else and coach the younger girls. In spite of that, she kept checking the clock, worried Dawn might not show.

Her cell chimed with a text from Natalie that Dawn's parents had arrived.

Cece turned off the music. "Okay, you two. I need to meet with Miss Natalie. While I'm gone, practice Clara's dance with the nutcracker again."

"Again?" they said in unison.

"Yes, again," Cece said, handing Jennifer and Brianna each a wooden nutcracker. She recalled the endless number of times she rehearsed the same dance. "And then again and again and again."

Cece headed to the office. The door was open. A man and woman sat in front of the desk, their backs to the door.

Natalie raised her chin. "Oh good, here's Cece."

The couple turned. Cece's stomach dropped. Heat permeated her body and she felt her face flush. Dawn's father was the man who had spilled her coffee at Nutmeg's.

"Hi." Cece managed to squeak out the one word.

The man's face registered instant recognition. He wore a dark suit with a white dress shirt and a tie loosened around his neck.

"This is Cece Camden," said Natalie. "She just started working with Dawn."

The man stood, extending his hand. "Brad Redmond," he said, a smile playing on his lips. His touch flustered her.

"Nice to meet you," Cece said, trying to hide her awkward reaction.

Dawn's mother stood. "I'm Pam."

Cece forced her eyes off Dawn's father onto the mother. She was stunning, with short blond hair and skin the color of pink rose petals. It took only a moment for Cece to notice a substantial diamond on her left hand.

"Hi, Pam," Cece said, shaking her slender hand. "Dawn is a lovely dancer. Very talented."

"Thank you, Cece," said Pam. "I appreciate your saying so... under the circumstances." Pam's voice was gentle and sincere, and Cece felt an instant rapport. What a slime her husband was.

"I'm sorry she's been so unreliable." Pam clasped her hands in front of her chest and turned to Natalie. "May I look at your chart?"

"Of course." Natalie got up and joined Dawn's mother.

Brad Redmond moved to the couch. He crossed his legs and nodded to Cece. "Pleasant surprise," he said, his voice low.

Cece returned the vague smile and went to stand beside Natalie. She tried to focus on the chart, but with the handsome *married* man who had asked her out to dinner sitting only a few feet away, she had trouble concentrating.

"Dawn's your only Sugar Plum Fairy," Pam said, pointing to the chart. "I feel terrible."

"We need her," Natalie said, motioning for Pam to sit on the couch. "I don't have another dancer for the role. At least not one nearly as accomplished as Dawn."

Dawn's father leaned forward, his elbows on his knees. He looked serious. "When she is here, is she focused? Does she work hard?"

Natalie looked at Cece. "What do you think?"

"Oh, um..." Cece reached for a curl but stopped herself. She needed to be professional and poised. "I've only worked with

Dawn one time, and just for a few minutes. She left when her boyfriend called."

"Her boyfriend?" Brad Redmond looked at his wife. "What boyfriend?"

Cece flinched. "Maybe it wasn't a boyfriend. It could have been just a school friend. The music was on, and I probably misunderstood." She squirmed, and she felt a drop of perspiration roll down her back.

"It's all right," Pam said. "There is no boyfriend."

Brad frowned. "Are you sure about that, because—"

"Brad," Pam interrupted him. "I'm sure. She spends way more time at my place than at yours."

Two homes? Cece glanced at Brad Redmond's left hand. No ring. Maybe she had misjudged.

Brad tightened his jaw. "Fine."

Pam's cell vibrated in her hand. She looked at it. "Dawn's here," she said, holding up the text. "I told her we'd be in the office."

"Good." Brad stood. "Let me handle this, Pam."

Cece didn't know if she liked his take-charge attitude. Perhaps he spent too much time in court being the boss. In this situation, though, she hoped it would work.

Dawn walked through the door. Her eyes widened when she saw her father. "Daddy? What are you doing here?"

Brad looked at his watch. "The question is what are you doing showing up over an hour late?"

Cece could tell Dawn felt trapped. She knew what it was like to be a teenager with a messed-up family. Her disapproval of Dawn lessened.

Brad walked over to his daughter. He put a hand on her shoulder. "This is very simple, Dawn. You either want to dance in the show or you don't. Tell us now, because if you choose not to, Natalie needs to find a replacement."

"Your dad's right, sweetie," said Pam. "You can't leave everyone hanging."

Dawn hung her head and picked at her black nail polish.

"On the other hand," her father continued, "if you choose to stay in the production, you will show up to rehearsals on time, dressed, and ready to go. You will give a hundred and ten percent. And if you don't do what's expected of you, I guarantee the consequences will be very unpleasant."

The room was silent, and Cece could hear her own heartbeat.

"Can I have a day to think about it?" Dawn asked, looking at her mother.

Cece held her breath. Every minute counted at this point. She looked toward Natalie who, she could tell, was thinking the same thing.

"Absolutely not," her father said. "The show opens in a matter of days, and from what I understand, the clock is ticking. I'm not going to lecture you, Dawn. You already know how I feel about commitments."

"But I—" Dawn started.

"Nah-uh." Her father stopped her. When he tightened his lips, Cece noticed the dimple near his mouth.

"Tell you what: your mom and I will step out so you can talk to your instructors. We'll be back in five minutes. If you have not decided by then, I'll decide for you. And I'll do it by flipping a coin." Brad motioned to Pam to come with him. "I highly doubt you want to leave such an important decision to chance."

Dawn's parents left the office, and the tension in Cece's body loosened.

"Do you have any questions?" Natalie asked. She stood a head above Dawn and looked down at her. Cece admired how intimidating her friend could be.

"Can I see the rehearsal schedule again?"

"Of course." Natalie pointed to the white board where she

had outlined daily rehearsals down to the smallest detail. Cece knew Dawn had to be at the studio almost every waking minute.

As Dawn studied the board, Cece watched her, intrigued. Her impertinent expression faded, giving Cece a flicker of hope.

At the five-minute mark, Dawn's parents re-entered. "Have you decided?" Brad Redmond asked.

"I think so. Can I talk to you outside for a second, Daddy?"

They stepped out. Pam sat on one of the chairs. She folded and unfolded her hands. "How's your mother, Natalie? Still fighting that bug?"

Natalie shifted. "She's better, thanks. Should be back soon."

Cece bit her lip. There was so much to worry about, she didn't know what to worry about first.

"That's good," Pam said. "Tell her we all miss seeing her."

The clock on the wall ticked as the minutes passed. Cece's anxiety level rose steadily.

"To be honest," Pam blurted out, "we're having a little trouble at home too. This business with Dawn isn't, well, a complete surprise."

Cece shrank. They were approaching the too-much-information point.

But Natalie leaned forward. "What's going on?"

Pam fidgeted with her large diamond. "My husband's two sons moved in with us. They're young and, well, incorrigible, so Dawn wants to spend more time at her dad's."

Cece was bowled over by Pam's openness. She chewed her lip. Definitely TMI.

"That is difficult," Natalie said.

"But," Pam continued, "Brad is out of town with work so much, it's just not feasible. And besides, our custody agreement is—"

"Pam," Natalie interrupted. "You don't need to explain. We understand, don't we, Cece?"

"Absolutely," Cece said. And boy, did she ever.

Pam looked tearful. "Maybe Brad and I can figure out a..."

The door opened, and Pam closed her mouth. Dawn and her father came back, their expressions giving nothing away. Cece squeezed the arms of her chair.

"What did you decide, honey?" Pam asked.

"I'll dance," Dawn said quietly.

Cece relaxed her hands and let her knuckles crack.

Relief washed over Natalie's face. She walked up to Dawn, getting a little closer than necessary, just like Ilana used to do. "I'm glad, Dawn, thank you. Now, you have a lot of work to do, so go get ready. You'll be here late tonight."

Dawn nodded. She picked up her dance bag and walked out the door.

"If there's any problem, Natalie," Brad said, "let me know." He folded his jacket over his arm. "Nice meeting you, Cece. Good luck with my daughter."

Cece watched the man leave, his ex-wife following him. More small-town intrigue—Patty would love it.

19

Cece rehearsed with Dawn until after dark and drove home in an exhausted trance. Only two days in Clearwater, and already she was overwhelmed.

Meeting Brad Redmond, or re-meeting him, had been unexpected, to say the least. It rattled her. What would happen if they crossed paths again? Did she need to explain why she was back in Clearwater? She had no obligation to, but she did want to avoid confusion. Already people were gossiping about the return of Cecilia Rose. The mothers in the dance studio figured out who she was in less than two days. She had heard whispers in the locker room about 'Miss Natalie's old rival.' It was important to Cece that everyone understood she was in Clearwater only temporarily. As soon as the show closed, she'd be headed home to LA.

∼

Phil put a grilled cheese sandwich and a mug of tomato soup on the kitchen table in front of Cece. "Here you go."

"My favorite comfort food. How'd you remember that?"

"You have any idea how many years you survived on nothing but grilled cheese? The soup I could change up now and then, but not the grilled cheese."

Cece took a bite and savored the smooth, gooey mouthful. "So good." She hadn't realized how hungry she was until she started eating. "Sorry I kept you up so late."

"Don't mind at all." Phil sat across from her. "Can you believe I haven't gotten the tree yet? Tom and I have been slammed at work, but I'm going tomorrow for sure. Getting a blue spruce, real big one."

"Sounds nice." Cece sipped at her soup and felt the hot liquid run down her throat.

"Julia and Ryan will decorate with us, okay?"

Cece looked at her father. "Of course they will. Why are you telling me that?"

Phil scratched the back of his head. "I don't know. I just want everything here to be the way you're used to it—make you feel like you're sixteen again."

Cece choked. "Dad, the last thing I'd ever want to be is sixteen again." She thought about what Natalie had said about all the current drama around the dance studio. "I have no desire to relive any part of my teen years."

Phil patted Cece's hand. "I understand. You want more soup?"

Cece stretched, cracking her neck and back. "No. Thanks for dinner." She got up and went to stand behind her father, leaning over his shoulders. "I am so happy to see you happy, Dad. You deserve it more than anyone."

Phil squirmed. "Don't you go getting all mushy on me. Most important thing in the world to me is still my kids, no matter how big you and your brother are."

Cece kissed her father's scruffy cheek. "I know that. I've known that my entire life."

She dragged herself upstairs. In the bathroom, she filled her childhood tub with hot water and bubble bath. The lavender scented bubbles foamed. Cece stepped in and sank into the water.

"Ahhh," she said. She leaned her head on the terrycloth pillow, closed her eyes, and imagined the music. She was the Sugar Plum Fairy once again, dressed in her favorite lilac tutu and satin bodice with nude tights and pointes. Her hair was fastened into a bun so tight it pulled her eyebrows back. Oh how she danced, flying as if she had wings. She was sixteen years old, and time melted away...

"Oh shit!" Cece woke when her head dropped forward and she inhaled a nose full of bubbles. She sputtered and jumped out of the cold water, shivering, and wrapped herself in a towel. Her fingers and feet were creased like road maps.

Cece put on her pajamas, got into bed, and passed out. She'd been asleep only a few minutes when her cell chimed. "Oh no." She answered, trying to sound wide awake. "Patty, hi."

"You forgot about me again."

"No, no I didn't. I was just going to call you." Cece glanced at the clock. It was almost midnight.

"Liar," Patty said.

Cece sat up. "You will never believe what happened today." She fluffed up her pillows and regaled Patty with the whole story about her surprise encounter with the man from the bakery and whose father he turned out to be.

"I can't believe Mr. Sticky-buns is that nightmare teenager's father."

"She's not such a nightmare," Cece said. "And please don't call him that."

"I'm calling him that. Live with it. Sheesh, you weren't kidding about small towns. Not safe for a minute there, are you?"

"No. It's crazy," Cece yawned. "I'm so tired, Patty. Talk tomorrow?"

"Wait," Patty said. "I have something important to tell you."

Cece's heart skipped. "Did we get another rent increase?"

"No, nothing like that. It's about Doug. He came by today."

That woke her up. "He did?"

"He did. He left his camera here the other night."

Cece remembered. It had been on the entry table beside the front door with thousands of dollars' worth of equipment in it. Doug never let it out of his sight. Whenever they'd gone anywhere, if it was in his truck, he took it with him—into restaurants, movie theaters, friends' houses. He never forgot it. At least not until the other night.

"He was a mess, Ceece. I'm sorry to tell you, but I just feel like I have to."

Cece felt her eyes sting. "It's okay. Did you talk?"

"A little. He looked like he hadn't slept in days. Anyway, and this was really weird, he went and stood in the doorway of your room for like five minutes."

That was strange. "Do you know why?"

"No," said Patty. "I've never seen anyone look so sad."

Cece had thought she had no tears left. But she had plenty. "Then what happened?" she asked, wiping her eyes.

"He lifted his camera bag and put it on his shoulder, you know, the way he always does, with a little twist of his neck?"

A sob caught in her throat. She could picture the exact movement Patty described.

"I think he was about to leave, but then he stopped, like something occurred to him all of a sudden, and he went back into your room and picked up your painting of the ballerina face."

"Rea...really?"

"Uh-huh. And he took it with him."

Cece felt a chill run down her back.

"I hope you're not mad, Ceece. He told me to ask you if it was okay, and if it's not, he'll bring it back. Do you want me to tell him to bring it back?"

Cece wiped her face. She reached for a tissue and blew her nose. The tears slowed. She was surprised how content she felt knowing that her painting was with Doug. And that he was with it. "No, no it's fine. It's good."

"Are you sure?"

"Yeah. Actually, I want him to have it."

Cece didn't pay attention to the rest of the conversation. She said goodnight to Patty, got out of bed, and padded to her dresser. She opened the drawer and removed the picture in the Tiffany frame. In the dim light, she studied the beloved photograph. She smiled at the way her body folded into Doug's, her back against his chest. She could feel Doug's arms around her, his lips on her neck, his kiss on her shoulder. An inkling of hope lit up inside her. The fact that Doug wanted her painting meant that there was still a chance. She knew it in her heart. They loved each other, and maybe this time apart was what they both needed to realize that their relationship was worth saving. She would call him in a day or two. They would talk everything over, and then, as soon as the show ended, she'd go home. She and Doug would be reunited in time to celebrate Christmas together. There would be a fresh start.

20

"*D*awn," Cece said, practically shouting over the strains of Tchaikovsky. "You're the Sugar Plum Fairy welcoming Clara into the Kingdom of Sweets! Show the audience what kind of queen you are."

They had been rehearsing for hours in the main studio, and Dawn's talent continued to impress Cece. However, she had no warmth in her smile, no glint in her eyes. Her facial expressions were non-existent.

Dawn stopped dancing. Her hands flopped to her sides and her shoulders drooped. "How am I supposed to do that?"

Cece sighed. She herself had wondered the same thing the first time she had the role. "You have to figure out what you want to convey, just like every dancer who has ever danced this part. I only know how I did it."

Dawn frowned. "You danced this part?"

Cece studied Dawn for a moment. "Of course I did." She turned off the music, opened two bottles of water, and handed one to Dawn. "I grew up dancing here. Miss Ilana was my instructor for ages."

"She was?"

Cece nodded. It surprised her that Dawn didn't know who she was. Everyone else did. "Miss Ilana was the greatest dance teacher in the world."

Dawn sipped her water. "We don't see much of her anymore."

"I know." Cece tipped her head back and drank some water.

"She scares me," Dawn said.

Cece snickered. "Hey, she used to scare me too. Dance instructors have to be intimidating. I think I need to work on that."

Dawn laughed. It was the first time Cece had heard her laugh, and it sounded sweet and girly. "Yeah, you really aren't intimidating at all."

"Guess I'm going to have to get tougher."

"Oh my God!" Dawn's eyes grew wide as she looked past Cece.

Cece turned. A teenage boy stood in the doorway. His lip was split, and blood dribbled from a gash near his eyebrow.

Dawn ran to the boy. "Gabe! Again?"

Cece was awestruck. Her Cavalier had arrived. Even with a damaged face, he was perfect—tall, muscular, dark skin, and piercing eyes. She dismissed his beauty and focused on his injuries. "What happened?"

Gabe looked at her. He tried to smile but winced when it stretched open the cut on his lower lip. His tongue touched the blood.

"Gabe, this is our new instructor, Cece, the one I told you about."

"Hi," he said, touching the back of his hand to his lip.

"Were you in a fight?" Cece asked.

"Kinda."

"Stay here." Cece went in search of Robby. She found him cleaning cubbies. "Robby, quick! I need the first aid kit."

"Who's hurt?"

"My Cava—I mean Gabe."

"Gabe?" Robby opened a cabinet. He grabbed the kit and followed Cece to the dance room.

"Whoa!" Robby gaped at him. "They got you good this time."

"Hey, Robby." Gabe wiped blood off his chin with his shirt sleeve. "Same ol' bullshit." Gabe glanced at Cece. "Sorry."

"That's okay," Cece said, dismayed to realize male dancers were still bullied. "I guess some things never change." She opened the kit and dabbed the cut on Gabe's eyebrow with antiseptic.

"Did you fight back?" Dawn asked.

Gabe laughed without smiling. "Hell, yeah. Got that douchebag right in the balls." His eyes went to Cece. "Sorry."

"Man," said Robby, "wish I could go back to school and be your bodyguard."

"Thanks Robby, but I got at least twenty pounds on you. Besides, I have Ryan on my side."

Ryan? That name caught Cece's attention. *My step-brother?*

"Yeah," Dawn said. "Ryan's usually with him."

Another fascinating conversation. They talked like Cece wasn't even in the room, which was both disturbing and fruitful.

"Listen to you," Robby said to Dawn. "Still like him, don't you?"

"Kind of," Dawn said. A shy smile crept over her face, and she lifted a shoulder toward her chin.

Jesus Christ, Cece thought. *No mistaking that body language. My Sugar Plum Fairy has a crush on my little brother.*

Cece cracked the instant cold pack. "Put this on your lip for a few minutes. Then we need to get back to rehearsing."

"You're making Gabe rehearse?" Dawn said. "He can't dance."

"Yes I can," Gabe stood up. He looked in the mirror. "I look pretty tough with this scrape by my eye, don't you think?"

Cece smiled. Maybe coaching teenagers wouldn't be so bad after all.

~

As the sunlight faded, so did Dawn and Gabe. Even Cece felt as if she'd been walking on rocks. But her mood was uplifted, heartened by the hard work of her students and the knowledge that Doug had wanted her painting. It was a sign. They would work everything out and get back together.

Cece looked at her Cavalier and her Sugar Plum Fairy. "Great work, you two."

"Are we done?" Dawn asked.

"Done for today," Cece said. "You're a trooper, Gabe, and a great dancer."

"Thanks." Gabe yawned and then yelped. "Is my lip bleeding again?"

Cece looked. "Just a bit. You'd better ice it more when you get home."

"Can we have tomorrow off? It's Sunday." Dawn stretched her shoulders, arching her lithe body.

"No," said Cece, "but let's sleep in. We'll start at eleven, how does that sound?"

"Good," Dawn said. She picked up her bag. "Oh hi, Daddy."

Cece turned. Brad Redmond was standing in the doorway. "Hi, sweetie."

Dawn's father gave Cece a nod. "Nice to see you again." He turned his attention to the kids. "Gabe, Jesus, what happened?"

"It's nothing, Mr. Redmond. Just a scrape."

Brad lifted Gabe's chin. "You'll have a fat lip there. Looks to me like a right hook caught your face."

"He's fine, Daddy," Dawn said. "You can drive Gabe home, right?"

"Sure." Brad put a hand on Gabe's shoulder. "Keep icing it.

It'll feel fine in the morning. Now, go get your stuff, you two. Car's out front."

"See you tomorrow," Cece said as the two teenagers left.

Brad put his hands in his pockets and rocked on his feet. "So…"

Cece picked up some CDs, averting her eyes from his handsome face. "So…" she repeated.

"So," he said again. "I had Chinese for lunch yesterday, and my fortune said I should prepare for an unexpected event. I believe your appearance might be that event."

Cece brushed some hair off her face. "Have to admit, you were quite a surprise as well."

They both smiled.

"Dawn did well today," Cece said, breaking the uncomfortable silence. "We finally connected, I think. I hope. She's a lovely dancer."

"I agree, but of course I'm biased." Brad took a step toward her. "I, uh, hope you don't mind my asking, but weren't you going back to LA?"

"Oh, I did. But I came back…obviously." Cece's hands grew clammy. "I'm an old friend of Natalie's. She's the one I was meeting the other day, you know, the day when we, uh, had coffee."

"I remember."

"Anyway," Cece said, "it's a long story, but I'm here just for a few weeks to help open *The Nutcracker*, and then I'm going home. Again."

"Well then, on behalf of the dance families, thank you. The Christmas show is very important around here."

"Yes, I am aware."

Brad smiled. "I'd better go see what those kids are up to. Get 'em home for dinner."

"Okay." Cece recalled Patty's nickname for him, Mr. Stickybuns, and she suppressed a smile. "See you next time."

Brad raised his chin. "I hope so."

Cece drove home wondering what Brad meant. He'd already asked her out once, and she'd turned him down. Still, he was a charmer.

She pulled into the driveway as Phil, Tom, and Ryan were sliding the Christmas tree out of the back of Tom's truck.

"That tree is gigantic," Cece said, getting out of her car.

Tom lifted the upper half and eased it off the truck bed while Phil and Ryan caught it and set it on the ground.

Julia came out and stood on the porch. She had on cowboy boots, jeans, and a green, crocheted poncho. "How on earth will that ever fit in the house, Phil?" Julia asked. "It's too tall."

Phil put his hands on his lower back and stretched. "Nope. Eleven feet, ten inches. You think I'd buy a tree without measuring it?"

Cece smiled. Her father never went anywhere without a tape measure. She walked up the steps and gave Julia a kiss on the cheek. "This is going to be fun to watch."

Julia put an arm around Cece's waist.

"You seem better."

"I am." She thought about her plan to go home and reunite with Doug. "I think Doug and I might work things out," she whispered. "I'll tell you about it later."

Julia gave her a quick squeeze. "Can't wait."

After dinner, they went into the living room to start the decorating process.

"Come on, come on everyone," Phil said. "Let's go. Tom, fill the stand with water."

"You want me to get the corn syrup?" Julia asked.

"Corn syrup?" Cece said.

Phil scratched his head. "I don't think so. Causes nothing but trouble."

Tom looked at his sister. "Last year Boomer kept drinking the sugar water, and he gained like three pounds."

Cece laughed. "Boomer, come here you silly boy." She rubbed the dog's face and kissed his nose.

Listening to Kenny Loggins belt out "Celebrate Me Home," the Camden family decorated their tree. The aroma of fresh pine filled the house, and for the first time since she'd arrived in Clearwater three days ago, Cece felt herself unwind. Rehearsals were going relatively well, and she had a definitive plan for fixing everything with Doug.

He missed her every bit as much as she missed him. She would call tonight and apologize for everything—her impatience, her control-freakishness, her hang-ups about money, and her outburst the night of her birthday. They both were still young, and there was plenty of time to think about marriage over the next few years.

Phil pulled strands of tiny white lights out of a box and wound them in and around the tree branches while the rest of them hung ornaments. With the five of them working, it took less than an hour.

"Okay, Ry," Phil said. "Light her up."

Ryan plugged in the light string, and the tree lit up, turning the room into a magical wonderland.

"Oooh," they all said.

"It is so beautiful!" Julia said, sliding her hand inside Phil's arm.

Cece felt an emotional tug at the sight of her family and their sparkling tree. It stood in front of a tall picture window, and visitors would see it before they even came inside. The Camden Christmas tree was always perfect, bursting with lights, colors, and dozens of ornaments set in between shimmering gold, ivory, and cranberry ribbons. There was a story behind each one.

Julia went to the kitchen and came back with coffee and

Christmas cookies. "Fresh baked," she announced. The men wasted no time devouring most of them.

"Hey! I want one," Cece said. She was sitting on the floor leaning against Boomer, using him as a backrest.

Ryan picked up a gingerbread Santa and brought it to her. "Here, Cece." He sat down beside her. Boomer lifted his head as if to see who had joined the dog pile. He gave Ryan a sniff and went back to sleep.

"Thanks, Ry," Cece said, biting off Santa's leg.

Julia started organizing the empty boxes. "Oh wait. What's this?" She opened a small box and removed a pink, blown-glass ballerina.

"Wow," Cece said. She hadn't seen the ornament in years, not since her mother had left.

Julia handed it to her, and Cece held it up by its string. The ballerina spun and shimmered in the light. "I'd forgotten all about this."

"It's nice," Ryan said. "Where'd you get it?"

"It was a gift." Cece felt a rush of emotion. "Given to me the first time I danced the role of Clara. I was nine." Cece realized that twenty years had passed. A lifetime. "I remember being so scared. I'd never danced a solo before." She looked at Ryan. "On opening night, I freaked out."

"You did?"

Cece nodded. "I did. So my dance teacher, Miss Ilana, asked me what I was afraid of, and I told her I was scared I'd disappoint her."

"But I thought you were a good dancer," Ryan said.

Cece laughed. "I was good. And I had practiced for months, but I still was really scared." Cece smiled at the sweet memory. "Miss Ilana said the only way I could disappoint her would be if I refused to dance. So, I just went out there and danced."

"I bet you were fabulous," Julia said.

"Not even close. I missed steps and even tripped over my

own feet at one point, but I kept going." Cece pictured herself pirouetting across the stage. She touched the delicate tip of the ballerina's toe shoe. "Then after our last performance, Miss Ilana gave me this ornament. I can still hear her saying, in that thick Russian accent, 'Cecilia Rose, you make me proud, so very proud.'"

"That's a good story, Sis," said Tom.

"It is, isn't it?" Cece got up and stood beside the tree. She lifted a branch and hung the ornament next to a little wooden nutcracker, the perfect spot for her pink ballerina.

21

*L*ater that night, Cece sat on the couch with Boomer curled up next to her, his head resting in her lap. The Christmas tree lit up the room, and the glass ballerina, catching the warm air from a heating vent, danced in the glow of the tiny lights. Cece picked up her cell, put it down, picked it up again. Her palms were damp, and her heart thumped. She hadn't spoken to Doug in four days, not since he'd walked out of her house leaving his camera behind. She placed the call and held her breath.

I'm being ridiculous, she told herself. *I know he wants me to call him, I know he does…*

"Hello?"

Cece gripped her phone. "It's me."

"Cece. Is everything okay?" His voice was low and a little shaky.

"Yeah," Cece fought back her tears, "sort of, not really. I, um, I just wanted to talk to you." Her voice cracked, and it was useless trying not to cry. Good thing she always had a box of tissues with her lately.

"Don't cry, Ceece."

Cece could tell by the raspy tone in Doug's voice that Patty was right. He wasn't doing well.

"I wanted to tell you, that…that I'm sorry." She took a trembling breath. "I'm sorry for everything I did."

"Please, Cece, stop. It's okay."

"Patty told me she saw you. She said you're not doing well."

"I'm not. It's been the worst week of my life."

"Me too, Doug. And when Patty told me that you took my painting, I just knew that…" she couldn't get the words out between her sobs.

"I'm glad you called."

"You are?"

"Yeah. I was going to call you."

"Really?" Her shoulders quivered.

"I need to tell you something."

"Okay." Cece's body tensed up. She put a hand over her eyes and willed him to say the words that would bring them back together.

"I'm going away."

Those were not the words.

"What?"

"I got a job, a photography job, with a nature magazine. You know it's what I've always wanted to do."

That was true. He had told her the very first time they met that he wanted to photograph animals in their natural habitats. "Where are you going?"

"Central America. We're starting in Costa Rica."

Cece looked at the lights on the Christmas tree. They appeared to be moving and looked like little white fireflies. She put her free hand across her stomach, feeling ill.

"Are you still there, Ceece?"

She cleared her throat. "I'm here."

"I can't stay in LA anymore, Ceece. It's too hard without you. And I need to figure some things out, you know?"

She wanted to beg him not to go. "How long will you be gone?"

"Couple of months, maybe more. If the publisher likes the series, we'll move to another location. I'm going to see the rainforest, babe, take pictures of insects and birds and…"

"Monkeys," Cece said. "You'll see lots of monkeys." She gave up trying to stifle her tears.

"I'm sorry you're so sad. It's killing me that we're apart, but I need to do this."

"I know," Cece said between hiccups. "It's just I was hoping that…that after I got home, we'd be able to go back, you know, to the way things were before my…" She could not continue.

"Please don't cry, Ceece. The truth is, if we were together I never would've considered the job. So, I don't know, in some twisted way, maybe the timing was right."

Cece tried to imagine what her life would be if only she could turn back time, undo one thing, change one decision. "You'll miss Christmas."

"I don't really care about Christmas this year."

Cece took a deep breath. She didn't really care about it either, not anymore. She got up and unplugged the Christmas tree lights.

"It's great you're doing this, Doug," she said, steadying her voice. "I mean it. It's always been your dream."

"Cece?"

"Yeah?"

"About the painting. I shouldn't have taken it, but for some reason when I saw it in your room, I just wanted it. I watched you paint it, and I loved the story that inspired it, you know?"

"I do know."

"I'll drop it off at your house before I leave."

"No," said Cece. "Don't. I want you to keep it."

"You do?" Doug sounded shocked. "Are you sure?"

"Yes. I'm completely sure." Mae's words swam in Cece's

mind. She wanted her work to matter, and it mattered to Doug. "Take it with you."

Cece could hear Doug's shallow breathing, and she pictured his face fighting back tears. Her handsome, masculine man was as heartbroken as she was, maybe more.

"You stay safe now, promise me," Cece said, her tone firm.

"I will."

"I hope you have an amazing time, Doug." She sniffed and dragged the back of her hand under her nose. "I really do."

"God, Ceece, this hurts so much."

"I'll always love you."

"Me too." Doug's voice broke.

"Bye," she whispered, ending the call.

In front of her eyes, the door to her chosen path in life closed, leaving Cece in darkness.

22

ece walked into the office and fell in a chair across from the desk. Natalie gave her a crooked smile. "Are you hung over?"

"I wish," Cece said, sipping on her third cup of coffee.

"Bad night?"

"Didn't sleep, that's all," Cece said. "I'll be fine."

Natalie gave her a worried frown. "Are you sure?"

Cece nodded. "I just want to work. Nothing else. Just work."

"Okay, then." Natalie turned her laptop around and showed Cece the calendar for the month. Every day was jammed. "Today's December fourth, and the show opens on the sixteenth. It's crunch time."

Only twelve days until opening night. Cece shook her head and tried to clear it. "Not much time, is there?"

Natalie rubbed her forehead. "No. If only my mother could help. Did you see her when you came in?"

"I didn't. I came through the back door."

"She's probably in the front," Natalie said.

Cece leaned on the desk. "Does she know I came back? That I'm working here?"

"I've told her every day, several times a day, so she should."

Cece hoped so. She hadn't seen Ilana since her visit the day after Thanksgiving. Just then, the door opened, and Ilana walked in.

"Vhere is my record, Natalia?"

"I have it, Mamma." Natalie took an album out of a drawer and handed it to her mother. It was in its original cover, the same one that Cece remembered from when she was a little girl.

"Look who's here, Mamma," Natalie said. "It's Cece."

Ilana turned.

"Good morning, Ilana," Cece said. She stepped forward and kissed Ilana on both cheeks.

Ilana looked confused.

"Mamma," Natalie said, "Cece's here to help with the show. Remember?"

Ilana nodded her head slowly, a slight smile formed on her lips. "Ah, yes. You are my Sugar Plum Fairy, Cecilia."

"Not exactly, Ilana. I'm coaching Dawn Redmond. She's our fairy this time." Cece felt her headache worsen. "She's a very good dancer. You'll be pleased."

"But I put Cecilia Rose on zee board," Ilana said. She went to the chart and began rearranging Natalie's sticky notes.

"Let's get the record player, Mamma, so that we can listen to the album." Natalie gently took her mother's hands off the chart and put the notes back where they belonged. "Cece would love to hear the old record we used to use, wouldn't you, Cece?"

"Sure."

As they walked, Cece watched Ilana. Her steps were short, unsteady, and she leaned heavily on Natalie's arm. It pained Cece to see how frail she'd become, seeming much older than her sixty-eight years.

Natalie opened the large closet just off the main studio. She pulled out the cart with the old turntable and speakers and rolled it across the room. As she passed by Cece she whispered, "Don't worry. She'll snap out of it."

Cece wasn't worried, just exhausted. She'd had three hours of sleep, maybe, and those were on the couch, sandwiched between the cushions and Boomer. She wondered where she could find Natalie's supply of headache remedies.

One of the French doors opened, and Teresa, Brianna's mother, walked in followed by Kendall, who was holding a costume wrapped in plastic.

"Good afternoon, everyone!" said Teresa. Her black hair was piled on top of her head in a tight bun, and she wore her signature flannel shirt and Levis. "Oh, my goodness, Ilana, how nice to see you. Did you have a nice trip?"

Ilana looked at her daughter. "Vhere did I go?"

Cece's eyes darted from Teresa to Natalie. Ilana looked confused.

"Nowhere, Mamma. You had a bad cold and stayed home for a while."

Teresa frowned. "Didn't you say she was out of town? Somebody said she was out of town."

"No. She just had a stubborn cold, that's all," Natalie said.

Kendall coughed loudly. "I think I'm catching it too."

Bad actress, Cece thought, but at least she's trying to help.

Natalie flashed an appreciative smile in Kendall's direction. "Thanks for getting the costumes, Teresa. How did they turn out?"

"Fabulous," Teresa said. "I brought in one of the snowflakes to show you." She took the costume from Kendall, lifted the plastic, and shook it out. Then she fluffed up the edges of the sparkly, white tutu attached to a long-sleeved bodice adorned with sequins. "How darling is this? We sequined all the tutus!"

Cece imagined little Olivia and all her friends dressed in glittery white from head to toe. They'd be adorable.

The door opened again, and Dawn Redmond came in. Cece

was surprised and pleased to see her arrive a half hour early. Except for the fact that she did not look happy.

"Dawn," Natalie said. "You're early."

"My mom and step-dad had to drop me off early so they could get to my step-brother's soccer game." The teenager rolled her eyes and slumped into a chair.

"Sit up straight!"

Dawn jumped to her feet when Ilana appeared in front of her. "Oh! Miss Ilana, I didn't see you. How are you feeling?"

Ilana stepped close to Dawn. "I am vell, thank you. Must I remind you zee importance of proper posture? You are ballerina."

"I know, Miss Ilana. I'm sorry."

Cece and Natalie grinned at each another, hearing Ilana sound like her usual imperious self.

"Ilana," Teresa interrupted, "do you want to see the snowflake costumes?"

Ilana harrumphed. "I do not. I must instruct. Zere is much work to do vith Sugar Plum Fairy."

Dawn looked nervously at Cece. "Um...okay. I'll get ready."

"Not you, my dear. Cecilia." Ilana put the record on the turntable and carefully placed the needle. The "Dance of the Sugar Plum Fairy" music began. She clapped her hands twice. "Cecilia Rose, vhere are your pointes?"

Teresa stared wide-eyed at Ilana. Dawn stepped back. Cece raised her eyebrows and looked at Natalie for help.

"Mamma," Natalie said, putting an arm around her mother's shoulder. "Cece's not dancing, she's—"

"Natalia!" Ilana interrupted her daughter. "I am sorry, but Cecilia Rose is better dancer, and she vill be Sugar Plum Fairy. You are disappointed. I am sorry."

Cece tried to scoot Teresa, Kendall, and Dawn out of the studio. "Natalie needs a few minutes," she whispered. "Let's go into the dance room and let her—"

"Cecilia! Vee must rehearse! I spoke vith your mother. Did she not tell you scouts from San Francisco come to see you dance?" Her words stopped Cece cold.

Ilana marched to the record player. She started the number over and turned the volume up. The "Dance of the Sugar Plum Fairy" blasted from the speakers. "Cecilia Rose!" Ilana shouted. "Dance!"

Without thinking or hesitating, Cece followed Ilana's orders.

The music she knew and loved filled her head. Thirteen years melted away, and she danced as if she were sixteen again, ignoring the open mouth stares directed at her. The only one who was not surprised was Madam Ilana Lurensky, her teacher and mentor, the one who knew what Cecilia Rose could have become.

The music and movements overwhelmed her, emotionally and physically sweeping her off her feet. Tears burned her eyes, and Cece felt her heart crack. She had lost so much, thrown it away, punished herself in order to punish her mother. How could she have been so foolish? Ballet had meant everything to her.

The music, like drops of water shooting from a fountain, heightened her senses. She remembered every *pirouette*, *arabesque*, and *entrechat*, just the way Ilana had taught her. The melody transported her. Her body and brain disconnected from each other, and she danced in joyful oblivion and complete surrender.

The music halted. Cece stopped, unable to process what had come over her. Natalie was standing beside the record player holding the disconnected plug.

Cece was jolted back to reality. "Natalie, I'm sorry, I just—"

Natalie put her hand up. "It's okay."

"Natalia, vat are you doing?" asked Ilana.

"Mamma," Natalie said, her voice soft and soothing. She took her mother's arm and guided her toward Cece. "Cecilia is twenty-nine years old, and so am I. We aren't teenagers, and we're not your students anymore. We're all grown up." She took a few steps with Ilana to the side of the room where Dawn and Teresa stood. "Now, this is Dawn. You remember her, right? She's danced with us for years. And she's our Sugar Plum Fairy. Do you understand?"

Ilana closed her eyes for a moment. She opened them and looked at Cece. "I am sorry, Cecilia. I am sometimes confused, and I do not…" She stopped and looked at her daughter. "I should rest now, yes?"

Natalie nodded, blinking back tears. "Come Mamma, I'll help you."

Ilana and Natalie walked out.

Cece looked at the other three, disbelief on their faces. Kendall and Dawn stood against the wall, jaws hanging open and eyes wide. Teresa had both hands over her mouth. Cece lifted her chin. There was no shame in what she had done. She'd been magnificent.

She looked squarely at Dawn. "Told you I was once a Sugar Plum Fairy."

Dawn stared at Cece as if she had just sprouted wings. "You're an amazing dancer, like, wow, totally incredible."

Before Cece could reply, Natalie reappeared. "We need to talk," she said to everyone.

Teresa uncovered her mouth. "Yes, we do."

Natalie sat in a folding chair, and the rest circled around her. She leaned forward, defeated. "My mother isn't well."

"Clearly," Teresa said. "And my guess is she hasn't been for some time."

Natalie chewed a fingernail. "You're right, Teresa. I was trying to keep it private. But, well, now that you all saw—"

"Stop right there." Teresa interrupted Natalie and pointed at all of them. "Nobody, and I mean nobody, can know what happened here today."

Natalie's head snapped up.

Cece was so shocked she bit her tongue.

"We five are going to be a team," Teresa said. "We have a mission, and that is to get our show opened on time and without a hitch. Every one of us has to be part of the plan. Agreed?"

Dawn nodded. "I can keep a secret. I promise."

"Me too. I haven't told anyone, and I've known for a long time," said Kendall.

"Good." Teresa looked at Natalie. "You need somebody to look after Ilana, at least until after the show closes. Do you have anyone?"

Natalie shook her head.

"No problem. My aunt is visiting, and she'll be happy to help. Besides, it'll get her out of my house, so you're doing me a favor." Teresa reached into her purse for her phone and started sending messages. "I'll take care of costumes, schedule at the theater, and other logistical items."

Natalie's head bobbed up and down. "That's good. I'll tell Robby he reports to you from now on. But what should I tell everyone about my mother?"

"Pneumonia," Teresa said. "Very common in people her age, and treatable, but serious."

Cece's head was spinning with Teresa's take-charge skill and no-nonsense approach. Within minutes, the plan was set. The five of them held hands.

Teresa's face was stern. "We have eleven days until the show opens and eighteen days until it closes. After that we'll sort out the rest of the situation. Until then, our sole objective is to produce the best *Nutcracker* this town has ever seen."

23

The mission gave Cece focus and a sense of order. Her days were scheduled from early morning until late at night. *The Nutcracker* filled her mind every waking moment and most of her sleeping ones, as well. She ate when food was put in front of her and didn't care when or what it was. The only things she wanted to do were teach dance and sleep.

The day after Ilana ordered her to dance, Cece went to the lake that gave Clearwater its name early in the morning. She walked to the edge of the shore, surrounded by thick, tall trees, their leaves creating a golden canopy overhead. The rising sun cut a shimmering path through the glassy water. Cece smiled at the sight of a small pier with a rowboat tied to one of the posts. It had been there forever, and the pier reminded Cece of all the summers she'd spent swimming and boating and playing at the lake.

Water lapped at the edge of the rocky shore. Cece kicked off her shoes and stepped toward it, cool mud under her feet. She moved closer and waited for the water to touch her toes. It felt like dipping her feet in ice water, but after a moment she got used to it and stepped in up to her ankles. As her feet went numb, she relived the moment. *Cecilia Rose, dance!*

In the water, Cece danced—music in her head, sand beneath her feet. The icy cold water splashed around her with every pirouette, splattering her clothes with mud and soaking her up to her knees. Warm tears streamed down her cheeks as she remembered the dancer she used to be. It was, for a brief moment, glorious.

～

On Friday night, five days after Teresa's plan had been put into action, Cece got home from the studio especially late. She found Julia and Phil alone in the kitchen lingering over dessert.

"Hi," Cece said.

"Hey, baby girl." Phil stood and hugged her. "You hungry?"

"Just tired." Cece trudged through the kitchen toward the stairs.

"Don't you want some dinner, honey?" Julia asked. "I made a pot roast."

"Maybe later."

As Cece walked slowly up the stairs, she could hear the whispers.

"I'm getting very worried about her," Julia said.

"Me too. I've never seen her so—"

Cece went into the bathroom and closed the door, shutting out the sound of parental concern.

After her shower, Cece went downstairs. She sat on the couch in the living room with only the Christmas tree lights on and stared into the fireplace. A small fire still burned, and she was mesmerized by the orange and gold embers. She felt numb. For a moment, ballet left her mind, and a vision of Doug popped in. She pictured him hiking in the rainforest, cameras hanging from straps around his neck, sunblock glistening on his tanned skin.

Julia came and sat down next to Cece, and the vision of Doug evaporated.

"Hi, sweetie." Julia handed her a bowl with a small serving of pot roast with vegetables and potatoes. "Just eat what you want."

"Thanks." She took a tiny bite of meat, rich with gravy.

"I wish there were something I could say to help, Cece, but I know what you're feeling, and there's nothing anybody can say to make you happy right now."

Cece appreciated Julia's understanding. "I'm so tired, and I'm so tired of being miserable."

"I know," Julia said.

"The other night when I called him, I really thought we'd... we'd get ba..." she hiccoughed, "...back together." A sob jolted her body.

"Oh, honey," Julia said.

"I just want to go to sleep and never wake up."

Julia rubbed her back. "Maybe it's a good thing you're so preoccupied with the show. Keeps your mind busy. And in a few weeks, you'll be better able to, well, adjust."

"If only I'd never said anything about getting married. That's what started the whole problem, that and my controlling, plan-for-everything obsession."

Julia put her hand on Cece's leg. "You're not being fair to yourself, honey. You did nothing wrong letting Doug know you wanted to marry him."

"You don't think so?"

"I don't. Perhaps your timing and method were a little awkward, but expressing what you want out of a relationship is, in my opinion, just plain smart."

Boomer pushed his head onto Cece's lap and sniffed at her

bowl. She plucked up a piece of meat with her fingers and fed it to him.

"I guess." Cece scratched Boomer's ears. "I just need to get through the next couple of weeks without falling apart. But I hate being so unhappy, especially around the kids."

"Then don't be."

Cece gave Julia a puzzled look. "What do you mean?"

"Just what I said. Be happy when you're around the kids."

"But I'm not happy."

"Doesn't matter," Julia said. "Act like you are. Pretend."

Cece almost laughed. "That's impossible."

Julia looked at Cece with a stern, motherly expression. "It's difficult, yes, but not impossible. And frankly, you owe it to those children. Listen, seven years ago when my husband took off with a younger, prettier version of me, I forced myself to put on a happy face for Ryan. I struggled with it for months, and there were days it nearly killed me. But as time passed, it became less of an effort. And as more time passed, it became less of an act."

A log in the fireplace cracked and fell, sending sparks up the chimney. Cece stared into the red-orange glow. She leaned into Julia's shoulder and cuddled against her, mulling over her stepmother's advice. "I hope someday, if I ever get to be a mom, that I'm the kind of mom you are."

"Oh goodness," said Julia, working Cece's damp hair into a braid. "There is no doubt in my mind that you will be a mother one day. And a wonderful one too."

Cece smiled. A genuine smile. Maybe she *could* act happy. It would be worth a try.

24

*L*ittle girls dressed as snowflakes giggled and danced in place as they lined up for inspection. It was their first time trying on their costumes, and they were so excited they could not stand still. Teresa and Robby herded them together.

"Hey, hey, hey!" Robby shouted. "Careful there. You're gonna get 'em dirty. Brooke, Whitney, don't sit on the floor!"

"Mith Thee-thee, look at me," Olivia broke away from the group and ran into Cece's legs. "I'm a thnowflake!"

Cece knelt down. She held Olivia's hands and spread out her arms. "Let's see your pirouette."

Olivia turned in her little slippers, her wide smile showing off tiny teeth buds breaking through her gums.

Cece laughed. "Excellent, Olivia, just perfect." She stood and clapped her hands at all the snowflakes. "Costume check, everyone!"

Kendall came in followed by six gray mice. "Come on guys," she said, trying to herd them. "Follow me."

"Quit pulling on my tail!" a little boy shouted.

Dozens of people filled the studio as the day wore on,

creating a controlled chaos that kept everybody energized with all the activity. Opening night was in less than a week, and Teresa had recruited a group of mothers to help check and fit every costume.

It took all weekend to complete the work, but Teresa had organized the schedule and assignments as expertly as a CEO running a Fortune 500 company.

~

By mid-afternoon on Sunday, the last of the parents and kids were gone. The costumes, safety-pinned with nametags and hanging on four rolling garment racks, billowed on both sides like huge, colorful clouds.

Cece found Natalie in her office. "You want to get some coffee?"

"Oh wow, yes." Natalie stood and stretched. "Two days of costume fittings and I'm wiped. Thank God for Teresa. She's an organizational genius."

They put on their jackets and stepped out into the cool, after-noon air. The sky was clear and sunny.

"What a beautiful day," Cece commented.

Natalie glanced in her direction. "You seem better."

"I'm working on it." Cece put her hands in her pockets as they walked toward Nutmeg's.

"Have you spoken with your boyfriend?"

"I think he's officially my ex-boyfriend now." Cece's voice wavered.

"Oh, hey, I'm sorry. I shouldn't have asked."

Two boys sped past them on skateboards, and they stepped to the side. "It's all right. I'm just sick to death of crying, you know?"

"Yeah, I know," said Natalie.

"But," Cece said, forcing her voice to sound chipper, "the

good news is I'm really enjoying the kids. Some of them are pretty special."

"They are, aren't they?" The sound of chirping birds came from Natalie's bag. "Hold on, that's my cell." She rummaged in her purse and pulled out her phone. "Hello?"

Cece stepped away. The afternoon sun was setting in an orange and purple sky, and the Christmas lights all over Main Street twinkled. There wasn't a pole or street lamp or store window that wasn't decorated. Green wreaths adorned with cranberries, colorful ribbons, tiny ornaments, and twinkling lights hung on every door.

"Cece," Natalie said, "I'm sorry. I've got to run home. It's Maria, Teresa's aunt. Something about my mom's medicine."

"Don't worry," Cece said. "Go on. I hope everything's okay."

"I'll see you tomorrow. Have a good night."

Cece watched Natalie jog back toward the dance studio. She stood still, not sure which way to go. She had listened to Julia and forced herself to act happy around the children. But nobody said she couldn't wallow when she was by herself. She took a few steps toward Nutmeg's, then stopped. Home sounded better. Maybe. She looked at her watch. It was close to four-thirty, and she hadn't eaten since breakfast. Her stomach growled. As if calling to her, the holiday lights around Nutmeg's window flickered and came to life, and the aroma of cookies fresh from the oven greeted her. Cece inhaled deeply, trying to decide what treat to order as she walked toward the door.

When she got inside, the sound of holiday music greeted her —Dean Martin's "It's Beginning to Look a Lot Like Christmas." It lifted her spirits. Trevor, her favorite barista and star of the basketball team at Clearwater High, was at the register. "Hi, Cece."

"Hey, Trevor," Cece said, looking up at him. "I'll have a pecan sticky bun, heated, and a large hot chocolate."

"Whipped cream?"

"Yes, please," Cece said. "On both."

Cece carried her snack to a table in the corner and sat, relieving her tired legs and feet. She lifted the oversized mug of hot chocolate to her mouth and closed her eyes as she drank.

"Did you know you got the last sticky bun again?"

Cece's eyes flew open at the sound of Brad Redmond's voice. She put her hot chocolate down.

Brad pointed to his upper lip. "You have some whipped cream on your, um, lip there."

Cece felt her face heat up. She grabbed a napkin, wiped her mouth, and tried to contain her discomfiture. "Hello," she said.

"May I sit?" Brad asked, motioning to the empty chair beside her.

"Um, sure," she said, regaining composure. She moved her plate.

"Don't worry, I won't knock it over."

Cece laughed. "It's good you showed up."

Brad's eyebrows rose as he set his coffee on the table. "Really? Why's that?"

"To prevent me from eating this entire thing all by myself. Still carrying silverware in your pocket?"

Brad laughed. "You," he said pointing at her, "are a funny lady."

"Thank you, I think."

"Absolutely meant as a compliment." Brad scooted his chair in. "I think I'll search the attic for my old Boy Scout mess kit with the folding cutlery. Something tells me it could prove useful."

Cece cut the sticky bun into bite-size pieces. "Number one rule of Scouting—be prepared."

"Don't tell me you were a Girl Scout."

"Of course I was. Little green dress and a sash covered in badges."

"Prima ballerina, Girl Scout, and straight A's, I'll bet." Brad helped himself to a piece of sticky bun with his fingers. "Can't imagine your SAT score."

"Very, very high, I assure you." Cece smiled with false bravado. "Quintessential over-achiever and stressed-out perfectionist. It's exhausting to be me."

He grinned, and the dimple near the corner of his mouth appeared. "I know the feeling." Brad took a sip of coffee. "I figured out who you are."

"Who I am? What do you mean?"

Brad rested his chin on his hand. "Years ago, the day we signed Dawn up for lessons at the studio, Ilana asked her to dance. Wanted to see if she had any talent, I guess. She put on some music, and my sweet little girl started dancing. I was standing right next to Ilana, and under her breath she whispered, 'just like my Cecilia Rose.' For some reason, what she said stuck in my mind."

Cece imagined Ilana saying the words. "She was the only person who ever called me by my full name. My mother sometimes called me Cecilia, but only when she was mad."

"It's a beautiful name."

Cece lifted a shoulder. "I never liked it. I was so happy when my little brother started talking. He pronounced Cecilia as Cece, and it just caught on."

Brad leaned back in his chair and crossed his legs. "Well then, I will call you Cece, or do you prefer Miss Cece?"

"Cece is fine." She laughed.

Brad popped another bite into his mouth. "I have to tell you, when you walked into Natalie's office last week, I was completely stunned."

"Imagine how stunned I was to see you with your lovely wife. And what? Less than a week earlier you had asked me out."

"To be clear," Brad said, "Pam and I have been divorced for a while."

LONG DANCE HOME

"Okay." She pressed her lips together, not sure how to respond.

Brad put his elbows on the table and folded his hands. His eyes were green, clear, and intense, his smile alluring. Cece could feel his gaze on her. She shifted in her seat.

"Am I making you uncomfortable?" Brad asked.

"Not at all," Cece fibbed. "I…well, maybe a little."

Brad leaned back in his chair. "I'm going to take a leap here, which I may regret, but I get the feeling your situation, your personal situation, may have changed." It was a question hidden in a statement.

Cece swallowed. She tilted her head and began twirling a curl at the base of her neck. "Rather perceptive of you."

"So it did?"

For a brief moment, Cece felt her eyes burn, but the feeling passed.

The seriousness of Brad's look disappeared, and his eyes softened. "There I go again. The first time we met I ruined your breakfast, and this time I've spoiled your, what is this? Lunch?"

Cece looked at him out of the corner of her eye. "Maybe we should avoid accidentally running into each other."

"Then why don't we run into each other on purpose? Have dinner with me Monday night."

Cece rubbed her palms on her legs and tried to keep her nerves in check. "Monday? Isn't that tomorrow?"

"Yes."

"Um, I don't know if…"

"It's just dinner, Cece," Brad said. "Not a big deal."

Cece took a deep breath, searching for a reason to turn him down. She came up with nothing.

25

"*A*re you kidding?" Patty asked. "Mr. Sticky-buns is taking you to dinner?"

"Quit calling him that. His name is Brad." Cece sat in a rocking chair near the Christmas tree.

"What are you going to wear?"

"That is a serious problem. I hardly brought any clothes, and I can't exactly go in a leotard and ballet skirt."

"I don't know," Patty said. "It's a good look on you."

Cece laughed. "Right."

"No, I mean it. Accentuates your *ass*–ets."

Cece rolled her eyes. "I have some jeans, and Julia said I could borrow a top from her."

"I hope she has something besides those flowery, peasant blouses."

"I do too," Cece said. "Otherwise I might end up in one of my brother's flannel shirts."

~

On Monday night, after spending the entire day and part of the night at the studio, Cece rushed home and cleaned up for her dinner with Brad Redmond. She leaned toward the mirror above her dresser and dabbed on pink lip gloss. The last time she primped for a date in her childhood bedroom, it was for senior prom. She put on the butterfly necklace Mae had given her. It went well with the dark blue Burberry sweater that Cece selected from the more than ten tops Julia had pulled out of her closet. It had a simple scoop neck, long sleeves with signature cuffs, and fit just snugly enough to hint at her curves. At first Cece hesitated to borrow something so expensive, but Julia had insisted.

"Don't be silly," Julia had said. "It looks lovely on you. Besides, I've waited half a lifetime to share my clothes with someone."

The sound of a knock on the door made Cece jump. "I can't believe I'm nervous," she mumbled as she headed downstairs. In the foyer, Cece looked in the mirror, fluffed her hair, and checked her makeup one more time before opening the door.

"Hi." Cece tried to look relaxed as her eyes fell upon Brad. Doug flashed through her mind, but she pushed him away. The man standing in front of her was beyond handsome.

"Hello," Brad said. He wore jeans, a blue button-down shirt, and a black North Face jacket. He smiled and presented her with one long-stemmed, red rose. "I know. So cliché."

"Not at all. It's lovely, thank you." Cece took the flower from him. "Come in."

Brad stepped inside. "Wow, that is one impressive Christmas tree," he said, looking at the giant tree with twinkling lights and dozens of ornaments.

"I know. My family is really into Christmas."

Brad followed her to the kitchen. He looked around as if somebody might jump out at him. "It's been a long time since I picked a girl up at her parents' house."

Cece laughed. "Now *that* I believe." She filled a vase and put the rose in it.

"Do I, uh, have to meet your father and, you know, hear the 'have my daughter home by midnight' speech?"

"Oh right, hold on a sec." Cece leaned on the banister and called upstairs. "Daddy, come down and meet Brad."

She watched Brad's face turn pale.

"Boy, are you an easy target." Cece laughed. "Nobody's here. They went out for pizza."

Brad smirked. "Good one. But just so you know, fathers generally like me. And I always make Dawn introduce me to her suitors."

Cece picked up her coat. Brad took it and held it for her. She slipped her arms in and looked over her shoulder at him. "I'm sure you do," she said, wondering if Ryan had been one of them.

They went outside and crossed the driveway. Brad opened the passenger door of his car, a small, black SUV, and Cece slid into the tan leather seat. Her heart beat a little too quickly, her palms grew damp, and she chided herself for feeling like a teenager.

"So where are we going?" she asked. "I hope I'm dressed okay."

"Absolutely you are." He put his hand on top of hers—the gesture both reassuring and scintillating. "And I hope you're hungry. I'm taking you to a place that serves the best steak in California."

Her nerves began to settle. She leaned back and tried to relax as they chatted all the way to the restaurant.

~

"That," Cece said, pushing her plate away, "was the most delicious steak I've ever had."

They sat next to each other at a small table close to a fireplace. The high ceiling boasted exposed beams and massive iron light fixtures. A fire flickered and popped, and it filled the intimate corner where they sat with a warm, yellow glow.

"I'm glad you liked it," Brad said. He wiped his mouth with a cloth napkin.

Cece lifted her wine glass. After two glasses of cabernet, her anxiety had vanished. "And this wine is sensational."

"Comes from a winery right up the road. One of my favorites." Brad tapped his glass against hers. "So tell me more about the gallery. Your friends sound like real characters."

Cece shook her head. "I have talked non-stop this entire meal. It's your turn."

Brad tore a roll in half. "Okay. What do you want to know?"

"I want to know," Cece said, taking another drink of wine and choosing her words carefully, "about your family, Dawn and the stunning Mrs. Redmond."

"*Ex*-Mrs. Redmond," Brad said, reminding her.

"That's right." Cece tightened her lips. "I just have to say, you two look pretty perfect together."

"We were perfect for a while, but things got complicated."

"Long story?" Cece asked.

"Of course." Brad refilled the wine glasses. "I'll give you the abridged version. But not until we order dessert." He motioned for the waiter, who rushed over.

"We'll have an apple dumpling, heated, with lots of whipped cream, please." Brad winked at Cece.

When the waiter left them, Cece raised her eyebrows. "You do know how to please a girl, don't you?"

Brad put a hand on her cheek, his thumb near her lips, his fingers lightly touching her neck. "You have no idea." His kiss was like melted chocolate—smooth, sweet, warm. Cece was caught off guard, but she closed her eyes and allowed herself to enjoy it, the first kiss from a man other than Doug in forever.

The abridged version took only a few minutes. They'd met

freshman year at UC Santa Barbara. "We were only twenty-one when Pam got pregnant, but completely crazy about each other, so of course we did everything in the wrong order. Had the baby, went to law school, then got married. It was insane."

Cece pictured his little family fifteen years ago—the handsome husband, beautiful wife, and darling baby girl. "How'd you end up in Clearwater? Not exactly a mecca for lawyers."

"Pam grew up in Oakland. When Dawn was born, we moved there so her mother could help out while we went to school. One weekend we went on a family outing, got lost, and stumbled into Clearwater. Looked like a great place to raise a family." Brad sighed. "We were happy then, when Dawn was little and everything revolved around just the three of us. But things change sometimes, even if you don't want them to."

Cece almost said, 'Don't I know it?' "It's sad when the fairy tale doesn't end up happily ever after, isn't it?"

"I don't much believe in fairy tales," Brad said. "Sorry if that makes me sound cynical."

Cece looked down at her lap. "Yeah, well, me neither." She leaned her arms on the table. Her eyes met his. "So what happened, if you don't mind my asking, to your happy ending?"

Brad rubbed the back of his neck. "You know, too much, too soon, too young. We were kids. And, well, we made mistakes."

Cece was not sure what that meant, but she had an idea.

"Anyway, Pam's a great mother," said Brad. "And we work things out, even if we don't agree on everything."

"Parents never agree on everything," Cece said, downing the last drop of wine. "Mine sure didn't."

"Exactly. But we both put Dawn first no matter what."

Cece recalled what Pam had said about her crazy household and Dawn's little step-brothers. Brad seemed like a great father; no wonder Dawn wanted to be with him.

The apple dumpling arrived—a big, round crust stuffed with warm, spicy apples—surrounded by mounds of whipped cream.

Cece opened her eyes wide, feeling like a child walking into a candy store.

"That looks divine." She picked up her spoon. "May I?"

"You may," Brad said, flashing his smile. Cece liked the way he responded to her, as if she charmed him with every word.

"You know," she said, her mouth full, "now I can't have a sticky bun all week, not after this dinner."

"Too bad. I was going to accidentally run into you there tomorrow."

"Nuh-uh," Cece said, taking another bite. "Remember we agreed, no more accidental run-ins."

"Oh, that's right. I certainly don't want to spoil any more of your meals."

"Or snacks." Cece put a large bite of apple dumpling loaded with whipped cream in her mouth. "Or desserts."

"Or desserts," Brad said, pushing his spoon into the dumpling. "Do you like this?"

Cece ran her tongue over her lips, licking off the cream. "What do you think?"

"I think you do." Brad touched her hand. "How could you not?"

A shiver ran up Cece's back. Whether it was the wine, which she was feeling pretty strongly now, or the attention, she did not know. She only knew that she loved the feeling. Brad filled her glass again.

"If you keep pouring me wine, I won't be able to walk out of here."

"Then I'll have to carry you." He rested his chin on his palm.

"You could leave me on my father's porch in a shopping cart, just like the guy did in *Animal House*."

Brad cracked up. "God, you're funny. And I love that movie."

Cece recalled the countless times she and Doug had watched

it. "Laughter's good, isn't it? Some days I think I have to laugh, or else I'd just have to cry."

Brad grew serious. He studied her face. "Is that how you feel right now?"

Cece looked at the crackling fire. "A little bit." She wondered how a man could be sweet, sympathetic, and sexy all at once.

Brad toyed with the tips of Cece's fingers. "I like you, Cece. A lot. I liked you the very first time we met."

Cece pulled her hand back. "Ah, yes, the time you spilled my coffee. Did I tell you about the dog on the sidewalk?"

"Cece," Brad said, his voice gentle, "I can tell you're not ready for anything…serious. That's okay. I just want to spend time with you while you're here, as long as you want that too. Okay?"

Cece blinked. She slid her hand back to where it had been and touched the tips of his fingers. "Okay."

---

26

*E*ight little snowflakes danced their way across the floor in front of the mirror. "Arms up everyone. Bend your elbows! Come on, we've done this a hundred times!" Cece tried to stay upbeat, but she was getting weary. "Brooke, Olivia, Taylor, and Emily, come up front through the middle and then turn. That's right."

The studio was in pandemonium every day with dancers and parents coming and going from mid-morning until seven or eight at night.

Cece helped Kendall with the younger kids each afternoon until Dawn showed up. Then the two of them would rehearse the dance of the Sugar Plum Fairy.

Natalie and Teresa had their heads together constantly, juggling every detail of the show while keeping Ilana's situation under the radar. Ever since the day Ilana had her breakdown, the five of them had bonded over the conspiratorial scheme.

By Tuesday afternoon, Cece had demonstrated the same *petit fouetté* at least a hundred times. She turned off the music and looked at her little snowflakes. "We need a little break, huh?"

"Yeth," said Olivia. "I have to tinkle."

"Me too!" said another tiny snowflake whose name Cece could never remember.

"Okay," Cece said. "But be quick. Miss Kendall will meet you in the big studio in five minutes."

The snowflakes disappeared down the hallway, and Cece went to get water. She bumped into Robby, who was pushing a cart loaded with more than a dozen poinsettia plants.

"What are you doing with those?" Cece asked.

"Natalie wants them all over the place. Not enough that we have the tree and all the lights out front and fake snow sprayed on the windows," Robby said. "Now I have to take care of these." He picked one up and put it close to Cece's face, as if to accentuate the extent of his burden.

Cece laughed and gave Robby a sideways hug. She had grown fond of him.

Robby backed away, blushing, and went back to his poinsettias.

Natalie was sitting at the desk sipping tea when Cece walked into the office. Her head was bent over a stack of paper. Behind her, raindrops dotted the large window. She looked up and smiled. "Cece, hi."

"Hey, Nat, how you doing?"

"Okay." Natalie shuffled some papers on the desk. "Just paying bills. Honestly, I don't know how my mother did it, teaching dance, running her business, taking care of my dad."

Cece recalled how Natalie's father had been sick off and on for years. He died shortly after Cece and Natalie finished high school.

"By the way, how's Teresa's aunt doing with your mom?"

"Maria is wonderful. Half the time my mother thinks she's her cousin, so she likes her a lot." Natalie picked up her coffee with two hands. "You know, this whole situation would be almost funny if it weren't killing me. I can't imagine what's going to happen when everyone finds out what's really going on."

Cece understood, and she worried about Natalie and the stability of the dance studio without Ilana. She felt a twinge of guilt. Pretty soon she'd be leaving Natalie and going back to LA.

"If we lose students, I'll be in..." Natalie stood up. "I'm sorry, Cece. I don't want to burden you with my worries; you've been a lifesaver already. How's our Sugar Plum Fairy doing?"

"Good, really good. Dawn's an incredible dancer. I think being in on the secret about your mom has made her more, I don't know, committed maybe?"

"I've noticed that too. And Teresa, wow, talk about rising to the occasion."

"I guess that's another silver lining," Cece said.

Natalie nodded. "Listen. I know I keep saying thank you, but I can't help it. You're my angel who saved Christmas."

"Hey, you're doing me a favor too, you know. If I weren't working here, I'd be in the unemployment line."

"I'm glad it worked out," Natalie said. "Oh, by the way, Pam called this morning. She spoke very highly of you."

"Really?" Cece said, recalling how nice Pam was the first time they'd met. "What did she say?"

"Just that Dawn likes you a lot and you're a great instructor. Nice, huh?"

"Very nice." Cece toyed with the lid on her coffee. "I'll tell you this, I sure have a new appreciation for your mother. I never realized how much work it was for her to mold and teach and train us. Ilana really was incredible."

Natalie sighed. She looked beyond Cece to the chart on the wall with all the colored slips of paper stuck to it. "She certainly was."

∾

Dawn and Cece rehearsed alone until Gabe showed up. Then they worked together perfecting the *pas de deux*. Cece felt like she could watch them forever, they danced so elegantly, the regal Sugar Plum Fairy and her handsome Cavalier in one of the most romantic and captivating dances known to ballet.

It was dark when Cece shut off the music. "Let's call it day. Don't forget, Thursday is dress rehearsal."

"Okay, Miss Cece," said Gabe, using the younger kids' name for her.

Dawn stuffed her pointe shoes into her bag. "Gabe, can you drive me home?"

"My brother took the car. Thought you said your mom was picking up."

"I never said that. I guess we could walk, but it's freezing. Cece, can you drive us?"

Cece looked up. "Oh, um, sure. Where are you going?"

"Just to my house," Dawn said. "It's really close."

Cece wondered whose house Dawn meant. "Um, okay. Let's go."

Gabe rode in front with Cece, while Dawn gave her directions from the back seat, directing her past Nutmeg's and toward the lake.

"Gabe," Dawn said, "did you talk to Ryan? Wasn't he going to study with us tonight?"

Cece's ears perked up at the mention of her step-brother. She looked in the rearview mirror at Dawn, who was texting with fast thumbs.

"I saw him after school," Gabe said. "He didn't say anything about studying."

Dawn raised her head. "He wasn't with that girl again, was he?"

Cece saw Gabe's chest go up as he inhaled. "Nope." His tone was crisp.

"I don't know why he ever hung out with her in the first place, you know?" Dawn said. "She's kind of a skank."

Gabe didn't respond. He looked straight ahead. Cece caught a flash of annoyance in his face. *Oh no,* she thought. *My Cavalier and my Sugar Plum Fairy. And my step-brother? This can't be good.*

Dawn directed Cece down a small street lined with attractive, newer homes. "It's at the end of the block. Gray house on the left."

Cece pulled into the driveway of a gray shingled house at the bottom of a cul-de-sac. The garage door was up, and Cece could see Brad doing something at the work bench. She rolled her window down, figuring she should at least say hello.

Brad looked up. When he saw it was Cece driving, he smiled and walked toward the car.

Dawn jumped out. "Hi, Daddy. What's for dinner? Me and Gabe are starving."

"Gabe and I," Brad said, correcting her grammar. He moved closer to Cece's open window. "I'm going to pick up Chinese. How does that sound?"

"Great," Gabe said, pulling his bag off the back seat. "See you tomorrow, Cece. Thanks for the ride."

"You're welcome."

Dawn thanked her, threw her ballet bag over her shoulder, and walked into the house with Gabe in tow.

Brad sauntered over to the driver's side window. He leaned an arm on the roof of her car and looked in. "You have an uncanny ability to show up at just the right time."

"I do?"

"Yes. I was just thinking about you. Would you like to come in?"

"That might be weird."

"Right," Brad said. "Well, have you had dinner?"

"Not yet."

"Meet me at Ming-Loo's. Do you know where it is?" Brad raised his eyebrows.

"Of course. I've been eating there my whole life."

"We'll grab a quick bite while I get take-out for the kids. Go on ahead. I'll be five minutes behind you."

"Um," Cece hesitated. They'd just had dinner together the night before. But so what? There were no rules, at least none she could think of. Besides, Chinese food sounded divine. "Okay," she said. "See you there."

Cece traveled the familiar streets to her favorite Chinese restaurant, feeling as if no time had passed since she'd last been there. She followed the route her father had shown her so many years ago: take the alley behind Harry's Hardware and turn right into Ming's parking lot. Phil wanted her to avoid a left turn at a corner with no stop sign. Harry's Hardware was long gone, and there was a new stop sign on the corner, but Cece still used her father's directions.

The dark glow of red lanterns lit up the Asian Christmas decorations. Cece sat in a booth with her face behind a tall plastic menu, hoping not to see anyone she knew.

The waiter came and filled her water glass. "Are you dining alone, Miss?"

"Oh, um, no. There'll be two of us." Cece motioned to the second glass. The aroma of fried wontons and hot sauce stimulated Cece's taste buds. "I'll have an order of eggrolls while I wait."

The waiter disappeared, and Cece texted her father she'd be home late, amused and chagrined that at twenty-nine years old, she was back checking in with Daddy.

The eggrolls arrived along with hot tea. Cece poured a cup and sipped.

"Starting without me?"

Cece inhaled sharply, and the tea burned her tongue. "You startled me."

Brad scooted into the booth across from her. He picked up an eggroll, dipped it into the sweet and sour sauce, and took a bite. "How'd you know these were my favorites?"

"They're everybody's favorite. Ming-Loo makes the best eggrolls in California." Cece ate hers in three bites.

The waiter took their order, and Brad placed the to-go order at the same time.

"What did you tell Dawn?" Cece asked. She did not want Dawn to know they were having dinner, regardless of how insignificant it was.

"Just that I had to make a couple of stops first, so it might take me a little longer than usual."

"Guess that's the truth. Sort of."

"I think so," said Brad. "I didn't say where I was stopping, so this table here counts as a stop, doesn't it?"

"Why not?" Cece poured Brad some tea.

He picked up the little round cup. "Perfect timing tonight."

"What do you mean?" Cece cut the third eggroll in half.

"If you'd arrived at my house one minute earlier, I'd have been inside and missed seeing you. Makes me think it was meant to be."

Cece licked a drop of sweet sauce from the corner of her mouth. "You're all about the 'meant to be' thing, aren't you?"

"Perhaps," Brad said, splitting his chopsticks. "But I think it's more that I'm the kind of a man who sees opportunities when they're presented."

Cece felt herself blush. Brad smiled, and she caught a glimpse of his dimple.

"Since we're short on time," Brad said, "I'm just going to put something out there. I haven't been this attracted to a woman in quite a while."

Cece's heart raced. She didn't know how to respond.

Brad leaned back and rested an arm over the pink leather

seat. He smiled and shook his head. "There I go again, making you uncomfortable."

"That's okay. I'm getting used to it."

Their food arrived—shrimp chow mein, broccoli beef, spicy chicken with green beans.

Cece smiled at the waiter. "Thank you. This looks delicious." She put a small amount of everything on her plate, avoiding Brad's eyes. He did make her uncomfortable. His intensity contrasted dramatically with Doug's easy-going manner.

"Cece, I—"

"Brad," Cece interrupted, "I really enjoy being with you, but it's a little bit, uh, I'm not sure how to put it."

"Too soon?"

"I think so. Sorry."

"No, I should apologize." Brad said. "I've been accused of coming on a little strong sometimes. It's the lawyer in me."

The conversation paused, and they started eating.

"However," Brad said, chow mein noodles hanging from his chopsticks. "You're only here a couple more weeks, so let's make the most of it. I want to take you to a place you've never been."

"I've been everywhere in this town."

Brad leaned toward her. "It's not in this town. But it's not far. Anyway, how's Thursday night?"

Thursday was only two nights away. That would be three dinners in one week. She came up with a good excuse. "I can't on Thursday. It's dress rehearsal. We won't finish until...I don't even know when."

"That's okay," Brad said, helping himself to more broccoli beef. "I don't care how late it is. Besides, Dawn will be with her mother. Come on, say yes."

Cece lifted some noodles with her chopsticks and looked at Brad. He was nothing if not persistent. And she had to admit, it was flattering. And distracting. "Well, okay. Yes." She put the noodles in her mouth.

The waiter arrived with the to-go order, and Brad handed him his credit card.

"This was a real treat tonight," said Cece. "I haven't been here in so long. I'd forgotten how good it is."

"I'm glad you enjoyed it." Brad kept his eyes on her while she continued to eat.

Cece glanced up at him. "Stop. You're making me nervous."

"Okay, okay, sorry," Brad said, returning to his own plate.

The waiter brought the credit card and receipt back to the table with two fortune cookies. Cece finished her dinner and picked up a cookie.

"Do we dare?" she asked.

"What the hell. Live dangerously. You go first."

"No, you go first."

"Fine." Brad cracked open his cookie. He ate the broken pieces and straightened out the little slip of paper. "Uh-oh."

"What's it say?"

"It says…" Brad frowned in mock seriousness, " 'Advancement will come with hard work. Pay close attention to business and avoid distraction.' Boy, I've already blown that one."

They laughed. Cece opened her cookie and looked at the fortune. She glanced at Brad. "It says, 'A tall, dark, handsome stranger will turn your life upside down.' "

"Really? That's your fortune?"

"No." Cece giggled.

"Guess I deserved that."

"Yes, you did," Cece said, smoothing the tiny slip of paper. "Here's what it really says: 'Big changes lie ahead. Open your heart and mind to something new.' "

Brad's eyes sparkled in the red lantern light. "Now that is one intriguing fortune."

27

*C*ece drove home in a quandary. She didn't understand how she could be attracted to Brad when she still was pining for Doug. It made her feel somehow disloyal to both of them.

She entered through the back door and saw Phil, Tom, and Julia sitting at the table finishing dinner.

"Hi, guys." Cece sat with her family. "Tommy, do you really have your own apartment?" She flashed a smile at her brother.

"Yeah," Tom said. "But when I moved out, Julia said I could come back for dinner anytime I wanted."

Julia put a hand on Tom's arm. "And we love having you here, honey."

Tom looked at his sister. "Told ya," he said, his mouth full. "Oh, um, did you go to dinner with Brad Redmond last night?"

Cece frowned. It sounded like an accusation.

"Who had dinner with Brad Redmond?" Phil asked.

Tom took a large swallow of beer. "Cece did."

Phil looked surprised. "You did?"

Cece ignored her father's question. "How do you know about that, Tommy?"

Julia got up. "Phil, I need some help in the kitchen."

"Huh? But I'm still—"

Julia squeezed his arm. "I need you in the kitchen, honey."

Phil gave his wife a confused look, but he followed her as instructed. Cece was grateful they had left her and Tommy alone.

"What's going on with you?" Cece asked.

"Nothin'. I just think you've been in LA for so long you've forgotten what it's like to be in a small town."

"Believe me," Cece said, "I have not forgotten."

Tom filled his mouth, chewed, and swallowed. He looked at his sister. "Friend of mine tends bar at the restaurant you were at. She texted me."

Cece picked at a fingernail. "So big deal, we went out to dinner. He's nice."

"Nice...suppose you could say that." Tom licked his fork. "And here I thought you were nursing a broken heart. Typical."

"What's that supposed to mean?" Cece suddenly felt defensive.

"Like you don't know?"

Cece studied her brother's face. "You know, when we were kids, I figured something out about you."

"Yeah? What's that?" Tom showed minimal interest.

"Whenever you act like an ass, like now, it has to do with something completely unrelated to the thing you're being a jerk about."

"That makes no sense."

"Of course it does." Cece knew her little brother better than anyone. "So, tell big sister what's bothering you."

Tom rolled his eyes. "All I'm saying is, what about Doug? Is that all it takes to get over the love of your life? Some good-looking guy in a fancy car wining and dining you?"

Cece sat for a moment and said nothing. Tom's eyes met hers. Then he looked away.

"Wait." Cece put both palms on the table, the light dawning.

"I knew this wasn't about me. It's about you and what's her name, isn't it? The hot little waitress you used to date."

Tom's jaw tightened, a telltale sign she'd hit the nail on the head.

Cece sighed. "Got herself a new boyfriend?"

"Fiancé," said Tom.

Cece raised her eyebrows. "Wow, you guys only broke up a few months ago."

"Yup." Tom stretched his neck. "Ran into her yesterday. She couldn't wait to flash her diamond at me—even thanked me for breaking up with her. Said if we were together, they never would've met."

Cece winced. Doug had said something similar. *If we were together, I wouldn't be going to Central America.*

Cece patted her brother's hand. "Sorry about that."

Tom shrugged. "Forget it."

Julia and Phil came back to the table.

"We didn't really like her," Julia whispered in Cece's ear.

"I heard that," Tom said.

"Well, we didn't," said Julia. "She was too controlling. Led you around like a puppy. Right, Phil?"

"Well," Phil said, "her looks kinda made up for that."

"Phil!" His wife pushed his shoulder. "Shame on you."

Tom finished his beer. "I gotta go. My landlord asked me to help him hang his Christmas lights."

He kissed Julia's cheek, hugged his father, and punched Cece's upper arm. "Listen, Sis, I won't tell anyone about Brad. But if you are trying to keep it quiet, good luck. Everybody knows everyone's business around here, and that's just how it is."

Cece watched her brother go, knowing he was right.

Later that night, as Cece helped Julia empty the dishwasher, she considered what Tommy had said about getting over Doug so fast. "Julia?"

"Yes?"

"Do you think it was wrong of me to go out with Brad? Like it's too soon or something? I mean, should I be wallowing more?"

"Absolutely not." Julia wiped the table with a towel. "Going to dinner with another man doesn't mean you've forgotten Doug, or that you don't still love him. It's just a distraction."

Cece leaned against the counter and twisted a ringlet of hair. "But I do like Brad Redmond."

"Of course you do. He's charming. And gorgeous."

"You know him?" Cece asked.

"Not really, but I've seen him around. And I think his daughter has a crush on Ryan."

Cece went to work on another curl. "Yeah, I heard something about that the other day. How do you know about it?"

"I'm a cyber-stalker. Ryan leaves his phone and laptop lying around. It's so easy to snoop these days."

"Does Ryan like Dawn?"

"That I'm not sure about." Julia filled a kettle with water and put it over a flame. "Get the teabags, sweetie."

Cece opened the tea drawer. "I haven't forgotten Doug, you know. Not at all."

"Of course you haven't. And you probably never will. We remember our first loves forever."

Cece looked at her step-mother. "Are you talking about Ryan's dad?"

"Heavens no—my high-school sweetheart. I was crazy about him." She laughed. "Anyway, go easy on yourself. You'll have Doug in your head for a long time. Even when you're attracted to other men."

Cece chewed on a chipped fingernail. "I don't get it though. How can I still love and miss Doug, which I do, but have these feelings for someone else?"

"Because nothing compares to new," said Julia, opening the

tea bags. "Attention from a man is flattering and fun, especially somebody different. Gets all those hormones pumping."

Cece recalled how she felt the first time she met Brad at Nutmeg's. She was attracted to him even then. "So, I shouldn't feel guilty going out with him? That's what you're saying?"

Julia poured boiling water into the mugs. "That's what I'm saying. For heaven's sake, you had one dinner."

"Two."

"Two?"

"We had dinner tonight, kinda last minute." Cece blushed. "I drove Dawn home, and he was there. Asked me to meet him at Ming-Loo's. It was great."

Julia waved a hand. "Okay, two dinners then." She set the mugs on the table, and they sat across from each other. "You are a young, beautiful, single woman, and you don't have to explain anything to anyone. Go out with Brad while you're here, and have some fun. He knows you're going back to Los Angeles, doesn't he?"

"Of course."

"So it is what it is—a little romp for the both of you. Sort of like a summer fling, just at holiday time."

Cece sipped her tea. A holiday fling. It made perfect sense.

28

For two days, Cece and Natalie could barely come up for air as the countdown to opening night began. On Thursday afternoon, dress rehearsal at the theater started early, went for hours, and ended in chaos.

"Kyle! What are you doing? Let go of Travis!" Cece rushed onto the stage to pull apart two young boys—one of the mice and one of the soldiers.

Robby intervened just in time. He wrapped a long arm around Kyle's middle and pulled him off of Travis.

"He pulled my tail!" Kyle cried.

Robby unhooked the tail from Kyle's backside and put him back on the floor. "I'm taking this before the entire costume is ruined."

"Travis! Leave your brother alone!" Their mother jumped into the fray, wrangling her two sons and dragging them away.

"Cece!" Kendall hollered. "Can you come here and help the snowflakes?"

Cece looked backstage to see a dozen little snowflakes squirming, some of them crying, some of them giggling.

"Mith Thee-Thee, I'm thtuck!" Olivia had herself twisted up in the sequined bodice of her costume, as did several others.

"It's scratchy," another little snowflake cried.

"Hold on, girls," Cece said. "We'll help you. Don't pull or you'll tear the costumes."

Cece and Kendall went to work getting the girls changed and the costumes on hangers. Robby helped the boys on the other side of a curtain, while Teresa pinned nametags on the backs of the costumes before hanging them on the rack. Natalie stood with a clipboard in the middle of the room talking to the two Claras. As the dancers left one by one, the theater cleared out until only Natalie and Cece were left. They collapsed into two front row seats.

Natalie heaved a sigh of relief. "That went better than I thought it would."

"Really?" asked Cece. "I thought it was insanity."

Natalie shook her head. "You should've been here last spring when we did Peter Pan. Somebody knocked the whole box of Tinker Bell's fairy dust out of the rafters, and it gave half the kids sneezing attacks. What a disaster that was."

"Think we're ready?" Cece asked.

"You know," Natalie said with a thoughtful nod, "I think we are."

"Me too." Cece checked her watch. She was meeting Brad at the studio for their late dinner date.

Natalie looked at Cece with an expression of curious amusement. "Is there some reason you keep checking the time?"

"No, not really. I'm just, well, I have a..."

"Date with Brad Redmond?"

Cece felt like she'd been caught with her hand in the cookie jar. "This is why I love Los Angeles. Nobody knows anything about you, and if somebody does know something, they're too self-absorbed to care."

Natalie stretched out her long legs. "Hey, it's okay with me. I'm thinking he might be just the thing that keeps you in Clearwater."

"Keeps me in Clearwater? What are you talking about?"

Natalie gave Cece a quizzical look. "Don't tell me you haven't heard. Everyone's asking if you're my new assistant director."

Cece had heard, but chose to ignore, the gossip. "That's ridiculous. I'm going back to LA."

"Can't blame them for wondering." Natalie got up. She walked onto the stage and over to the Christmas tree, a thick, six-foot Douglas fir decorated with old-fashioned candles, huge red bows, and swooping rows of silver garlands. She leaned over and unplugged the fake candles.

It struck Cece how beautiful and genuine Natalie was. She had always been that way, and Cece had not always appreciated it. "I hope I don't seem ungrateful, Natalie. I've loved working with you."

Natalie turned. "No, of course not. It's just that, well, the situation with my mom—I'm afraid it's going to get complicated."

Cece understood what Natalie was trying to say. "I know," she said, wishing she could be more helpful. "But my life is in LA. I love living there."

"Even with..." Natalie stopped. "Sorry, that was over-stepping."

"It's okay. Not like I haven't wondered about it myself. But yes, even without Doug."

Natalie walked toward Cece with an extended hand and pulled her out of her seat. "Understood," she said. "But if you change your mind, the job is yours."

They put on their heavy coats and went out the back exit into a misty night. Cece inhaled and looked down Main Street.

Taking in the beauty of the decorations, she had to admit that no place had Christmas spirit quite like Clearwater.

Natalie tucked her hand inside Cece's arm. "And as far as you dating Brad Redmond…"

"I'm not dating him. We've just gone out a couple of times."

"Right," said Natalie, "but remember what it's like here. Small town gossip is unavoidable. That's why my love life is far away."

Cece turned to her old friend as they crossed the street. "Your love life? You have one?"

Natalie laughed. "I do, and it is in the city, far away from the gossip mill in this town."

"Do tell," Cece said, intrigued.

"Older, divorced, grown children. Very uncomplicated and low maintenance."

"Sounds perfect," Cece said.

"Perfect? Nothing is ever perfect. But it works for us."

"I get that."

They climbed the front steps of the old Mayfair Hotel and went inside. Cece followed Natalie through the studio and into the office.

"I have a little something for us," Natalie said, dropping her jacket on the back of a chair. She went to a cabinet and unlocked one of the doors, revealing a small refrigerator.

"You really do like secrets, don't you?" said Cece.

"Doesn't everyone?" Natalie lifted the cover on the mini freezer and pulled out a tall, slim bottle of vodka.

"Stolichnaya." Cece grinned. "And *Elit,* no less."

"I am Russian, you know." Natalie poured the ice-cold vodka into two cut crystal glasses. She handed one to Cece. "To Tchaikovsky."

Cece clinked her glass against Natalie's. "To Tchaikovsky."

~

Brad pulled up in his SUV as Cece was putting her dance bag into her trunk. She locked her car and jumped into his. "Woo, it's freezing out there," she said.

Brad smiled and looked at Cece with warm eyes. "Hi," he said, his voice low and relaxed. "You look nice."

"Thanks." Cece had changed into jeans, flat black boots, and a gray, nubby sweater.

"So, how did rehearsal go?" Brad asked.

"Good. Exhausting. The Beckwith brothers got into it again." Cece pulled her seatbelt over her shoulder. "Pretty chaotic, but I think we're ready for tomorrow night."

"And my daughter? Did she show up on time?"

"She did." Cece brightened thinking about Dawn. She had become a joy to work with. "Danced beautifully, as expected."

"Good." Brad leaned toward her. His lips touched hers, warm and moist. "You," Brad licked his lips, "have had a drink. Vodka maybe?"

"Stoli *Elit*." Cece giggled. "It's Russian."

"It certainly is," Brad said. "I like it." He kissed her again, leaving Cece short of breath.

Brad backed his car out of the parking lot, turned the corner, and headed down Main Street. "I'm taking you clear out of Clearwater tonight, okay?"

Cece leaned back against the leather seat. "Absolutely."

They drove for over half an hour, deep into Napa Valley. Brad parked and looked at her. "This will be fun."

They got out of the car. He took Cece's hand and guided her into a noisy, crowded bar inside of a renovated barn. There was a band on a small stage in the front playing "Hotel California."

"I love this place," Brad shouted. "Great food, and I never run into anybody I know!"

Cece squeezed Brad's hand. How did he know that she needed to disappear? The hostess seated them at a round table tucked into a dimly lit corner. Large candles burned on every table and in sconces on the walls.

"Kinda like a haunted house." Cece looked around as she scooted into the curved, red leather booth.

"Are you scared?" Brad asked, sliding in next to her.

"Me? No way. I love haunted houses. My favorite ride at Disneyland."

"No kidding? Mine too."

The waiter came, and Brad ordered.

"Two vodka martinis, please, dry with extra olives." He looked at Cece. "Okay if I order your dinner for you?"

She nodded. "That'd be great."

Brad looked back at the waiter and shouted. "Two classic burgers and a side of sweet potato fries."

It sounded delicious, and Cece felt her stomach gurgle. "You must think I eat enough to feed a horse."

Brad put an arm over the back of the booth. "It's refreshing. Do you have any idea how boring it is to take a woman out and all she orders is green salad with dressing on the side?"

Cece laughed. "Can't say that I do. I come from a long line of very big eaters."

The waiter came with their drinks—cool, clear liquid filled to the edges of large, frosty martini glasses. Cece leaned over and took a sip. "Yum," she said. "So good."

Brad tapped his glass to hers. "To opening night," he said.

"Ah, yes," Cece said, returning the tap. "To opening night."

They drank and talked and sang with the band until the waiter brought them their enormous hamburgers and a bucket of fries.

"This looks fabulous!" Cece ate a fry. Then she had a few more.

Brad ordered a glass of pinot noir for them to share. Cece ate, and drank, with abandon.

"How do you like it?" Brad asked.

She looked up, her mouth full. "So, so, so good!"

The band returned from a break, and the female vocalist took the mike. She had blond hair cut short and wore tight jeans, a red tank top, and cowboy boots.

"Isn't she cute?" Cece asked.

Brad gave the singer an appraising look. "Not nearly as cute as you."

Oh Jesus, Cece thought, *did I set him up for that?* She bumped him with her shoulder and drank some more wine.

"We got a request!" the singer said. She had a strong voice and a Southern drawl. "From this gentleman right here in front. He and his lovely wife are celebratin' their anniversary!"

Everyone applauded.

"How many years y'all been married?" The singer held the microphone in front of the man's face.

"For twenty-two years," the husband said, "I've been married to my high-school sweetheart, the love of my life!"

"Isn't that the sweetest thing ever?" Cece said.

Brad nodded. "Pretty sweet."

"Twenty-two years! How 'bout that folks?" The singer stepped back. "And she is still the one!"

The music swelled, and the band played *You're Still the One.* It sounded as if Shania herself was singing.

Cece swallowed hard. The song, about the kind of love that lasts a lifetime, made her eyes burn. The pain in her chest caught her by surprise.

"Going to the restroom!" She shouted to Brad above the noise.

She scooted out of the booth and maneuvered through the crowd of drinkers and dancers.

The bathroom was crowded, and she waited in line for a stall. A large woman bumped into her, a young girl stood too close, and two teenagers argued with each other.

Cece finally got into the stall and stayed put until her

breathing calmed. When she felt certain she wouldn't burst into tears, she exited and washed her hands.

Cece looked in the mirror. She wiped a bit of mascara from underneath her eyes then freshened her lipstick, hopeful her abrupt exit hadn't caught Brad's attention.

As she made her way back to the table, the band was playing *Oh What a Night*. Cece smiled. "Much better," she said to herself.

Brad looked up as she approached. She gave him a confident smile, picked up her martini, and drank.

"Almost empty," she said, putting the glass on the table and taking her seat.

"You want another?"

"Yes, please," she said.

"Want to share a bowl of chili, too?" He motioned to the server to bring two more drinks.

"God, no, I couldn't eat another bite." She picked up a couple of fries and held them out. "You have to finish these." He ate them from her hand.

"Wait," Brad said, gently taking hold of her wrist. "Ketchup." He licked the tip of her finger, his tongue lingering. It sent chills up the back of Cece's neck. She picked up her martini, downed the last drop of it, and turned her face toward his.

He leaned in and kissed her. She felt the tip of his tongue brush over her lips. Whether it was the vodka, the sensuality of his kiss, or both, Cece didn't care. She pushed Doug out of her head. Her lips parted, and Brad responded in kind.

The sound of a throat clearing interrupted them. "Here you go," the server said as he put two fresh martinis on the table."

"Ah, great," said Brad. "Thank you."

They laughed, clinked their glasses, and drank.

"This is the best drink I've ever had," Cece said. She took a big swallow of it.

"You're kinda supposed to sip it," Brad said.

"That so? What if I prefer to gulp it?"

Brad's green eyes reflected the candlelight. "Then you can do that, too."

Cece giggled. She drank more, feeling the cold, spicy vodka fill her mouth and run down her throat. She gazed at Brad over the rim of her glass.

"But maybe you ought to slow down just a little." Brad's expression held a hint of concern.

"I don' think so," Cece said. Getting drunk was working just fine. It made her carefree, uninhibited. "I can sleep late t'morrow."

"That's good," Brad said, "because you'll need to."

Cece moved closer to him. "You...you're nice."

Brad rolled his eyes. "Oh, that's just great."

"What?"

"Come on, you know nice guys finish last."

Cece ran a finger around the edge of her martini glass. "That's not necessarily a bad thing."

"No?" Brad's smile looked tempting, seductive. "How's that?"

"Depends wha' they're doin'." Cece realized her words screamed innuendo. She drank again.

Brad laughed out loud. "You're killing me, Cece. You have no idea."

She placed her hand on his knee. "Di' you know tha' you are a good kisser?" Cece could hear her words slurring.

"You think so?"

"Uh-huh," she said, stretching the word.

"Would you like more kisses then?"

"Uh-huh," she said again.

Brad lifted her chin with one finger. He put his mouth next to her ear. She felt his breath on her skin. "Good," he said.

She shivered as his fingers moved her hair out of the way and his lips brushed over her ear to the soft skin behind it. He kissed her there, and she felt the light touch of his tongue. Cece leaned her head to the side and allowed his kiss to trail down her neck.

A summer fling in winter—what an intriguing idea.

29

*C*ece woke up with a headache that reminded her of her twenty-first birthday. Boomer, snoring loudly, was sprawled over more than half the bed. She glanced at the clock—only a little past nine, and she didn't have to be at the studio until three. Cece turned over, threw an arm around Boomer, and went back to sleep.

At noon, her cell phone rang. Cece grabbed it and opened one eye to see that Patty was calling.

"Hey."

"Hey, yourself," said Patty. "You sound like you just woke up."

"Yeah, you woke me."

"Oh goody! How was last night?"

Cece put a hand over her eyes to shield them from the light. "Oh yeah, last night. It was…good."

"Drank too much, did you?"

"Waaaay too much."

Patty laughed, and it made Cece's head throb.

"So tell me," said Patty, "did he sweep you off your feet?"

"Kind of." She pushed back her covers.

"Do you really like him?"

"Do I like him?" Cece pinched her eyebrows together to relieve the pain, but it didn't work. "Yeah, we have a great time together."

"I hear a 'but' coming," Patty said.

Cece sighed. "But it's not going anywhere. I'll be home in a couple of weeks, so there's no point in getting all excited about a few dinners." Cece recalled the feel of his lips on her neck and his hand on her back.

"Hey," Patty said, interrupting her thoughts, "I almost forgot —Barbara called. It's looking good for the gallery to reopen in January."

Cece perked up. "Really? That's great. Thank goodness for Mae."

"And," Patty said, "I'm guessing Barbara talked her sister into another infusion of cash. Come January, everything goes back to normal. I can't wait."

Well, Cece thought, *not quite everything.*

She tried to stand, but she couldn't quite make it. "I'm a little hung-over."

"I can tell," Patty said. "I wish I were. I'm bored to death without you."

"Are you going to Dallas for Christmas?"

"Still figuring that out."

The sound of hammering came through the phone and assaulted Cece's ears. "What the hell is that?"

"Someone's building a frame behind me."

"You're at work?"

"Yeah, I'm at work," Patty said. "And shouldn't you be? Doesn't the show open soon?"

"Tonight."

"Tonight? Wow, good luck! Are you excited?"

"Actually, I am," Cece said. "I think it's going to be great."

"Take pictures. And get one of Mr. Sticky-buns and text it to me."

"Yeah, right. Talk to you later. Love you."

"Love you more. Bye!"

After a long shower, many Dixie cups of water, and Tylenol, Cece got dressed and headed downstairs. "Hello?" she called. "Anybody here?" She went into the kitchen where Boomer was lying on his bed. He lifted his head.

"Too bad you don't drive, big boy."

Boomer whined as if he agreed. Cece picked up the phone and called her brother.

"Hey, Tommy. Where are you?"

"I'm doing a job just east of town. Why?"

Cece squirmed. "I…I need a ride."

"You got car trouble?"

"Um, kinda."

Tom laughed. "I'll be there in twenty minutes."

〜

The cast assembled at the theater three hours before curtain, and the pre-show pandemonium began.

Two hours before curtain Cece realized she hadn't seen Dawn. She stopped Kendall, who was painting whiskers on the mice.

"Do you know where Dawn is?" Cece asked.

Kendall looked up. "You know, I did see her, but not in a while. Maybe she's putting on her makeup somewhere."

"I just saw her," one of the mice said. "I think she left."

"Left?" Cece felt a surge of panic.

"She went out that way." The little mouse pointed toward a side door that let out into a courtyard.

Cece ran toward the door and threw it open. Outside, she saw Dawn sitting on a bench. She had her arm wrapped around a crying boy. He couldn't have been more than six or seven.

"What's wrong?" Cece asked. The boy was wearing the top half of a soldier costume.

Dawn looked up. "Henry's scared."

Cece exhaled with relief.

"Henry's in my little brother's class at school," Dawn said. "And this is his first show."

Cece's heart melted. She hardly recognized the little boy, but she recognized his fear. "Dawn, why don't you go on in and finish getting ready? I'll take care of Henry."

Dawn stood. She patted Henry's shoulder. "Don't worry, Henry. Miss Cece will know exactly what to do."

Henry wiped his eyes with the backs of his hands. Cece sat next to him. She rested a hand on his thin arm.

"Why are you scared, Henry?"

"I...I'm scar...scared I'll mess up."

"Really?" Cece said. "You know, I totally get that."

"You...you do?"

"Sure I do. Let me tell you about the first time I was Clara."

"You were Clara?" His eyes got big. "But you're so old."

Cece laughed. "Well, it was a really long time ago..."

~

Cece lost herself in a flurry of kids, costumes, and nervous anticipation. Everyone had poured their hearts into Clearwater's annual Christmas production of *The Nutcracker*. Cece thought about Natalie and how much she had riding on it. If the performances went well, it would make things much easier for her when the situation with Ilana became public knowledge.

A horrible cry coming from the dressing room sent Cece running. Behind the partition, little Olivia, dressed in her snowflake costume, had blood dripping down her chin onto the front of the white sequined bodice. The adorably chubby Emily stood next to her biting down on a trembling lower lip.

"What happened?" Cece tried to hide her horror at the condition of the costume.

Olivia extended her hand and held out a tiny, bloody tooth. "Mith Thee-thee," she sobbed. "Emily crashed into me and...and..."

"And my hand hit her in the mouth." Emily started to cry too. "And knocked out her tooth!"

"Look at my coth-tume Mith Thee-thee." Olivia's face scrunched up like she'd eaten a lemon. "I'm tho thorry!"

"It's okay, honey," Cece said, kneeling down. She hugged Olivia, smearing the little girl's blood on her own white shirt.

"Miss Cece," Emily said, "she can have my costume."

"Oh, Emily, sweetie, don't worry. We'll get Olivia fixed up. Now, you find the other snowflakes and Miss Kendall, and let them know Olivia will be there in a few minutes. Would you do that for me?"

Emily nodded, her face serious. "Yes, Miss Cece." She turned and ran off to complete her mission.

"Robby!" Cece shouted. "I need you!"

Robby, with a mouth full of safety pins and yards of royal blue tulle wrapped around his neck and shoulders, appeared. When he saw Olivia, he spit the pins into his hands. "Oh fu... fudgy-wudgy!"

At the sight of the tulle on Robby, Cece forgot about Olivia. "Oh no, is that—"

"Yup, Mother Ginger's skirt tore, but I've got it under control," Robby said. "I'm a magician with safety pins."

"What about me?" Olivia asked.

"Oh yeah, Olivia," said Robby. "It's all good. I'll work my magic and poof! You'll have a fresh snowflake costume." He turned and trotted away, dragging a train of blue tulle behind him.

Cece sat on the floor and looked at Olivia. "Come here, sweetie."

With her shoulders still quivering, Olivia sat in Cece's lap.

"Where's your tooth?"

Olivia opened up her fist.

"Is the tooth fairy going to come for it?"

"Uh-huhhh," Olivia sniveled.

"Then we don't want to lose it. How about I hold it for you until after the show, okay?" She plucked the little tooth from Olivia's palm.

Olivia nodded. "Do you think Robby will make me a new coth-tume?"

Cece hugged Olivia. "I'm sure of it."

Olivia smiled her utterly adorable toothless smile.

Behind the heavy velvet curtains stage left, Natalie and Cece stood together. The first dancers—Party Guests, the Maid, the Butler, and the Stahlbaum family—lined up in order, chirping excitedly.

"Okay, you guys," Natalie whispered, fixing Fritz's twisted suspender, "this is it, curtain time. You all look fabulous, and I'm so proud of you!" She had tears in her eyes as she turned to Cece. "Thank you. I could never have pulled this off without you."

Cece's eyes burned. "I'm glad I'm here, Nat. I really am."

The overture swelled, the curtains opened, the lights came up, and as her dancers took the stage, Cece realized that she felt happy, truly and genuinely happy.

30

One performance ran into the next. Each show was thrilling, nerve-racking, and heartwarming. There were mistakes, mishaps, and missed cues, but far more triumph and joy than anything else.

For three days straight, Cece and Natalie lived between the studio and the theater. Following each performance, they reviewed their notes like football coaches after a game, making changes and adjustments.

On Sunday afternoon following the matinée, they sat on the couch in the office with their feet up.

"I may never move again," Natalie said.

"Me neither—three shows in two and a half days. Was it this hard when we were younger?"

"God, no," Natalie said, kicking off her shoes. "We're just old now."

Cece leaned her head back and looked at the ceiling. "Could you believe Dawn's dancing? She was spectacular."

"Thanks to you."

"Yeah, well," Cece laughed, "I'll take a modicum of credit."

Natalie pulled her legs underneath her and turned to Cece.

"When Dawn first started dancing with us, like five or six years ago, my mom was watching her. She took my arm and said, 'Natalia, one day zat one vill be Sugar Plum Fairy.'"

"Whoa, you sounded exactly like her," Cece said.

Natalie gazed toward the old armoire that held Ilana's memory books. "I don't know what I'll do without her."

Natalie looked like a weary soldier, and Cece had no idea how to cheer her.

"She'll be okay," Cece said with empty assurance. "After the doctors figure out—"

"No." Natalie shook her head. "It's bad, Cece. They're pretty sure it's Alzheimer's."

Cece froze. She had been hoping for better news. "I'm so sorry."

Natalie went to the white board. She crossed off days with a red marker. There was little joy in doing so. "Without my mom, the magic is missing."

Cece wanted to say that it wasn't so, but it was. The Lurensky Dance Academy was not the same without Ilana.

"She's the inspiration behind everything." Natalie turned. "This studio was her dream, and now it's mine. But the dream is fading, and I don't know what to do about it."

Cece knew all about fading dreams, and it pained her to see Natalie so distressed. "I wish there were something I could do to help."

Natalie sighed. "Me too, but unless…" She waved a hand as if dismissing the thought.

The clock on the wall chimed six times.

"Hey, you want to get some dinner?" Cece asked, pushing herself off the couch.

"Actually, I'm going to the city."

"You are?" Cece was intrigued.

"Yeah, just for dinner."

Cece gave her a sidelong glance, grateful for the change in subject. "How long have you been seeing this mystery man?"

"Three years."

"Really?" It was the same amount of time she and Doug had been together. "And no plans to, you know, take the next step?"

Natalie went to the desk and thumbed through a stack of mail that had piled up over the last week. She pursed her lips. "No. He won't ever marry again."

"But you stay with him?"

"I do. We broke up one time, because he thought I shouldn't give up the possibility of marriage and babies."

"And now you have?"

"Maybe. I don't know. Not sure I'm even cut out to be a mom." She tossed a few envelopes in the trash. "I'm not like you that way."

"Like me? What are you talking about?"

"Remember your toy stroller?" Natalie asked. "You used to stuff it with dolls and walk down Main Street pretending to be the mommy."

"Oh my God," Cece said, picturing herself. "I did do that, didn't I?"

"Yes you did," Natalie said. "And it was so you."

"So me? Come on."

Natalie straightened her back and looked at Cece quizzically. "You don't remember much of our childhood, do you?"

Cece thought about her mother and the havoc she had wreaked on their family. "There's a lot I chose to forget."

"But you do remember what you always said you wanted to be when you grew up, don't you?"

Cece leaned her head back and looked at the ceiling. She remembered vividly. "I said, 'First I am going to be a ballerina, and then I am going to be a mommy.'" Cece could almost hear a clock ticking inside of her. "I blew the ballerina part, didn't I?"

Natalie pushed her feet back into her shoes. "You will be a mother one day, Ceece. I'm sure of it."

Cece hoped Natalie was right. "Thanks." She stood and put an arm around Natalie's waist. "I have to tell you, putting on the Clearwater Christmas show has been more fun than I thought it would be."

They walked through the main studio, passing the Christmas tree in the corner, the poinsettias placed all around the room, and the windows framed with lights.

Outside on the porch, Natalie locked the door, and they headed back toward the theater where their cars were parked. On the corner, as the street lamp flickered and a cold wind whipped around them, Natalie turned and faced Cece.

"I want you to know something," Natalie said.

Cece tucked her hands into her pockets. "What?"

"I was never the dancer you were. I worked my ass off trying to make my mother as proud of me as she was of you. I'm not saying this to make you feel bad, Cece. You had more talent, the perfect ballet body. Jesus, even your feet were the right size."

Natalie laughed, but Cece could see tears clinging to her lashes.

"When we were, what, sixteen, and you quit dancing, part of me was happy. Finally, my competition was gone, and I could be the star."

Cece shifted her feet. A deep confession was not what she had expected.

Natalie looked to the sky. "But you know what? It didn't happen. When you left, my dancing diminished, and it wasn't because I got lazy without the competition. I just felt uninspired." Natalie wiped the tears off her cheeks with her hand. "I'm sorry. I know it sounds ridiculous."

"It doesn't." Cece thought about how she had no desire to paint anymore. "It doesn't at all."

"Anyway, these last few weeks with you here, I have a

feeling inside that I haven't felt in a long time, a renewed energy. It's like that old glimmer is back."

"Maybe it's the Christmas lights all over town," Cece said, trying to lighten the mood.

Natalie pursed her lips and shook her head. "Christmas decorations come out every year. The only thing different this year is you."

Cece got the message. Ilana's magic was fading. And she had brought some of it back.

31

"I'm home!" Cece shouted as she walked into the kitchen Sunday evening.

"There she is!" Phil swooped her into a big bear hug. "We are so proud of you. The show was spectacular!"

Julia joined the hug. "Oh my God, best *Nutcracker* we've seen in years, honey, and I'm not just saying that."

Cece swelled with pride. The whole family had attended the Sunday matinée, and it had been the best performance so far.

Tom walked in, his face red from the cold. "Hey, Sis. Show was great, really great. Congratulations." He gave Cece a kiss on the cheek. "And Ryan, how about that Sugarplum? You've got good taste." He gave Ryan a playful slug on the arm.

"She's not my girlfriend," Ryan said, his mouth full of potato chips. "I keep telling you that."

Phil put a fatherly arm around Ryan. "You know, Tom can help you out with that. He's got quite a way with the ladies."

"Stop it you two, you're embarrassing him," Cece said, trying to stifle a laugh.

"We are not." Tom pulled him into a headlock. "Are we Ry?"

"Go away," Ryan said, wriggling free. "I'm hungry, Mom. When's dinner?"

Julia pulled a pan of lasagna from the oven and placed it on a trivet in the middle of the table. "Right now, honey."

The five of them sat down to the family meal.

"So," Julia said, "no show tomorrow?"

Cece blew on a fork full of hot lasagna. "Right. We take Monday off. Then we'll have a full dress rehearsal again on Tuesday, need to practice a couple of changes, and then shows the rest of the week."

"All the way through Christmas?" Phil asked. "That Natalie's a real slave driver, isn't she?"

"Not all the way, Daddy. Closing show is the night before Christmas Eve."

Julia gave Ryan a second serving of green beans. "That's right. And I have tickets for all of us, including you, Tom."

"I have to go again?"

Cece punched him. "Don't you want to?"

"Do you have any idea how many times I've sat through *The Nutcracker*?"

Phil put down his wine glass. "Not as many as I have, Son."

Cece gave her father a look. "Daddy!"

"But I've enjoyed it every time, baby girl, every single time."

~

It was after ten when Cece awoke Monday morning. She meandered into the kitchen wearing her purple robe and a pair of sweat socks she'd found in the clean laundry pile. She poured herself a cup of coffee. It appeared that nobody was home, which she appreciated. A lazy morning was exactly what she needed.

She made herself a piece of toast and jam and sat down with her Christmas gift list. She had gifts for almost everyone thanks to the items Barbara had given her. Only a few things left, and she would pick those up today. Her cell chimed.

"Hey, there."

"Good morning," said Natalie. "I didn't wake you, did I?"

"No, I'm up. What are you doing?"

"I'm heading out to the dry cleaners with a few costumes that need stains removed. I wonder if you could do me a favor."

Cece drank some coffee. "Sure," she said, thinking it had something to do with the show.

"There's a little problem with my mom, and I was hoping you could run over there and help Maria."

"Of course. What's the matter?"

"Maria just said my mom is disoriented." Natalie sounded worried.

"More than usual?" Cece asked. Ilana was confused most of the time now.

"I'm not sure, but it makes me nervous, and I'll be gone about an hour."

"Just to go to the cleaners?"

"I take costumes to that fancy one across town. The one by the studio makes a mess of beads and sequins. Anyway, I'll drop everything off and come right back. I'd just feel better if Maria had some help until I get there."

"No problem."

"Thanks, Ceece."

"You're welcome." Cece stood and took her dishes to the sink. "I'll leave here in ten minutes."

"You're a lifesaver."

"That I am." Cece put down her phone. She took a deep breath and went upstairs to get ready for her visit to Ilana.

Cece knocked on the door of the yellow, ranch-style house. She couldn't remember the last time she'd stood there.

Quick, heavy footsteps approached. The door opened a crack, and a slightly built, older Hispanic woman greeted her. "Cece?"

"Yes, that's me."

Maria pulled the door open and ushered Cece in. "Thank you for coming. Señora not good today."

She followed Maria into the living room where Ilana sat staring blankly at the wall in her pink silk robe. Cece approached her. She wondered if it was more serious than Natalie had thought.

"Ilana? How are you feeling?"

She looked at Cece, and her face lit up. "Cecilia, you are here. Natalia!" she called loudly. "Cecilia here to play. Come!" She turned back to Cece. "Cecilia, you should vant to eat. I make you grill cheese, yes?"

"No thank you, Ilana," Cece looked at Maria. "How long has she been so disoriented?"

"One hour, two maybe. This morning she tired. Now she confused. She think I her cousin."

"Has she had her medication?"

"I give her this morning."

Ilana stood. "Petrov? Vhere are you?" She began speaking Russian.

Cece could not understand a word, but she could tell that Ilana was searching for her dead husband, Petrov.

"Maybe she need to see doctor," Maria said, standing beside Ilana with a worried frown.

Ilana stepped toward Cece, still rambling in Russian. Then she switched to English.

"Cecilia Rose, vhere is your mamma? I call her to talk but I not hear back. Too busy vith boyfriend, I think." Ilana sneered when she said the last part.

Cece cringed. Even the confused Ilana remembered her mother's affair. "Maria, do you have the doctor's number? I think we need to let them know what's going on."

"Si, I have right here." Maria picked up a pad of paper. "I go call from other room."

Cece took Ilana's arm and coaxed her back to the couch. They sat next to each other, their legs touching. Ilana had stopped looking for her dead husband, and her face took on a grave expression. She picked up Cece's hand and looked at her with penetrating eyes.

"Cecilia, you vill go to San Francisco. You vill be part of real ballet company."

Ilana's voice was calm. She smoothed Cece's hair and cupped her cheek with a cool hand, and Cece felt herself transported back half a lifetime ago.

"I vill miss you, my dear, but your talent is too much now. You grow beyond vat I can do." A single tear rolled down Ilana's cheek. "Cecilia Rose, you vill be shining star."

Cece tried to stop her own tears, but she couldn't. What would her life have been if she hadn't quit ballet?

"Yes, Miss Ilana, I'll go. And I will make you proud of me."

Ilana moved Cece's hair out of her eyes and kissed her forehead. "My dear, you make me proud every day, every dance, since you vere little girl."

Cece hugged her beloved teacher and mentor. She felt Ilana's arms around her. Ilana, who seemed frail and thin, held her with an embrace full of strength and comfort.

Maria returned and tapped Cece's shoulder. "The doctor say to bring her," she whispered.

Cece disentangled herself from Ilana's arms. She looked into the woman's watery blue eyes.

"Ilana," she said softly, "you need to get dressed. Natalie will be here shortly, and she's going to take you to see the doctor."

"Vhy?"

"Um, I'm not sure," said Cece. "Just to check your medication, I think."

"Very vell. I go to see zee doctor. But first I must give Petrov his lunch." Ilana walked toward the kitchen.

Cece reached for Ilana's arm. How could she let her go into the kitchen and prepare lunch for a man who had been dead for more than ten years? But something swished around her ankles, making her jump back. "Holy shit!"

A huge white Persian cat looked up at her. "Meowwwww…"

"Petrov!" Ilana's voice was cheerful. "Zere you are, my boy." She scooped the cat into her arms and carried him off to the kitchen, speaking to him in Russian the entire way.

32

*C*ece and Natalie sat at Nutmeg's on Tuesday afternoon before rehearsal. With only three performances left, Friday's closing show sold out, and Christmas in five days, Cece could be back in LA in less than a week.

She sipped at her steaming black coffee. "So, how'd everything go with your mom and the doctor yesterday?"

"Okay," Natalie said, lifting her foamy latte. "He said it's normal for her to have good days and bad days. In fact, she seemed better this morning. I don't know, maybe I'm just looking for signs of normal behavior."

"I can't blame you. I really thought she'd lost it yesterday, until I realized she was talking to the cat and not your dad."

Natalie laughed. "It was so bizarre when she named him Petrov, but I think she just missed saying my father's name."

"I get that." Cece stretched her back and shoulders. Her return to the world of dance was straining her muscles.

"So, what's happening with you?" Natalie asked. "Any more late-night dinners with the handsome Mr. Redmond?"

Cece glanced around Nutmeg's, half expecting Brad to pop up. "Actually, I haven't heard from him in a few days." Cece thought about their last dinner together—the drinks and the kisses and his hand on her back. "I might've freaked him out though. Drank a teensy bit too much last time."

"It would take a lot more than that to scare him off."

"What do you know about him?" asked Cece.

"Very little," said Natalie, "except that he does not date women in Clearwater. You, however, are evidently the exception."

Cece brushed it off. "We're not dating. We've gone out to dinner a few times, that's all."

"Hey," said Natalie, "you don't need to explain anything to me."

Cece's cell vibrated. She glanced down. "Speak of the devil." Natalie winked at her.

Cece got up from the table. "Hello?"

"I'm sorry I didn't call sooner," Brad said. He sounded rushed. "I had to go to Sacramento."

"That's okay," Cece said. The pleasure she felt surprised her.

"I'll be home in a couple hours. Are you free for dinner?"

"I am," Cece said. "But I'm not going to let you get me drunk again."

"Aww, but it was so much fun," he said. "Shoot, I gotta grab this call. Pick you up at eight."

The call ended before Cece could say goodbye. She returned to Natalie.

"Well?" Natalie asked, her eyebrows raised.

Cece smiled. "Another late-night dinner with the handsome Mr. Redmond."

As Cece shampooed her hair, she calculated the number of times they'd been out. The fabulous steak, the impulsive trip to Ming's, and the bar where she drank too much. Three dates, not counting the times they'd bumped into each other at Nutmeg's.

Cece soaped her legs and shaved quickly. *Dinner number four,* she thought. She figured he probably expected her to sleep with him by now. She shaved under her arms. *Maybe tonight. Maybe, maybe, maybe.* There was no denying she found Brad Redmond desirable, and sleeping with him would probably be amazing, but she was a relationship kind of girl. Every man she had slept with, and there had not been many, were boyfriends first.

She got out of the shower, grabbed her towel, and looked at herself in the medicine cabinet mirror. "You're twenty-nine," she said to herself. "What are you waiting for?"

Her cell buzzed. She answered and put it on speaker.

"Hi, Patty."

"Hi, Ceece."

"What are you doing?" Cece asked.

"Stalking this really cute guy on online. He ordered a frame the other day, so I snagged a copy of the receipt to get his name. I'm looking at all his Facebook photos."

Cece laughed and dried her feet. "You're dangerous."

"I know. Oh wow, just found a link to his webpage. He must be a model or something...Shit, he's a god! I'm sending you the link."

"So that I can stalk him too? You and I are going to end up in jail together someday."

"I hope so," Patty said. "What are you doing?"

"Getting ready to go out."

"Mr. Sticky-buns?"

"Dinner number four."

"Hope you shaved your legs."

"Yes, Patty, I did."

"Pits, too?"

"Patty, stop." Cece laughed.

"Well, I'm just trying to figure out where you're going with this."

"I'll let you know." Cece wrapped the towel around her body and went to her room, taking the phone with her.

"Call me after," said Patty. "I don't care what time it is. And look at that link I sent. His pictures will get you going for sure."

"You're disgusting."

"I try. Talk later. Bye."

Cece tossed her phone onto the bed and got dressed. She put on a pair of black jeans and another shirt borrowed from Julia—a cream colored, gauzy thing with long sleeves. It was funky with a low cut, scoop neck that showed just a peek of cleavage. She dabbed some perfume behind her ears and went downstairs.

Phil was at the back door putting on his jacket.

"Where are you going?" Cece asked.

"I'm meeting Julia at the hospital. We're delivering Christmas presents to the children's wing."

Cece put her coat on a chair. "That's so sweet."

"Yeah, it's nice." Phil looked at Cece. "You going out?"

She grinned at her father. "Out to dinner."

Phil smiled at his daughter. "Good. I'm glad you're having some fun. And you look very pretty." He kissed the top of her head. "G'bye, baby girl."

Cece stood at the counter and organized her purse. She dropped a lipstick on the floor and bent down to pick it up. As she stood, Ryan's laptop caught her eye. It was sitting open on the kitchen table. She finished organizing and sat down at the computer.

It had been weeks since she'd been online. She logged into Facebook, and a photo jumped out at her. It was from a party she and Doug had gone to over a month ago, and the picture was of the two of them standing with another couple and laughing. It looked as if someone had just told a joke.

Her fingers hesitated over the keyboard as she contemplated opening the album their friend had posted. She turned to look at the clock on the wall. Fifteen minutes until Brad would get there. With a shaking finger, she clicked.

Scrolling through dozens of photos, Cece took deep, calm breaths. Three weeks had passed since the night they broke up. She couldn't even remember who broke up with whom or who was at fault or how everything unraveled so quickly.

Part torture, part catharsis, she continued. She and Doug were in the background of dozens of pictures, holding hands, leaning against each other, smiling at one another. She stopped on a candid in which she was talking to somebody, and Doug was standing off to the side. He was looking at her with a slight smile and adoring eyes, the soulful, brown eyes Cece knew so well. Eyes that revealed every emotion, from love to heartache.

Tears blurred her vision. "This is so stupid!" Cece closed the laptop with a slap of her hand. She grabbed a tissue and blotted her eyes. For the next five minutes, she chastised herself for even looking at the pictures. She went to the refrigerator to see if there was an open bottle of wine. None. She opted for a glass of Ryan's chocolate milk.

By the time Brad arrived, she had her emotions in check.

~

They walked down a quiet, tree-lined street in St. Helena, a small town in Napa with old inns, wineries, and spas. They had just eaten at a romantic French bistro.

"You okay?" Brad asked.

"Of course. Why?"

"You seem kinda quiet tonight."

Cece looked up at him and smiled. "Just tired. I think all the rehearsals and performances have drained me."

That much was true. Cece felt like she was running a marathon she hadn't trained for in advance.

It was cold and windy, and the air smelled of pine and

burning wood. Brad picked up Cece's gloved hand. He pulled her glove off, lifted her hand to his lips, and kissed it. Then he wrapped his own hand around hers and tucked it inside his coat pocket.

"Is there any chance you'll stay through New Year's? One of my clients throws a huge bash every year, and I, uh, need a date."

"You need a date?"

"Well, I want a date. And I want my date to be you."

Cece moved her hand around in his pocket, feeling his warm skin against hers. "I don't know yet."

Her tentative plan was to leave right after Christmas, but what for? New Year's Eve in LA without Doug would be miserable. "I might still be here."

"Just keep it in mind," he said.

They turned the corner, and an older couple bundled in heavy coats passed by slowly.

"Evening," the old man said. "Nice night."

"Yes, sir," Brad responded. "Merry Christmas."

"Merry Christmas," the husband and wife replied together.

The brief interaction touched Cece. How romantic it must be to grow old with the love of your life. Doug's face flashed through her mind. She untangled her hand and pulled it out of Brad's pocket.

"What's wrong?"

"Um, where's my glove?" The red cashmere gloves had been a gift from Doug.

"Right here." Brad handed it to her. "I wasn't going to lose it."

"I know. I...I just wanted to put it back on."

"Okay." They continued walking. Stars sparkled in a cloudless sky.

"Are you cold?" Brad put an arm around her shoulder. He pulled her close, and her body involuntarily stiffened.

Brad stopped and turned to face her. He furrowed his brow. "What just happened here?"

Cece forced a smile. "Nothing."

"Really? I might be a guy, but I'm not completely dense."

Cece bristled. "It's nothing, Doug—" she caught herself, "Brad."

Brad said nothing for several seconds. "Did you just call me Doug?"

Cece felt hot in spite of the freezing temperature. "I can't believe I did that. I'm so sorry, it's just that I was...I wanted my glove because..." Tears filled her eyes, and she turned away.

"Hey, hey." Brad wrapped his arms around her. "It's okay. Doug's a good name."

Hearing Brad say Doug's name only made her cry more. "I'm so embarrassed."

He turned her around. Cece looked up at him.

"Did you know you cry black tears?" Brad teased.

Cece laughed and cried at the same time. "God, I must be a mess."

"If I were a true gentleman, I'd have a handkerchief in my pocket to give you."

Cece fished through her purse. "I don't even have a tissue." She wiped her eyes with her glove, smearing mascara onto the red cashmere.

Brad pulled her toward him. "Come on, let's get inside."

Cece sniffled against him like a child while he guided her toward an espresso bar down the block. Brad opened the door, and warm air greeted them. They walked past an old-fashioned Christmas tree garlanded with strings of popcorn and fresh cranberries. A guitarist sat on a stool singing "White Christmas."

Brad took her to a small table by the window. He pulled out a chair. "Sit," he said. "Coffee or tea?"

She sat and slipped off her coat. "Tea."

As Brad went to the counter, she pulled a few napkins from

the holder and blew her nose, mortified she had called Brad 'Doug.' With another napkin, she wiped underneath her eyes to remove the mascara smears. "I must look like shit," she said to herself.

"Not really."

She looked up to see Brad standing over her holding a teapot and two mugs.

"If there were a hole full of quicksand here," Cece said, "I'd jump in."

"Then I'd just have to rescue you. And I'm wearing my good shoes."

Cece laughed, even though it hurt. Brad set the cups on the table and poured the tea. The waitress brought over a large lemon square and placed it between them.

"No sticky buns here," Brad said. "I hope you like lemon bars."

Cece nodded and sniffled. "I love them."

Brad cut the lemon bar into four pieces and popped one in his mouth. "You want to tell me who Doug is? Although I probably can guess."

"I can't believe I cried in front of you."

"Don't worry, I'm used to it. I have a teenage daughter, you know."

Cece straightened her back, forcing herself to pull it together. She did not want to be reminding Brad of his daughter.

"I feel the need to review," he said.

Cece blew her nose again. "What do you mean?" She nibbled on a piece of lemon square. It was creamy and tart.

"If I recall correctly, the first time we met, you said you were in a relationship. Then a week later you were back in Clearwater and, evidently, not in a relationship."

"Yes," Cece said, avoiding his eyes. "That pretty much sums it up."

"So, what happened?"

Cece circled the rim of her cup with one finger. "We just weren't on the same page anymore."

"That's vague."

Cece brushed a few strands of hair out of her eyes. "There's nothing more to say. We had a disagreement about something. Something big."

"I see." Brad took another bite, and Cece watched him chew. She could see him ruminating. He crossed his arms and leaned them on the table. "I'm going to guess, then, that one of you wanted to take it to the next level, and one of you didn't."

Cece wiped her mouth with a napkin. "Right." It didn't take a genius to figure that out. There was an edge to her voice that she hadn't intended.

He scooted his chair back and turned to the side, crossing his legs. "I see." His gaze was intense, a mix of curiosity and annoyance.

"It was a horrible breakup, and I..." she cleared her throat, "I don't really want to talk about it."

"Do you want to get back together with him?"

His question caught her off guard.

"Why would you ask me that?"

"Because I want to know."

She glanced down at her hands, thinking she might tell him that she was sorry, but it was none of his business. Cece spoke softly. "You know I'm going back to LA, so what difference does it make?"

Brad inhaled through his nose, and Cece caught a fleeting look of irritation, or hurt perhaps, in his expression. She felt awful.

"The show closes in two days, and I have to get back to my life."

His chest rose as he inhaled. "Got it. Sorry if I overstepped." His relaxed, confident face returned. "We should get going. I have an early appointment tomorrow."

33

Cece balanced the phone against her shoulder, pulled on her pajama pants, and got into bed.

"And then we left," she said to Patty.

"Just small talk the whole way home?" Patty asked. "That's it?"

"Pretty much. And some very awkward silence." Cece said. "It was like he just flipped a switch. But come on, why would he ask me about Doug?"

"Because he really likes you, that's why."

Cece could not deny that he did. She was the one with ambivalent feelings.

"And because he needs to know his competition. It's a guy thing. Just like those elephant seals you told me about."

Cece pictured the gigantic male bellowing and attacking the other males to keep them away.

"Oh, hey," said Patty. "Not to change the subject, but good news. One of my new buddies at the framing place invited us to a New Year's Eve party."

Cece shifted the phone to her other ear. "I'm not sure I'll be home. Brad asked me to go to a party with him. Although now—"

"No! Please come home. I miss you so much."

Cece sighed. "Maybe. Let me see how the next few days go. I'm too exhausted to make any decisions right now. I'll call you later."

"You'd better.

The Wednesday night performance was not well attended. Cece had noticed that many of the parents were missing, including Brad.

Afterward, Cece and Teresa sat next to each other on the sofa in the office going over ticket sales, while Natalie reviewed her notes.

"Maybe I scheduled too many shows," Natalie said.

Cece shook her head. "It's probably just a middle of the week lag, Nat. And tomorrow's the last day of school before Christmas break."

Teresa opened her laptop. "Look here, Natalie, tomorrow night we're eighty percent full, and Friday's closing show is sold out. We'll be fine."

Natalie gave Teresa a grateful smile. "Thanks, Teresa. You have been so much help to me, you have no idea. And thanks for managing the rumor mill about my mother."

"You're welcome," said Teresa. "Although I have to tell you, people know something's wrong. She hasn't been at even one of the shows."

Cece listened without comment. It was a delicate subject.

Natalie leaned back in her chair. "Might be time for me to address the elephant in the room, huh?"

"I think so," said Teresa.

Natalie looked at Cece. "What do you think?"

"I think," Cece chose her words carefully, "that people imagine things to be worse than they are when they are kept in the dark. Parents need to know that Lurensky Dance Academy is going to be just fine. No matter what."

Teresa pointed at Cece. "I like this one," she said to Natalie. "Can we keep her?"

Natalie's mouth twisted to the side. "I wish."

~

Thursday night was a disaster. The Mouse King rolled his ankle and couldn't finish his dance. The Beckwith brothers got into another fight, and Cece found Dawn backstage crying right before her big number.

After the show, Cece spotted Dawn sobbing into her father's shirt. Brad, patting his daughter on the back, caught Cece's eye and smirked, as if to say: "See? Told you I'm used to it."

Cece returned the smile, then looked away. They hadn't spoken in two days, and her embarrassment had not subsided. His New Year's Eve invitation remained unanswered, and Cece wondered if he wanted to rescind it.

Cece glanced back. Dawn's mother had joined them, and they comforted their daughter together. Mother and father whispered to one another. For a moment, Cece imagined them as the family they used to be. She stared, almost in a trance. Her own family had once looked perfect too.

Cece turned away, feeling like an intruder. She went backstage for her jacket and then headed toward the side exit.

As she reached the door, an arm brushed against her and opened it for her. "May I walk you to your car?"

She looked over her shoulder to see Brad behind her. "Sure," she said, putting on a smile that belied her discomfort. "Dawn okay?"

Brad sighed. "Crying over some boy again."

"Sorry to hear that," Cece said, hoping it had nothing to do with Ryan.

They took a few steps toward the corner, and Cece noticed for the umpteenth time the town's abundance of holiday decorations. "You didn't decorate your house," she said.

"What?"

"The first time we met at Nutmeg's, we were drinking coffee outside, and the workmen started putting wreaths on the street lamps. You said that you wanted to decorate your house this year."

"I did?"

Cece nodded. She tucked her hands into her pockets. "You did."

Brad shrugged. "Guess I forgot. Besides, what's the point? Dawn spends most of Christmas with her mom, and I'm not home that much."

Cece looked up at him. She felt a rush of emotion, realizing his was a lonely life. "I'm sorry about the other night."

"Hey, no, I'm the one who should apologize. I got a little ahead of myself."

They continued walking.

"I'm thinking about staying for New Year's," Cece said, "if you still want me to go to that party with you."

"I do," he said. "I'd love it."

Cece looked up at him. His profile was perfect. "I just need to find something to wear. And then tell Patty of course. She'll be upset. She's very attached to me."

"I don't blame her," Brad said with a suggestive smile. "Listen, you can let me know. New Year's is still nine days away."

"I don't want to leave you hanging."

"Don't worry. It's not like there's anyone else waiting to be asked."

Cece laughed. "That cannot be true."

"Well, maybe a few women are pursuing me, but I'm a little caught up with something else right now."

They rounded the corner onto the quiet side street where

Cece had parked. Brad leaned against her car. Cece stood in front of him and put her hands on his shoulders. He wrapped his arms around her waist and pulled her closer. Looking into her eyes, he slipped his hands underneath her sweater. He rubbed her lower back, and Cece felt the heat of his skin on hers. She leaned against him, her body pressed against his, and felt him adjust his hips.

"Uncomfortable?" she asked.

"That's not exactly the word I'd use."

Cece kissed him, softly at first, then harder. His hand slid up her back along the side of her waist and around to the front.

"What are you wearing?" Brad laughed.

Cece laughed too. "It's my workout bra. Sorry."

"You are adorable." Brad bent her backwards and kissed her like Rhett Butler kissing Scarlett O'Hara. The idea of a holiday fling was sounding better all the time.

34

*W*ith standing room only, the theater turned into a whirlwind of excitement as the entire town of Clearwater poured inside. Nobody wanted to miss the last performance. Backstage in the dressing room the performers darted back and forth as they readied themselves for the closing show. Cece looked around. She grabbed Robby's arm as he ran past her.

"Have you seen Natalie?"

Robby shook his head and sped off, just as Natalie entered with Ilana.

Cece breathed a sigh of relief.

"We're here," Natalie said, exhaling audibly, "finally."

Ilana looked tired, but other than that, just like herself. Cece hugged her. "I'm so glad to see you."

"Vell, I could not miss final show, my dear." Ilana wandered off with Maria following her like a protective shadow.

"She seems better, Natalie."

"Yeah, a little, but I brought Maria just in case."

"Good idea."

Cece felt a light touch on her arm. She turned. "Dawn, hi. You look magnificent."

"I'm sorry about last night, Cece. I know I let you down."

Cece rested her hands on Dawn's shoulders. "You did not let me down. Besides, last night's performance is over, and I want you to forget about it. Tonight, beautiful girl, you will be amazing." She kissed Dawn's forehead the exact same way Ilana used to kiss hers.

To Cece's surprise, Dawn threw her arms around Cece's neck and held onto her. "I wish you didn't have to go back to LA. I'm really going to miss you."

Cece's eyes burned. "Me too, Dawn."

Dawn released her. "You will be proud of me tonight. I promise."

Cece picked up a few strands of hair that had fallen from Dawn's bun and put them in place. "I already am, sweetie."

Dawn gave her a delighted smile. "Thanks." She turned with a fluid, graceful step and pirouetted back to her friends.

"Hey, Sis!"

"Tommy?" She turned toward her brother. "Why are you back here?"

"I need to talk to you for sec. Come here." He motioned with a curved finger, and she followed him to stage left.

Cece's mouth dropped open. "Patty!"

Patty jumped on Cece, practically knocking her over. They squeezed each other until Cece ran out of air.

"What are you doing here? I thought you were going to Dallas!"

"Well I didn't go, flights were outrageous. Besides, I wanted to see you more."

"Lucky me!" Cece said.

"That's right, lucky you!"

Cece gave her best friend a tearful smile. "I'm so happy to see you."

"Me too, Ceece. You know I'm lost without you. And I'm dying to see this show, among other things..."

Cece smacked Patty on her little rear end. "Naughty girl. Go take your seat, and I'll see you afterwards."

"But wait, I need to see—"

"Come on you, let's go." Tom wrapped an arm around Patty and swooped her away.

Cece stood between the curtains, clinging to the fabric, as Dawn, resplendent in a lilac tutu, sequined bodice, and sparkling tiara, took her place on stage. She was the Queen of the Land of Sweets, presenting her kingdom to her guests. Dawn danced exquisitely, bringing applause from the audience at several turns. She held herself with regal authority, yet her face portrayed the queen's generosity and kindness. The transformation since their first rehearsal was remarkable.

From her spot just off stage, Cece glanced at Brad. He was sitting next to his ex-wife in the third row, watching his daughter with a proud, beaming smile. Seeing them together reminded Cece of what a beautiful couple they must have been. She turned her attention back to Dawn, who pirouetted *en pointe* with quick, precise steps, her arms as graceful as wings, and a smile that lit up the stage.

Cece felt Natalie standing next to her. She looked at her friend and saw tears in her eyes. "She's spectacular," Natalie whispered.

Cece nodded, wiping away her own tears. "Yes, she is."

They put their arms around each other and watched Dawn finish her solo. The audience rose to its feet, and a deafening roar filled the theater. Clearwater hadn't seen a Sugar Plum Fairy so glorious and captivating in a very long time. Not since the days of Cecilia Rose.

~

A crowd swarmed Cece and loaded her arms with flowers. Cece accepted hugs and kisses and congratulations from everyone.

Mothers, fathers, grandparents, and friends stopped to tell her how wonderful the show was. She reveled in the praise, thrilled the closing show had been close to perfect.

Off to the side, Ilana greeted all of Clearwater as if she were as lucid as ever. But Cece could see confusion hiding behind the plastered-on smile.

"Excuse me," Cece said to the crowd around her. She handed her flowers to Julia and went to Ilana's side.

Ilana turned. She blinked, and the blank stare disappeared as she recognized Cece. "Cecilia, all zees people. I cannot remember. I know zem, but…" She clasped Cece's hand.

"I'll stay with her," Cece said to Maria. "Come with me, Ilana. I'll help you remember."

"Thank you, my dear." Ilana tucked her arm through Cece's. They took a few steps, then Ilana stopped and pulled on Cece's arm. "Ah, my Cecilia Rose, you dance like an angel tonight. An enchanting angel."

Cece looked into Ilana's eyes and saw a mix of the woman she once had been and the confused, aging woman she had become. Her heart was breaking again—only this time in a different place.

35

"*H*ere, wrap this one." Cece handed Patty another bracelet.

It was Christmas Eve day, and the two of them sat on the floor in Cece's bedroom surveying the windfall Barbara had given them.

"I've got enough bracelets for every little girl at the studio." Cece held up one that was almost all pink. "This one's for Olivia."

Patty glanced at her through narrowed eyes. "They're growing on you, aren't they?"

"Who?"

"The kids—Olivia, Gabe, Dawn. You haven't talked about anything else all day." Patty pulled a long piece of ribbon off the spool and snipped it with sharp scissors.

"I know what you're thinking, Patty, and I'm not that attached. On January second, you and I are hitting the road back to Southern California." Cece pinched Patty's cheek.

"Good. Because I won't go back without you." Patty tied a bow. "Hey, did you tell Natalie about what Ilana said last night?"

"Yeah, I did this morning." Cece sighed. "I'm nervous for

her. Some of those dance moms are nuts. When they find out what's been going on, it won't be pretty."

"Girls!" Julia's voice floated upstairs. "Lunch is ready."

Patty's face lit up. "Coming!"

The two of them bounded downstairs like little kids on Christmas morning.

They spent the rest of the day in the kitchen preparing food for the annual Camden Christmas open house. They expected dozens of friends to come by for champagne, eggnog, and Julia's famous cooking.

The sun was just setting when Phil drove up with Tom and Ryan. Tom had a few last minute jobs, and Phil, who normally took Christmas Eve off, helped him finish. On their way home, they picked up Ryan from his father's house.

"What's to eat around here, Mom?" Ryan grabbed a few cookies off a big platter that Julia was arranging.

"Hey!" said Julia. "Those are for tomorrow. Didn't your father feed you?"

"Yeah, but I'm hungry again. I'm always hungry."

Tom grabbed Ryan in a great bear hug and pretended to punch his shoulder. "That's what happens when puberty kicks in, big guy."

Ryan blushed. "Puberty kicked in three years ago. How long is it supposed to last?"

"Don't you worry, Ryan," Cece said. "Tommy's only giving you a hard time because his voice squeaked until he was twenty."

"It did not," Tom said, purposely raising his voice.

Phil came in carrying a bottle of wine as if it were a newborn baby. "2006, Silver Oak, Cabernet Sauvignon. Been saving this one for a special occasion!"

The family sat down at the long farm table in the kitchen that was set with straw placemats and big white dinner plates. Patty helped Julia dish up her traditional Christmas Eve spaghetti and meatball dinner. Cece inhaled deeply and sighed. She looked at her family, her amazing, wonderful, wacky family, and her heart swelled. Everyone in the world that she loved was with her, close enough for her to touch, hug, and kiss. Almost everyone.

"There are enough presents under that tree for the entire town," Julia said. "What did you girls do, rob a store?"

Phil and Julia sat on the couch drinking tea with Boomer snuggled between them. Patty and Cece were on the floor beside the Christmas tree arranging the gifts. Ryan and Tom had gone upstairs to watch a movie.

"Let's just say we stumbled into a great sale," Cece said, winking at Patty.

Boomer lifted his head. He jumped off the couch, padded to the front door, and perked up his ears. At the sound of a knock, the dog barked and jumped up.

Cece stood. "I'll get it." She pushed Boomer aside and opened the door.

"Hi there," Brad said, standing on the front porch holding a big pink bakery box. He smiled his irresistible smile, dimple and all.

Cece stepped outside, closing the door behind her. "Hi yourself. What are you doing here?"

"Just thought I'd bring you some sticky buns for Christmas morning." He held out the bakery box.

Cece's eyes lit up. "You do know how to please a girl, don't you?"

Brad grinned. "Didn't you say that to me once before?"

"I believe I did. And I liked your response."

He put the box down and pulled Cece into his arms. His lips, cold from the night air, pushed against hers. His hand went to the back of her head, and he wound his fingers into her hair. Cece caught her breath, as his smooth, cool tongue slipped around hers.

Brad groaned. "How long are you going to make me wait?"

Cece heard a note of jest in his voice. She leaned back and looked into his expectant eyes. "Rhetorically or literally?"

Brad laughed. "I'll take either."

"Would you like to come in?"

"Nobody's home?" His tone was hopeful

"Everyone's home."

"Well, shoot," he said with exaggerated disappointment.

"Sorry. But come in anyway."

"I shouldn't. I'm on my way to a friend's house up north for a few days. Dawn's with Pam, so I thought I'd get away. Too quiet at my house."

Cece toyed with his fingers, realizing again how lonely he must be, especially around the holidays. She remembered her father's brooding after her mother left. "Just come in for a minute. Nobody's going to bite you."

Brad picked up the box. "I wouldn't mind if you did."

Cece slapped his arm. "Oh wait, Patty might bite. She's not very well behaved."

Cece pushed open the front door. Boomer greeted Brad by jumping up and almost knocking the box out of his hands.

"Oops." Cece rescued the box and put it on the table beside the front door. "Forgot about the dog. He's not so well behaved either."

"That's okay, I'm a dog person," Brad said, giving Boomer a scratch behind the ears.

Just one more reason to like him, Cece thought.

In the living room, everyone turned, their faces registering surprise at the unexpected visitor.

"Dad, Julia," Cece said. "This is Brad."

"Hello," Phil said, getting up from the couch. The men shook hands.

Julia welcomed Brad with a warm smile. "I'm so happy to finally meet you."

"Thank you, Julia, likewise."

"And this," Cece said, extending her arm with a flourish, "is Patty."

The corners of Brad's mouth turned upwards into an amused smile. "Ah, the roommate and best friend. I've heard about you."

Patty nearly fell over herself looking at Brad, and her mouth dropped open as she stared.

Cece rolled her eyes. "I told you she has terrible manners."

Brad was unruffled. "Very nice to meet you, Patty."

"This is Mr. Sticky-buns?" Patty said.

"Patty!" Cece wanted to crawl into a hole.

"Mr. Sticky-buns?" Brad looked at Cece.

Phil chuckled as he took Patty by the arm. "I'll get us some drinks. Come on, Patty, you're going with me."

Julia rested a hand on Brad's arm. "Patty's a bit of a character."

"I can tell," he said. "And I guess I earned that nickname, didn't I?"

"Well," said Cece, her face flushed, "you did just show up with an entire box of them."

"Guilty as charged," said Brad.

Julia laughed. "Brad, I'm surprised we've never met. Clearwater is such a small town."

"I travel quite a bit for work. My firm's main office is in New York, so I'm on the East Coast a lot."

Cece didn't know that about him. He'd never mentioned it. Not that it mattered.

Patty and Phil came back with glasses of eggnog on a tray.

"Thank you," Brad said, taking one. "Merry Christmas."

"Merry Christmas," said Phil. "Patty, do you have something to say."

Patty looked chagrined. "I apologize for my rude behavior, Brad. I was caught off guard by your devastatingly handsome face."

Cece gave Patty a light shove. "Go sit on the couch with Julia. You may not speak again."

Brad winked at Patty as she sat down. "Patty, you are beyond charming."

Patty opened her mouth as if to reply, but Julia lifted her chin and closed it.

"Mom!" Ryan's voice could be heard as he came downstairs. "I'm hungry. Is there anything to eat?" He walked into the living room and stopped dead in his tracks. "Mr. Redmond?"

Brad stood. "Yes?"

"What are you doing here?" Ryan asked.

"Ryan," Julia got up. "That's no way to—"

"Am I in trouble?"

Brad turned to Cece. "Who is he?"

Cece covered her eyes. "Oh no," she whispered to herself. She took a deep breath. "He's my step-brother, Ryan Bailey."

Brad's face went from utter loss to vague confusion to clarity in a split second. "*You're* Ryan Bailey? Dawn's b—uh, friend?" He looked at Cece then back at Ryan.

"Me and Dawn," Ryan said, "we're just friends. I swear it…I think."

Julia the diplomat stepped up. "Ryan, Mr. Redmond is a friend of Cece's. He came by to…to bring us sticky buns."

Patty got up and stood next to Cece. "You know, people would pay good money to see this."

"Shush!"

"Why did he bring us sticky buns?" Ryan asked.

"For Christmas, of course," Patty interjected.

"I told you to keep quiet," Cece hissed.

"Mr. Redmond," Ryan said, "are you here to talk to me?"

Brad gave Ryan a hard look. "I wasn't, but now that I know who you are, maybe we should talk about Dawn."

"Dawn?" Phil said. "Who's Dawn?"

Julia touched Phil's arm. "The Sugar Plum Fairy, honey, in *The Nutcracker*. Remember how extraordinarily she danced? Especially closing night, right Phil?"

"Oh yes. She was spectacular, fabulous." Phil turned to Brad. "You know her?"

"She's my daughter."

"Oh," said Phil. "Okay, I think I'm getting this, but maybe not."

"Ryan," Brad said, his voice controlled, "I'd like to know if there is something going on between you and Dawn."

"Nothing, sir. I swear, nothing."

"Then why has she been crying over you?"

"Over *me*?"

"That's right."

"Now hold on there a minute," Phil began.

Julia rolled her eyes and went to stand between Cece and Patty. "What a fiasco," she said.

"I am so loving this," Patty said.

"Phil," Brad said, "your boy Ryan here has caused my daughter considerable heartache."

Phil put an arm over Ryan's shoulder. "I'm sure there's a perfectly reasonable explanation for everything. Ryan is a good kid."

"Then why is Dawn crying her eyes out? Do you know what it's like to see the daughter you adore suffering with a broken heart?"

"As a matter of fact, I do," Phil said.

Patty squeezed Cece's arm. "I'm in heaven."

Brad took a swig of his drink. "Yeah, well, my daughter is

only fifteen. Yours is what, like…" He glanced at Cece. "I don't even know how old you are. Thirty?"

"Jesus Christ, twenty-nine. I'm twenty-nine."

"God, I love him," Patty whispered.

Phil turned to Ryan. "I didn't even know you had a girlfriend."

"I don't!"

"Well then," Phil said, "this is very confusing. Why is the Redmond girl crying over you?"

"I don't know," Ryan said. "I like Dawn, I do, but…but Gabe's the one that *really* likes her."

"Gabe?" Brad said. "Gabe Martin?"

"Yes, and he's one of my best friends."

Phil looked at Julia. "Do we know Gabe?" he whispered.

"Yes, Phil. We know Gabe."

Cece looked at Patty. "See why I hate small towns?"

Patty sighed. "I'm never leaving this place."

Brad looked flabbergasted. "Well, that's interesting."

"What's interesting?" Tom entered the living room. "Whoa. Brad Redmond?"

Brad looked at Cece. "Your house is a circus."

Cece felt a headache coming. "You think?"

"So, Brad, I hear you're making the moves on my sister."

"Who's your sister?"

"Sheesh," Cece said, "I am."

Patty practically jumped up and down. "This just keeps getting better and better."

Tom straightened his back and extended a hand toward Brad. "Tom Camden," he said, his voice low and authoritative.

Brad shook his hand slowly. He frowned at Tom, studied his face. "That name's familiar."

"Same last name as Cece's."

"No, that's not it." Brad frowned and rubbed his chin.

"Maybe we've crossed paths," said Tom. "I do a lot of the electrical work in town."

"Wait, wait." Brad pointed at him. "Tom Camden. Tommy Camden! You used to play football, didn't you?"

Tom nodded. "Yeah, in high school."

"I used to watch you play! Wide receiver, my God, you were great. I remember your last game, had to be about eight years ago. You caught that Hail Mary pass. Came at you from outta nowhere, and you scored the winning touchdown!"

"You were there?" Tom said, his face beaming.

"Hell yeah, I was there!"

Brad slapped Tom on the shoulder. "What happened to you, man? Thought for sure you'd get recruited."

Tom lowered his head and swung it back and forth. "Ah shit, went to Berkeley and blew out my knee before the season even started."

Brad tightened his lips in sympathy. "What a rip."

"Hey, Brad," Phil said, "come into the den, and I'll show you the photo of my boy catching that ball."

"You still have that, Pop?" Tom asked.

"What are you kidding? Of course I do."

The three men headed into the other room.

"Um, Mr. Redmond?" Ryan said. "Are we...are we, like, done?"

Brad nodded. "I think so. Sure. Did you want me to, uh, you know, say anything to Dawn about..."

"That's okay. I'll just see her back at school."

"Good then." Brad squeezed Ryan's shoulder. "Great. I like you."

Ryan's Adam's apple bobbed in his skinny neck. "Thank you, sir."

Brad followed Tom and Phil. Ryan collapsed onto the couch. Cece picked up the bakery box from Nutmeg's and opened it. "Sticky bun, anyone?"

36

"Your family's great, Cece. What a riot in there," Brad said as they walked down the steps toward his car.

"Uh-huh," Cece said, still embarrassed by the scene, "a regular comedy act."

"I can't believe I used to watch your brother play football. What a small world."

"What a small town," Cece said. "It's one of the reasons I left —everybody knowing everyone else and their business. I could not wait to get out of here and run off to the big city."

Brad put an arm over Cece's shoulders. "And I grew up in the big city romanticizing about living in a small town."

Cece sighed. "Funny how that works. What we don't have somehow becomes the ideal." The thought sobered her.

"Is living in Los Angeles your ideal?"

"Absolutely," Cece said. "Is living in Clearwater yours?"

"For now."

"Maybe you'll follow your daughter wherever she goes to college."

"Maybe I will," Brad laughed. "Wouldn't she just love that?"

The sky was clear, the stars sparkled, and Phil's extravagant Christmas lights illuminated the entire front yard.

"This house could win one of those contests, with all these lights and decorations," Brad said. "Especially the reindeer."

"My dad loves to decorate. We used to have this Santa and sleigh thing on the roof, but Julia nixed it. Too dangerous."

"That's actually very sweet," said Brad.

"It actually is."

They continued their slow walk down the driveway, gravel crunching under their steps.

"So," Cece said, "how long will you be at your friend's house?"

"Just a couple days. Will you be here when I get back?"

"Yes," Cece smiled up at him. "I decided to stay through New Year's."

"Did you, now?"

"I did. And I'll go with you to your fancy party. If you still want me to, that is."

Brad stopped and faced her. He put his arms around her and kissed her. "I absolutely still want you to." He kissed her again, his hands on both sides of her face. She stood on her toes and parted her lips, inviting him into a deep and sensuous kiss.

There was an old picnic table to the side of the driveway nestled in amongst some tall trees. Cece stepped backwards in the direction of the table, bringing Brad with her. She boosted herself up and sat on the end, her legs dangling.

"So, what should I wear?" She gave him a flirtatious smile.

"That is a loaded question if I ever heard one," Brad said, a glint in his green eyes.

"Well, I expect some of your colleagues will be there. I would not want to be underdressed."

"I wouldn't mind."

"Then I'd be cold."

"Then I'd warm you up." Brad stood in front of her and

looked down, his eyes sexy and mischievous, and removed his heavy jacket.

"What are you doing? It's freezing out here."

"Shhh…" He wrapped it around Cece's shoulders, lowered her onto the table, and leaned over her, his hands underneath her head. He kissed her with an urgency Cece hadn't felt before. He nestled his nose into her neck and inhaled. "You are driving me crazy, Cecilia Rose."

Cece wound her fingers into his hair. His kisses on her neck made her skin tingle and her breaths shorten. The stirring inside her stomach brought back a memory, but she pushed it away. Brad Redmond was here; he was now, and the way he wanted her made her body ache.

She put her hands on his shoulders and gently pushed him up. He lifted his head and looked at her, his eyes questioning. Cece said nothing. She ran her tongue over her lips, and unzipped her jacket. Brad's muscular arms were on either side of her, supporting his weight. She watched him breathe deeply.

"Don't move," she said, her eyes trained on his. She wriggled out of her jacket. "Just watch."

Brad swallowed. "Yes, ma'am," he whispered, one corner of his mouth rising, his dimple showing.

She began unbuttoning her shirt. Even on her back, vulnerable and unable to move, she felt in control. She watched his eyes trail downward as she released the buttons one by one. When she reached the last button, she opened her shirt, revealing her lacy, black bra. "You did say you'd warm me up, didn't you?"

Brad's smile was brighter than all the Christmas lights in Clearwater.

~

Cece stretched and yawned as she woke up the next morning. She could hear quiet whispers floating up the stairs. Patty snored softly next to her. Cece jumped on her. "Merry Christmas, little girl!"

"No. Too early." Patty opened one eye. "What the hell were you doing outside so late last night?"

"Just hanging out on the picnic table." Cece ruffled Patty's hair.

Patty yawned. "Doing what?"

"You're a nosy girl," said Cece. "Mostly talking. I told him I'd stay and go to that New Year's party with him. Sorry."

"That's okay," said Patty. "I'm staying too."

"What? Don't you have to go back to work?"

"Nope." Patty rolled onto her back. "I got fired."

"Fired? Why?"

"The assistant manager said I assaulted him with the hot glue gun."

"Did you?" asked Cece.

"No! Well, not exactly. Okay, kind of. He was stupid and incompetent and constantly telling me how to do things."

"So, you shot him with hot glue?"

Patty scowled. "It was an accident, and besides, it was just one drip. I get that stuff on my hands all the time. Look." Patty held up her hand to show Cece several faded scars. "What a whiny wimp he was."

Cece pushed Patty out of bed. "You are a scary girl. Come on, I hear the boys scurrying around. Let's go see what Santa brought!"

For Cece, Christmas day unfolded like a scene out of a storybook.

Julia had made enormous Christmas stockings stuffed with chocolates, homemade treats, mittens, and matching Santa hats for everyone. They sat for hours in front of their huge, magnificent tree opening gifts, drinking coffee, eating sticky buns, listening to the "Yule Log" on the radio, and laughing and delighting in every joyful moment.

By the time they finished opening presents, the floor was littered with wrapping paper, ribbons, and scrunched up balls of tape. It was almost noon when Julia stood and clapped her hands. "Okay, everyone, clean-up time. We got company coming!"

Countless friends, friends of friends, and family of friends filtered in and out of the Camden house all afternoon and into the evening. They had a roaring fire in the fireplace, white lights twinkling on the tree, Christmas music playing, and everyone eating, drinking, and toasting.

Cece stood against the wall watching the joyful chaos. She felt a tickle on her back.

"Happy?" Julia wrapped an arm around Cece's waist.

Cece hugged her. "You know what? I am."

"Good." Julia smoothed Cece's hair out of her eyes. It was a sweet, maternal gesture, and Cece liked it. "Did you notice that your brother is paying quite of bit of attention to Patty?"

Julia pointed to the far corner of the living room where Patty was sitting on Tom's lap. Cece smiled. "About time he made a move. I practically wrapped her up and gave her to him for Christmas."

"Well, I just hope the feeling is mutual," Julia said. "I'd hate to see him get hurt again."

A loud clatter in the kitchen sent Julia running. Cece stayed where she was and watched her brother and Patty. She could read Patty as easily as a children's book. Her eyes shined, her head tilted to the side, her smile enticing and coy. She's interested in him, Cece thought, very interested.

Finally, the crowd started to thin. Cece was about to sit down in front of the fire when one of Julia's friends approached.

"Cece, I just wanted to tell you how much we loved the show. It was spectacular. One of the best productions in years."

"I'm so glad," Cece said, forgetting the woman's name. "Thank you for coming to see it."

"I haven't missed a show in twenty-five years." The woman touched Cece's elbow. "But I heard disturbing news about Ilana Lurensky. What a shame. How's she doing?"

The question surprised Cece, and it made her uncomfortable to discuss Ilana with anyone, especially someone making idle gossip. "She's, uh, actually doing better, I think. I'm sorry, but would you excuse me?"

"Oh, of course, I—"

Cece didn't listen to the rest. She had to get away. Just thinking about Ilana and the hurdles facing Natalie made her squirm. She was about to sneak upstairs, but Tom stopped her.

"Ceece, got a sec?"

"Sure. What's up?"

"Uh, I just, um, well, I was thinking..."

Cece raised her eyebrows at her brother. "Is this about Patty?"

Tom grinned. "Yeah. I'm thinking about asking her to go out with me on New Year's Eve."

Cece squeezed his muscular arm. "That's a great idea."

"Really? You don't mind?"

"Of course not. Now go ask her before you chicken out."

"Thanks Sis," Tom said, giving her a quick kiss. He headed off in search of Patty.

Yep, Cece thought, *everyone wants to be in love at Christmas time.*

37

*I*n the days following Christmas, a sense of calm settled over Cece. It felt as if all of Clearwater had taken a deep breath and let it out. The frantic tension leading up to the opening and closing shows was gone. The teen drama evaporated, and when the news about Ilana went public, the pressure of keeping it hush-hush vanished. The fallout, however, landed hard.

The show had closed only four days ago, and the dance moms were on the warpath. Natalie Lurensky had concealed vital information. They divided themselves—some in support of Natalie, and some against her. One of the mothers even started a petition to allow a rival dance center to take over the studio. Thankfully, it didn't gain traction because Brad Redmond intervened on Natalie's behalf. The Lurensky Dance Academy was a privately-owned entity, and there was no legal basis for a petition. Word was Brad had scolded the woman for wasting everyone's time, and then he told her she was making a fool of herself.

Still, Natalie's situation was grim.

~

Cece tapped on Natalie's office door as she pushed it open. "Hi."

Natalie stood. She walked around her desk, arms spread wide. They hugged each other. "At the risk of repeating myself for the hundredth time, I couldn't have done it without you."

"Repeat all you want." Cece smiled at her old friend. "I loved doing it. Maybe I'll come back next year and do it again."

Natalie released her. "Right now, I'm not sure there'll be a next year for the studio."

"That bad, huh?"

"Let's see, they're calling it everything from subterfuge to deceit to fraud."

"You've got to be kidding." Cece could hardly believe it. Despite the seriousness of the situation, that sounded a little over the top.

"Wish I were. I should never have brought her to the closing show." Natalie shook her head.

"What about Teresa?" Cece asked. "Can she help calm everyone down?"

"There's only so much she can do. The other parents are her friends, and I can't expect her to take the heat for me. Anyway, I do have a few parents still on my side." She opened a desk drawer and took out a white envelope. "Here," she said, handing it to Cece. "I wish I could pay you more. Your work with Dawn was extraordinary."

Cece fiddled with the envelope. "She is a talented girl."

Natalie rubbed the back of her neck. "She's a beautiful, talented dancer, but you took her to a level beyond expectation. Everyone's saying so."

"Come on," said Cece, flattered. "I didn't do that much."

"Yes, you did. You're a fabulous instructor." Natalie leaned against the desk. "I know this business, Cece. I've seen more ballerinas and dancers and teachers than I can remember. It's the rare athlete who becomes the great coach. And you're one of them. Or at least you could be."

Cece didn't know what to make of Natalie's assessment or how to respond to the praise. "Well, I guess your mother had something to do with that."

Natalie gave her a knowing smile, as if she could tell she'd made Cece uncomfortable. "Speaking of my mother, I'm taking her to Scottsdale for New Year's. I might not be back before you leave."

This was it. Time to say goodbye. It wasn't like she and Natalie wouldn't see each other again, but there was a sense of finality to the moment. A tear dropped onto Cece's cheek, and she whisked it away.

"Don't you dare," Natalie pointed at Cece, "or else I'll start to cry." She pinched the bridge of her nose and closed her eyes. When she opened them, she lifted her chin, and her radiant, confident smile returned.

"Oh, I almost forgot," said Natalie, opening her purse. She removed a small photograph with crinkled edges. "Did you ever see this picture?"

Cece took the photograph from Natalie's hand. She stared at it.

It was her ballerina, the Sugar Plum Fairy. The face Cece had painted with painstaking care stared at her. Standing next to the ballerina was nine-year-old Cece, her wild brown curls wider than her body. In the photo, she was looking up at the dancer, enchanted and reverent. The ballerina was looking at the camera and smiling just with her eyes.

Cece turned the photo over. On the back in Ilana's recognizable scrawl it said:

San Francisco Ballet - Cecilia Rose and Sugar Plum Fairy

Cece's hand trembled. She looked at the picture again. The image took her back in time to a moment she would never forget.

"Do you remember that day?" said Natalie. "We had so much fun."

Cece nodded. "I do."

"You can have the photo if you want it."

"Thank you," Cece said. Natalie had no idea how much it meant to her.

Natalie put an arm around Cece. They took slow steps toward the door. It felt surreal.

"Good luck with everything, Natalie."

"It'll be fine, probably, maybe," Natalie said, her voice soft. "And good luck to you too. I hope everything back home works out the way you want it to."

"Thanks." Cece squeezed Natalie's hand. "I really, really do feel bad leaving you with such a mess."

"Please don't feel bad. I wish you could, or would, stay, but LA's your home. That's where your life is. And you need to be there."

Cece nodded. She gave up on not crying and allowed the tears to stream down her cheeks. Natalie gave in as well. They hugged for a long time before Natalie pulled away. It was difficult for Cece to let go.

~

The house was empty when Cece got home. She plugged in the Christmas tree, and the twinkling lights came to life. Her ballerina ornament glimmered. Cece touched its delicate toe and watched the figurine dance among the lights. She thought of Dawn and herself and the Sugar Plum Fairy in the photo she held in her hand.

Upstairs in her room, Cece slipped the photograph into the frame of the mirror above her dresser. It looked as if it had been there for twenty years.

Boomer, snoozing on her bed, snored softly. Cece sat beside him and stroked his warm fur. He lifted his head and looked at her, his dark brown eyes full of love. Something stirred inside her, the creative urge. Cece reached under the bed for her sketchpad and art pencils. "I'm going to draw you," she said to the dog.

Cece opened her old art box. Beside her pencils was her beautiful sable paintbrush. She'd forgotten all about it.

The hair was supple and shaped to perfection. Cece studied the tip, gently rounded, not a strand out of place. The handle, long and thin with a maroon lacquer finish, gleamed. She rested it on the palm of her hand and thought about Doug finding the page she had marked in the catalog. To Cece's surprise, no tears came, only an intense desire to paint with the magnificent brush.

The back door slammed. Boomer jumped off the bed and raced downstairs.

"Anyone home?" Phil's loud voice echoed.

Cece tucked her paintbrush into its case and went to greet her father. "Hi, Daddy. Where's Julia?"

"Mahjong, I think. Why aren't you with Patty?"

"She's out with Tommy."

"Is that so?" Phil grinned. "Have you had dinner?"

"Not yet," Cece said. "It's too late to start cooking. Why don't we make popcorn and watch a movie, just like we did when Tommy and I were kids."

"Good idea." Phil pulled a large pot out of the cupboard. "Boy, did Kathryn get mad whenever I gave you two popcorn for dinner. 'Children need nourishment,' she used to say."

The mention of her mother rattled Cece. She couldn't even remember the last time they'd talked about her.

Phil poured oil into the pot. "We actually had a good laugh about that not long ago."

"Who? You and Tommy?"

"No." Phil glanced over his shoulder. "Me and your mom."

Cece grasped the back of the chair. "You talked to my mother?"

"Yes, honey," her father said. "Your mom and I do talk now and then."

Something intangible, yet monumental, shifted. "Why?" Cece asked. "I thought you hated her."

Phil frowned. "I never hated her, Cece."

"Of course you did! We all did!" She shouted at her father.

Phil objected, his head shaking. "I'll admit I was angry, but I didn't hate her."

Cece tried to absorb what her father had said. If he didn't hate her mother, had never hated her, what did that mean? Had she been wrong all these years? Panic rose in her chest, as if an earthquake were shaking her foundation. "Why didn't you tell me?"

Phil put the lid on the popcorn. He seemed surprised by her reaction. "Tell you what, Cece?"

"That you were in contact. I thought…thought she was out of our lives."

"She wasn't," Phil said. "We had two children together. Your mom and I always had things to discuss. Decisions about you kids."

Cece closed her eyes, as if to shut herself off. How could she not have known this about her parents? "I don't understand. My mother had nothing to do with me after she left."

"Actually, she did. A lot. She helped me help you move on."

Cece's legs went weak. She sat down, her mind spinning with questions. She grabbed one. "What about Tommy? Does he talk to her?"

"On occasion. I know she calls him on his birthday."

A chill crawled up Cece's back, scraping at her skin. The call on her birthday, every birthday. And every few months in between—an unknown number, a missed call, no message, a stalker. "I can't believe you never told me," Cece said, her voice barely audible.

"Never told you what, honey?"

"That I could stop being mad. That you'd forgiven her."

Phil removed the pot from the stove. He turned the burner

off, and the flame went out. Phil looked at Cece, his face serious. "We forgave each other."

"Each other? You didn't do anything wrong!" She felt like she was clinging to a rope that was unraveling.

Phil leaned against the counter. "Our divorce wasn't only your mother's fault, honey. I carry my share of blame."

"That's not true," Cece said, unwilling to accept any contradiction to what she had believed for so long. "My mother had an affair, and she walked out because she wanted to get away from us. It was that simple."

"Nothing is that simple, Cece. Marriage is complicated, it takes work. We both could've worked harder. I was devastated when she left, and caught off guard, to say the least. But as time passed, I stopped being angry. I had to. For my own sake, I just had to."

Tears blinded her. For thirteen years, every decision she made had been shaped by the knowledge that her mother had betrayed them. And now she was supposed to wrap her brain around a new version of the events?

"I'm sorry we didn't discuss this sooner, Cece. But you never wanted to talk about your mom when you were younger, and I didn't want to push you. And more recently, I don't know, everyone has moved on, so I figured, what's the point?"

"What's the point?" Cece repeated her father's question, astounded he would ask it. "The point is I quit dancing because of her. I left Clearwater because of her. I'm an uptight control freak because of her!" Hurt and anger bubbled inside her. "I would have been a prima ballerina if it hadn't been for my mother."

Phil took a deep breath. "And she would have been one if it hadn't been for me."

Cece felt dizzy. Missing puzzle pieces swirled, as if filling the gaps in her mind. Her mother's drive, her control, her need for Cece to achieve what she did not. "That's not true," said

Cece, clinging to thin threads of the story she wanted to believe. "My mother told me she wasn't good enough."

"Kathryn was more than good enough. But she made a choice. She chose me." Phil gazed at his daughter, his eyes full of concern. And something else. Disappointment? "You're not a victim, Cece, none of us are. This may sound harsh, but you need to own your decisions, even the ones made in anger."

His words hit like a slap. Cece did consider herself a victim —damaged because her mother had traumatized and deserted her. The wounds were deep inside and could not be healed. Staying angry was the only way to ease the hurt. It felt good. It felt right. And it was easy. Easier than owning her decisions. Easier than facing truths. Easier than trying to forgive.

38

*T*he unknown number became known. Her mother's voice, while familiar, had changed. It was softer. She spoke slowly, as if considering each word. They made only small talk, but it was a start. It was a step.

~

The café in Sonoma was known for its afternoon tea. When Cece was little, her mother used to take her to English high tea at the Fairmont Hotel every Christmas, and Cece had somehow thought that being in a familiar situation might ease the churning emotion of seeing her mother for the first time in years.

They exchanged pleasantries, nibbled on crust-less sandwiches, and sipped tea with cream and sugar. Kathryn was living in Monterey, working at an exclusive dress shop, and volunteering at a community theater where the local ballet studio performed *The Nutcracker* every Christmas.

Cece tried to act casually, as if sitting at a table across from her mother were an ordinary, everyday event. But the tension was suffocating. Cece skipped the hot tea and drank several glasses of cold water.

When they ran out of small talk and an awkward silence settled between them, Kathryn took a deep breath. She folded her hands and leaned toward her daughter. "I'm sorry," she said. "So terribly sorry for what I did thirteen years ago."

Cece swallowed. Her gaze drifted down and then back onto Kathryn's face.

"I hurt you and your brother, and I will regret it until the day I die. But I never forgot about you and, God knows, never stopped loving you. That's why I called you so many times. I just wanted you to know I was still there for you, even if you didn't want me in your life." Kathryn patted her lips with a white napkin; a bit of pink lipstick stained the cloth. It was like putting a period at the end of the sentence.

She had aged, Cece noticed, but in a good way. How old was she now? Cece calculated. Fifty-two. She'd been only twenty-three years old when Cece was born. Her brown hair was cut to just above her shoulders, and her bangs fell to the side. She wore dark blue pants and a crisp, white shirt. A strand of pearls encircled her slender neck.

"You look good, Mom."

Kathryn just smiled. She knew Cece well.

"Right," said Cece. "That was kind of a non-sequitur."

"It was." Kathryn's quiet laugh was the same as Cece remembered. "But that's okay." She poured herself more tea from the porcelain teapot, added a drop of cream, and stirred it with a tiny spoon.

Cece watched her mother lift the cup with two hands. Kathryn's nails were short and painted red. Her eyes settled on Cece's face, and she waited, patient and gentle.

Something stirred in Cece's chest, and she recalled her father's words. *We forgave each other.*

"I...I accept your apology," Cece said. She drank more

water. She could not tell her mother that all was forgiven. Not yet.

"Thank you."

Cece ate a cucumber and cream cheese sandwich. "I have questions," she said.

"I have answers." Kathryn straightened her back. "And plenty of time."

There were so many questions, but Cece didn't have to ask them all today. She knew now there would be other days.

"Why did you tell me you weren't good enough?"

Kathryn did not have to ask what she meant. "Because I wasn't."

"Dad said you were."

Cece's mother laughed. "That sounds just like him. I might have been good enough for a while, a good-enough ballerina, anyway. But I got tired. I missed my parents. I hated the travel. And..." She paused and dusted some crumbs off the white tablecloth with her hand. "And I fell in love. I chose your dad. And that is something I will never regret."

Cece was stunned. "Then why did—"

Kathryn stopped her. "What happened when you were a teenager was between your father and me. But I want you to know, it had nothing to do with you kids. Not one thing."

In a strange way, Cece accepted Kathryn's response with relief. There was only so much she needed, or wanted, to hear.

Kathryn stretched her hand across the table and touched Cece's fingertips, the first physical contact between them in years. Cece's hand went warm.

"I have a long list of regrets," Kathryn said.

Cece smiled thinly. "Yeah, we all do."

"But," said Kathryn, "I do not regret that I stopped dancing. By the time I did, I was mentally drained, emotionally stretched beyond my limit. I might have been as talented as you, but I was never as strong. You had focus and motivation that was rare. I saw it. Ilana saw it. It was almost instinctive."

Cece had never thought about it that way. Instinctive. "I am a good teacher," said Cece.

"I'll bet you are."

The waiter came by and placed the check on the table. Kathryn looked up. "Thank you very much. Here, let me give you my card." She handed the waiter her credit card without looking at the bill.

Cece didn't remember her mother being so...so refined. Another question that would wait until another day.

Kathryn studied Cece. "You're beautiful, Cece. Inside and out. I'm very proud of you."

"Thank you," Cece said. She had not expected such a compliment.

"And I hope we can see each other again. I actually get down to LA every so often."

Her mother in Los Angeles. Another revelation. "I'd like that."

They finished up. It had been just enough—the right amount of questions and answers, confessions and vulnerabilities. After signing the check, Kathryn stood and put her handbag over her shoulder. "Ready, Princess?"

Cece could tell by the look on her mother's face that the term of endearment, her pet name for Cece from babyhood, had popped out unintentionally.

"Oh, I..." Kathryn looked flustered. "I didn't mean to..."

"It's okay, Mom." Cece took a deep breath and got up from table. Her eyes burned just hearing it, but she brushed it off, as if it had meant nothing. But it meant something.

Kathryn walked with Cece to her car. They stopped on the sidewalk, under a tree. Cece removed her keys from her purse. "Thank you for tea. It was nice."

"Thank you for seeing me."

Cece sensed her mother's desire to hold her. She resisted at first, until her need to be held took over. And then she gave in. Her mother's arms were strong, her hold fierce and full of love, sadness, relief. It filled cracks in Cece's heart she hadn't even known existed.

39

*F*rom that moment forward, Cece allowed herself to recall memories of her mother that were happy. Little ones, a few at a time. Forgiveness was a process. It would not be rushed.

The weight from all the anger and resentment Cece had carried for so long began to subside, as if she were emptying small stones from her pockets one by one.

~

Patty was perched on a tiny round stool in the fitting room at Julia's favorite boutique. She pulled the Christmas lollipop out of her mouth with a slurp. "That dress is perfect on you."

"I have to agree," Julia said. "It is stunning."

Cece had tried on a dozen little black dresses. "I don't know," Cece said, turning in front of the mirror. "It's so clingy, though."

"Perfectly clingy," Patty said. "You look fabulous."

It was a classic LBD. It hugged Cece's body in all the right places. "You don't think it's too sexy?"

"Heavens, no," Julia said. "Very Audrey Hepburn, alluring and classy."

"And expensive." Cece held up the price tag.

"It's a birthday present." Julia unzipped the dress. "Now hurry up and get changed. Shopping with you two has worn me out."

After dinner, Cece went upstairs to her room and tried on the dress again. She pirouetted in front of the mirror like a little girl.

It is such a gorgeous dress, she thought. *Doug would love it on me.*

Cece froze. The thought had come out of nowhere. He was never far from her mind, but he wasn't a constant presence anymore either. Annoyed with herself, she removed the dress, hung it in the closet, and forced herself to think of something other than Doug. Something like Brad.

Brad Redmond, the man taking her to the party in her beautiful new dress. They hadn't seen each other since Christmas. He had called to let her know he was in San Francisco on business. And to tell her he was looking forward to New Year's Eve.

Cece sighed, anticipating a night with Brad outside of Clearwater, where nobody knew her. It would be liberating. And fun. As she turned to go back downstairs, she banged her toes into Patty's open suitcase.

"Ouch!" Cece grabbed her foot. She shoved the suitcase out of the way, tipping it over and uncovering an enormous stack of unopened mail.

"Patty!" Cece hollered as she picked up the mail and stomped down the stairs. She dropped the mail onto the dining room table. "Where are you?"

"She's outside with Tom," Julia called from the kitchen.

Cece peered out the front window. She could see them sitting on the tire swing, Patty's tiny body wrapped up in her brother's arms, his heavy jacket around her. She sighed. They were adorable together; but not that adorable.

Cece threw open the door and stepped onto the porch.

"Patty! Get in here."

Patty turned. "Can't you see I'm busy?"

"Yeah, well, you're going to get a lot busier now. I just found the pile of mail that you didn't bother to open all month!"

"Crap," Patty said. "I totally forgot I brought it."

Tom released her. "Thanks a lot, Sis."

"Sorry Tommy, but little Patty's in big trouble."

Tom gave Patty a swat on her behind. "See you tomorrow, cupcake."

Patty giggled as she skipped up the front steps. Cece held the door open for her. Jesus, cupcake?

"Oh my God, your brother kisses like—"

"Don't say it."

"An animal. All luscious lips and swirly tongue and—"

"Patty! Don't make me think about how my little brother kisses. It's disgusting." Cece closed the door. "Wanna tell me why you brought a suitcase full of unopened mail with you?"

"Because it needs opening?" she said, as if it were the most obvious thing in the world.

"Why did you ignore it all these weeks?" Cece asked.

"You know I don't do mail, Ceece. That's your job."

It was true. Cece did handle the bills. The two of them operated like an old married couple.

They went inside and sat on the floor of the living room in front of the coffee table. Patty tore open the envelopes, pulled out the bills, and pushed them toward Cece. Cece checked the dates and sorted them into stacks: 'past due,' 'pay soon,' and 'deal with when home.'

"I hate mail," Patty complained. "Sooo boring."

"Yeah, well, lucky for you I take care of it. Any more bills?"

Patty shuffled through some junk. "Think we got them all. Oh, wait." She picked up an envelope. "It's for you."

Cece yawned and stretched. She extended her hand. "Let me see." The block printing on the front made her gasp.

"What is it?" Patty asked.

"It's from Doug." She scrutinized the postmark. Costa Rica, December 16th. Cece swallowed. Her hand shook.

"Are you gonna open it?" Patty asked.

"I'm afraid to. I've been trying not to think about him. I don't want to slip backwards."

Cece put the letter on the table. She pushed it away with one finger, as if it had germs.

"I brought you girls a pot of tea." Julia placed a tray on the table. She looked their faces. "What happened?"

"Cece got a letter from Doug," Patty whispered.

"What's it say?"

"We don't know," Patty said, still whispering.

Julia sat on the couch. "Why don't we know?"

"Because she's scared to open it."

"I see," Julia said, her voice low.

"It's from Costa Rica," Patty said. "Mailed two weeks ago."

"Would you two quit talking about me like I'm not in the room?" said Cece. "Just give it to me."

Julia put her hand on the envelope and slid it across the table. Cece picked it up, tore the seal, and pulled out a folded piece of white notebook paper. A small photo fluttered out of the note. Cece picked up the picture. She inhaled, her chest trembling. It was Doug standing in front of a tree in the middle of a cloud-covered forest. Above his head, dangling from the branches, were four monkeys. Cece stared at the picture. She knew his face so well, the broad smile, the sad eyes.

One of Doug's companions had taken the picture. His own camera was slung around his neck, his right hand holding the lens, one finger over the lens cover. Cece had seen him in this exact position a thousand times.

"He made it to the rainforest," she said calmly. She handed the picture to Julia, who looked at it and then handed it to Patty.

Cece unfolded the letter and read it aloud.

Dear Cece,

I've been in Costa Rica only a few days, and already I love this place. It's beautiful, pristine, like I've gone back in time. I hope it's okay that I'm writing to you. I'm not even sure I'm going to send this letter, but I need to write it. Every day I see, hear, and smell things I wish I could share with you. A thousand times I've turned and looked for you, thinking I felt you at my side. I dream about you every night. And I think about you every hour. I'm so sorry Ceece. I never meant to disappoint you. I hope someday you'll be able to forgive me. I'm trying to believe our breaking up was for the best, because I'm finally a photographer in the rainforest. I just wish I could also have been everything you wanted me to be. I don't know, maybe I will be that man someday. But it'll be too late by then. My timing always did suck.

Cece lost focus. Her tears dropped from her chin onto the paper, smearing the ink.

If I send this letter, and if you're reading it, my guess is you're crying. I know this because I'm crying too. I haven't cried since I was eight years old, but in the past couple of weeks, I've cried a lot. The guys I'm traveling with think I have bad allergies, and one of them keeps making me drink this tea that he concocts from leaves and some root thing. It tastes like shit.

. . .

Cece stopped. She smiled through her tears. She almost laughed.

I guess I just want you to know I'm alive. We're here another week, and then we move on, not sure where. I hope things are going well for you, wherever you are now and whatever you're doing. They say that time heals all wounds. If that's true, I can't even begin to imagine how much time it will take for me to get over you.

His letter stopped there. Cece looked at Julia and Patty, their tears flowing as much as hers.

She left the table and climbed the stairs to her room. Cece sat on her bed and read the letter again. The sorrow that had steadily retreated over the last few weeks came rushing back like a strong wave. A wave with an undertow dragging her down. Cece crumpled Doug's letter into a ball and threw it into the wastebasket. She blew her nose and tossed the tissue on top of it. They were broken up, for better or worse, and Cece needed to move forward, no matter how difficult it was.

But the letter tormented her. She retrieved it from the trash and reread it...*I hope someday you'll be able to forgive me,* Doug had written. But there was nothing to forgive. Doug had done nothing wrong. And neither had she. Cece crossed another regret off her list.

40

The dress enveloped Cece like a smooth glove as Patty pulled the zipper up. The back draped in soft folds over her shoulder blades. Her hair was swept up into a loose bun with thin tendrils hanging around her face and down the back of her neck.

"You look, like, elegant, Ceece, in a very hot and sexy way."

"Exactly what I'm aiming for." Cece faced Patty. "And you, little girl, look downright naughty."

Patty did a turn. She had on a tight, black mini-skirt, high-heel, over-the-knee black boots, and a sparkly silver tank top with plunging neckline. She shimmied her shoulders. "I'm wearing my new push-up. It's like magic—who even knew I had boobs?"

Cece laughed. "Everyone will know now."

Patty spritzed perfume into her top. "Want some?"

Cece turned, and Patty sprayed the back of her neck. She sniffed the air like a dog. "We smell delicious."

"Yes, we do," Cece said.

"So, is tonight the night you and Mr. Sticky-buns will…"

"Stop right there. My New Year's resolution is to live in the moment." Cece waved her palm through the air as if seeing it in lights. "No more compulsive, controlling, plan-everything-ahead obsession. If it happens, it happens."

Patty smirked. "Oh, it's gonna happen."

Cece raised a shoulder. "I did get that bikini wax yesterday. Can't leave everything to chance."

"That's the Cece I know and love." Patty pursed her lips. "But," she said, furrowing her brow, "you know you don't have to, don't you?"

"Don't have to what?"

"Sleep with him," Patty said. "I know you, Cece. Casual sex isn't your thing."

Patty was right. She knew Cece better than anyone. But things had changed. Many things. Ever since seeing Kathryn, Cece felt lighter, as if freed from a burden she hadn't been aware of. She was not the same girl she had been a month ago. Not even close.

"Maybe it can be," said Cece.

Patty shook her head. "I don't think so. You're a hopeless romantic, Ceece." Patty gave her a serious look.

Cece frowned. "Not anymore I'm not." She toyed with one of her dangly earrings.

"Bullshit," Patty said. "Listen, I'm not telling you not to sleep with him. I'm just telling you to be sure it's what you want. You've been hurt enough."

Cece waved off Patty's admonition, but appreciated the love behind it. "Listen, I have to play it by ear. See how the night goes. Not over-think it."

"You not over-think?" Patty patted her shoulder. "Good luck with that."

Boomer barked and ran downstairs. The front door opened and slammed shut.

"Hello?" Tom's loud voice echoed throughout the house.

"Sounds like your date has arrived," Cece said.

They walked downstairs together. Cece watched her brother's face light up when he saw Patty, and it made her heart swell. Tom gave Patty a slow kiss on the lips. This relationship, Cece thought, will bloom like a flower in spring. Or crash and burn like a Roman candle on the Fourth of July.

"Nice boots," Tom said, pulling Patty into a hug. "What we could do with those later…"

"Christ Tommy, I'm standing right here."

"Hi, Sis," Tom said, giving Cece a kiss on the cheek. "Where's Dad and Julia?"

"Left about an hour ago," Cece said. "They're spending the night in the city with friends where they do the happy-new-year at nine, drink 'til ten, be asleep by eleven thing."

"Please," Patty said. "Smack me if I ever get that boring."

"Are you kidding?" Tom yawned. "I'm ready for that now, and I'm younger than you are."

There it goes, Cece thought, *crash and burn.* She gave Patty a quick hug. "Get out of here you two. Have fun."

Patty hugged Cece. "You have fun too. And remember what I said, okay?"

"Maybe." Cece winked at her.

"Oh, and I won't be back tonight. I'm sleeping at Tommy's, just so you know."

"Thank you for that." Cece shuddered.

She stood in the doorway and waved. They walked toward Tom's truck, and Cece smiled as she watched two of her favorite people in the world go off into the starry night, full of hope and excitement and alarmingly poor judgment.

∼

The valet opened the car door, and Cece stepped out in front of a Georgian mansion in Napa Valley. The private estate included the mansion, winery, and vineyards on over two hundred acres of land.

"This is magnificent," Cece said. "Like out of a movie."

"Wait 'til you see the inside." Brad took her hand. They climbed the steps and entered through cascading lights and giant poinsettias.

Cece felt Brad's hand on the small of her back as he escorted her into the party. In his black tuxedo, he looked like a leading man. His fingers dusted over Cece's shoulders as he removed her coat, giving her goosebumps. He leaned in and whispered in her ear.

"Have I told you how gorgeous you look tonight?"

Cece gave him a sidelong glance. "You have. Three times."

"I'm glad you're keeping track."

A waiter carrying a tray of champagne glasses stopped beside them. Brad took two flutes. "Thank you." He handed Cece a glass. "Happy New Year, Gorgeous."

Cece touched her glass to his. "That makes four." Cece sipped, her eyes steady on his. "Mmmm, it's the good stuff."

Brad did not leave her side. He introduced her to the people he knew, his hand on her back or around her waist or lightly caressing the skin on her bare shoulder. With every touch, Cece was reminded that she was the date of Brad Redmond, the most desirable, attentive, sexy man in the room. Her regrets and memories melted away with each kiss and sip of champagne. She was living in the moment.

The house was spectacular—marble floors, winding staircase, and huge Christmas trees in three different rooms. The guests looked as if they'd been selected by a casting agent. Handsome men in tuxedos, striking women in lavish, designer outfits, and enough diamonds on display to stock a jewelry store.

"This place could be in a magazine," she said.

"It has been," Brad said, eating an olive. "Several times."

"And you know the owner?"

Brad laughed. "Of course I do. Mitch is one of my clients."

They stood eating appetizers at a tall cocktail table draped with a gold cloth—sushi, shrimp, tiny lamb chops, caviar. A handsome, distinguished-looking man with gray hair and a Rolex watch that sparkled with diamonds stepped up to join them. He was holding a cut crystal glass filled with amber liquid and ice.

"Finally, our illustrious host appears." Brad shook the man's hand. "Good to see you, Mitch. Great party."

"How are you, Brad?"

"Excellent. I'd like you to meet Cecilia Camden."

Cece held out her hand. "So nice to meet you."

"The pleasure is mine," Mitch said, his eyes admiring.

"Your home is breathtaking."

"Breathtaking." Mitch repeated the word, as if it felt good to say it. "As are you."

Cece's heart pounded as Mitch brought her hand to his lips and kissed it softly. "Brad, I must warn you to stay close to this lovely lady. She has caught the attention of a number of gentlemen already."

Cece blushed.

"Believe me," said Brad, "I intend to."

Mitch released her hand and stepped back. He patted Brad's shoulder. "You two have a great night. Cecilia," he said, "I'm delighted you could be here. Finally Brad shows up with a date of whom I approve."

Mitch nodded to Cece with a charming smile and disappeared into the crowd.

"A date of whom he approves?" Cece eyed Brad.

"That's just Mitch. Has an opinion on everything, especially women."

"Now I get it, you wanted to impress Mitch," Cece teased. "So that's why you've been pursuing me all these weeks."

Brad picked up his champagne and drank it down. He put a

cool hand on the back of her neck and leaned in close to her ear. "I've been pursuing you for many reasons."

Cece lost track of how much champagne she'd consumed. Brad's friends flocked around them, and it became obvious that there was no shortage of women who were interested in Brad Redmond. Blissfully tipsy, she laughed and chatted, charming the women as well as the men. Between the alcohol and the flattery, she felt seductive and adventurous.

After dinner, they went outside for some fresh air. They stood at the edge of the courtyard where a waiter brought them two vodka martinis.

"Oh no," Cece said. "Remember what happened last time?"

"I do. Do you?"

Cece gave him a look. "Did something happen that I should remember?"

"Maybe…"

Cece frowned. "Really?"

"No," Brad laughed. "Only that you fell asleep on the way home."

"That's a relief. I hate it when something fabulous happens and I'm too drunk to enjoy it." She looked at him over the edge of her glass.

He looked at her in mock seriousness. "Does that happen often?"

Cece lowered her chin and fluttered her eyes. "Yes, doctor, what should I do?"

Brad cracked up. He pulled her close and kissed her lips, running his hand down her back, over the fabric of her dress. His arm wrapped around her waist and stayed there. They looked out beyond the courtyard to a long, rectangular reflecting pool with fountains at both ends. Colored lights turned underneath, transforming the droplets of water into dancing rainbows. Cece looked beyond the pool, out to the vineyards, which were illuminated by glass-covered torches. Rolling, grassy hills stretched behind the mansion for what seemed to be miles.

"I had no idea there was this much money in wine," Cece said.

"Wine, champagne, and olive oil."

"Olive oil? You're kidding!"

"Nope," Brad said. "It's—"

"Well," a woman's voice interrupted them. "Brad Redmond, what a surprise."

Brad turned toward the voice. He looked at the woman with his debonair smile. She was striking, late thirties, tall and slender. Her dark hair curled around her shoulders, framing an exotic, heart- shaped face with sapphire blue eyes. She had smooth, dark skin, accentuated by a strapless, turquoise cocktail dress.

"Katrina," Brad said. He gave her a polite kiss on the cheek. "I didn't expect you to be here."

"Well, here I am."

Cece waited for Brad to introduce her, but he didn't.

Katrina eyed Cece for a moment, then turned her attention back to Brad. Cece took a sip of her drink and watched.

"I was hoping I'd run into you. Haven't seen you in a while." She put a hand on his arm and leaned closer. "You still have my number, don't you?"

"I'm sure I do."

Cece was surprised, and intrigued, by Katrina's audacity, coming onto a man who was clearly with another woman. Brad remained impressively composed.

Katrina took a sip of her wine. "Well then, you should use it." She glanced at Cece again. "When you tire of little girls, I'd love to hear from you again."

"Happy New Year, Katrina," Brad said. "Enjoy your

evening." He turned away from her just enough to imply that they were finished.

Cece watched Katrina walk across the balcony. A short, balding man put his arm around her and offered her a cigarette, which she accepted smoothly.

"Now that was interesting." Cece licked her lips. "She's stunning."

"Yes, she is." Brad offered nothing more.

"You dated her?"

"Briefly."

Cece drank. She was enjoying needling him. "My goodness, you don't have much to say about her. Let me guess, bad in bed?"

Brad laughed. "You are feisty tonight, aren't you?"

"I'm trying to be." Cece moved closer to him. "You like feisty, don't you?"

He kissed her, and she felt his cool tongue on her lips. "What are you trying to do to me here?"

"Just making sure you have a good time," she said.

"I'm definitely having a good time. Are you?"

"Absolutely." Cece finished her martini and gave the glass to a passing waiter. "What time is it?"

Brad looked at his watch. "Twenty to midnight."

"I'm going to run to the restroom."

"Don't be long," said Brad. "You're my midnight kiss, you know."

"If I'm not back in time, I'm sure Katrina would happily take my place," Cece teased.

"I would probably jump into the fountain before I let that happen."

"Then I'd better hurry," Cece said, running her hands down the lapels of his jacket. "I'd hate to see you ruin your lovely tuxedo."

Cece walked toward the house and stepped inside through

the French doors. She found the powder room in an alcove off the foyer. Two attractive women stood beside the closed door chatting.

"Hello," Cece said with a friendly nod.

"There's a line," the blonde woman said, smiling apologetically. She wore a simple red dress, her hair pulled back into a perfect bun.

The other woman said nothing, her face pretty but pinched. She had an unusually small nose, short brown hair, and puffy lips. In her black, sequined halter-top, black velvet pants, and fabulous silver sandals, she reminded Cece of a super-hero. A diamond the size of an almond dangled just above her substantial cleavage.

Cece stepped back and waited.

"Well, from what I heard," the blonde woman said, continuing the conversation Cece had interrupted, "the production was a huge success. Everyone's been talking about it."

"Doesn't matter," the brunette said, shrugging. "*The Nutcracker* is over, and if Ilana Lurensky is as batty as I've heard, that studio will never survive."

Cece felt the blood drain from her face. She leaned against the wall.

The brunette continued talking, her voice grating. "After the holidays, our director is going to contact some of Lurensky's best dancers."

"She's going to poach them?" the blonde asked.

"Poach?" the brunette laughed. "That's an ugly word. She's going to offer them an opportunity."

Cece looked to the side, pretending she wasn't listening. Her heart pounded as discomfort gave way to anger.

The brunette toyed with the diamond resting between her obviously fake breasts. "Anyway, with Ilana gone, her daughter will take over. I hear she's very good, but she has no support."

"My goodness." The blonde shook her head. "It's very sad. The Lurensky Studio is one of the best."

"It *was*," said the brunette. "Really though, how could anyone hope to have a successful business in that little nothing of a town?"

Cece clenched her fists. *First the woman belittles my dance school, and now she's insulting Clearwater?*

"Bottom line? Natalie Lurensky is screwed."

"You're wrong." Cece was surprised by the sound of her own voice.

"Excuse me?" the brunette said.

Cece stood tall, fueled by anger and alcohol. "Your assumption is incorrect. Natalie Lurensky will do just fine."

The brunette raised her penciled eyebrows. "And how do you know?"

Cece felt her knees go weak. How did she know? "Well, I know because...because she's hiring an assistant director."

"So what?" The brunette rolled her eyes. "Who on earth is she going to find who can replace the great Madam Lurensky?"

Without thinking, Cece blurted out, "An extraordinary dancer by the name of Cecilia Rose." She straightened her back and raised her chin.

"I've heard of her!" The blonde's eyes opened wide.

Cece focused her attention on the blonde. "I'm sure you have. She's practically famous in Clearwater, danced with Madam Lurensky for years." Cece leaned in as if she were about to reveal a secret. "And I heard she was accepted by the San Francisco Ballet at the age of sixteen."

Cece turned and walked away, leaving the brunette with her mouth hanging open. Her head spun, and she thought she might pass out. *Oh my God,* she thought. *What have I done?*

41

"There you are," Brad said. He was standing in the alcove in the midst of all the guests. Cece walked toward him. She missed a step and stumbled, but Brad reached out and caught her arm. "Are you okay?"

"I...I'm fine," Cece said, trying to hide her anxiety. She smoothed the front of her dress, regaining composure, and laughed at herself. "For a dancer, I can be really clumsy sometimes. Let's get some champagne."

Across the foyer, guests were beginning to congregate. Cece could not run into those women again. The sooner she and Brad had their midnight kiss, the sooner they could leave. She peered out of the alcove into the crowd.

"Cece, what are you doing? Are you sure you're okay?"

She took Brad's hand. "I am fabulous." Quickly, she led him to a corner of the living room behind a giant Christmas tree. She pointed. "There goes the champagne! Grab some before they run out."

Brad dashed into the crowd, got two glasses, and returned to their spot behind the tree. "Here you go," he said, handing Cece hers. She gulped half of it down.

"You are really acting strange."

No kidding, she thought. She needed to take control of the situation. And she needed to make sure Brad would want to leave the party even more than she did. She licked her lips and looked up at him, fluttering her lashes. "It's because I'm a little nervous."

He looked confused. "Why are you nervous?"

She slowly backed him into the wall and leaned against him, tucking them both further behind the tree. "Because…because I want you to make love to me."

Brad's Adam's apple bobbed up, then down. "Oh. Really?"

Cece nodded her head. In her heels, she was almost as tall as he was. She pressed her body against his. With her right hand, she toyed with a button on his vest. She tilted her head. "Would you like to?"

"Absolutely," he said, his voice low and raspy.

Cece kissed him with wet, parted lips. She untucked the back of his shirt and slid a hand up inside it, feeling the muscles in his back tighten at her touch. His skin was smooth and hot. Anxiety and champagne mixed with the feel of Brad's strength and the smell of his cologne. As the crowd started to count down toward midnight, her adrenaline soared, stirring her passion. Brad pulled her closer, tighter, and the guests started the countdown to midnight:

"TEN…NINE …"

She felt his desire for her…

"EIGHT…SEVEN…SIX…FIVE…"

One of his hands reached around and squeezed…

"FOUR…THREE…TWO…"

Cece looked up at him.

"ONE! HAPPY NEW YEAR!"

Brad grabbed her wrist and pulled her toward the door.

"Wait, my coat!" Cece reached out. "That one," she said to the coat checker.

They sailed through the foyer amidst the joyful celebration of partiers howling and singing and dancing to the live music. Brad handed the valet his ticket, then he pulled Cece behind a tall tree. With his body pinning her against a concrete planter, he kissed her lips, her throat, her neck. His hands went everywhere, searching her body through the thin fabric of her dress.

"Your car, sir," an embarrassed voice interrupted them. Cece giggled as they jumped in and sped off.

At the end of the road, Brad stopped at a stop sign, and Cece practically crawled into his lap. To hell with what Patty said, casual sex was fantastic! She had never had it before, and she wanted it.

"Where are we going?" Cece asked in between kisses.

Brad took her face into his hands. "I booked a room at an inn...just in case." His tongue entwined with hers, and a moan escaped her throat.

A horn honked at them. They both laughed, and Cece fell back into her seat.

The inn was only a few minutes away. Brad pulled into the parking lot, and they jumped out of the car. He took Cece's hand as they climbed the steps and entered the cozy lobby. A Christmas tree stood beside a crackling fire.

A young man stood at the reception desk. Brad slapped his credit card down. "Checking in," he said.

While the man typed into his computer, Brad slipped his hand under the hem of Cece's dress. She felt his fingers on the back of her thigh. She shivered.

"Your name, sir?"

"Brad Redmond. It's right there on the card."

"I...I'm terribly sorry, but there's no reservation."

Brad leaned on the counter. "I made it five days ago. Look again." His voice was edgy.

The young man cleared his throat. "I'll get my manager." He disappeared into the back.

Brad winked at Cece. "They'll figure it out."

Cece moved closer to him. "Okay," she whispered.

The manager appeared. He was only slightly older than the first man.

"Mr. Redmond, I'm afraid we don't have a reservation under your name. Did you call directly or book it online?"

"Online," Brad said.

The man went to another computer. "Just a minute, please."

Cece grew nervous. The champagne was wearing off.

"Ah, I see what happened. The reservation was not confirmed. You should have received an email informing you that—"

"I never got any email," Brad said. "But forget it. I'll take any room you've got."

"Sir, we are booked solid. I'm sorry."

Cece could tell that Brad was getting angry. "Brad, it's—"

He ignored her. "Find me a room. If you don't have one here, call someplace else."

"Mr. Redmond," the man said, "it's New Year's Eve. Every place around here is completely sold out. I'm terribly sorry."

The man stepped back as if to say: *please leave.*

Brad's jaw clenched. Cece grew more nervous, worried Brad would explode. He turned and picked up her hand. "Let's go."

They walked to the car. Brad opened Cece's door and let her in. She bundled herself up in her coat. Brad got in on his side and slammed the door. He looked at her. A slight smile formed around the edges of his mouth. She blinked at him. He started to laugh. Cece looked at him with amused puzzlement.

"You're laughing?"

Brad laughed louder. "I'm laughing!"

Cece started to laugh too. "But what's funny?"

"I've wanted to get you into bed since the day I knocked your coffee over, and here I was so close, and I blew it."

Cece was relieved that his frustration had turned to humor. She rubbed his leg. "Maybe we need to come up with a Plan B."

"And what would 'Plan B' be?" he asked, grinning at her.

"Your house?"

"Nope. Dawn's at my house. Having a party."

Cece was shocked. "You let Dawn have a party when you're not home? Are you crazy?"

"Relax. My nephew and his wife are chaperoning."

"Phew. I was about to think you had lost your mind."

Brad leaned over and ran a hand up her leg and underneath the hem of her dress. "Is there such thing as a Plan C?"

Cece cupped his face with both hands. "My dad's house is completely empty."

"Is it now?" Brad started the car. "I can't remember the last time I went home with a girl to her daddy's house." He glanced in Cece's direction. "Makes me nervous just thinking about it."

"Well," Cece said, "I've never done it in my daddy's house."

Brad licked his lips and threw the car into reverse. "It's about time you did."

As Brad drove, Cece kept glancing at him. She imagined what it was going to be like to make love to him. But as the alcohol worked its way out of her system, reality edged her fantasy aside, and she recalled the announcement she'd made in front of the two women by the bathroom.

How was she ever going to undo that? And what on earth would she say to Natalie?

"What are you thinking about?" Brad asked, interrupting her anxious deliberation.

"Huh?"

He squeezed her hand. "You look preoccupied."

She took a deep breath. "I'm good," she touched his cheek. "Great, actually."

This was no time to think about anything other than Brad.

She was about to take Brad home and have sex with him. But

then what? Would they just go their separate ways? Forget about their holiday fling? Patty was right. Cece was a planner, a thoughtful, reflective woman. And a hopeless romantic to boot.

They stopped at a red light, and he pulled her into another deep kiss.

Her body shuddered with desire. What the hell was she afraid of? Tomorrow did not matter. Her resolution was to live in the moment, and that was exactly what she intended to do.

Brad glanced at her. "I hope this doesn't freak you out, but just so you know, I haven't put all this effort into pursuing you for just a holiday fling."

Had he read her mind?

"You want to keep seeing me?" she asked, a bit more hopefully than she would have liked.

"Why not?" Brad said. "It's only a one-hour flight to LA."

"So, like a long-distance relationship thing?"

Brad chuckled, tapping the steering wheel. "Relationship's a big word. Maybe something in between."

Cece frowned. "There's a lot of wiggle room between fling and relationship."

Brad took a deep breath, his chest rising. "Why don't we just see where this goes? Not everything has to be part of some big, long-term plan."

Again with the mind-reading. Cece shifted in her seat and composed herself. In the last month, nothing had gone according to plan. In fact, there was no plan, not anymore.

"You're absolutely right," she said. "Let's not overthink this."

Brad's foot hit the accelerator. "Works for me."

42

*T*hey made out like teenagers at every stoplight. There would be no turning back.

Cece thought about how everything would play out. Would she offer him a drink first? Would they go straight upstairs, removing articles of clothing along the way? Would he scoop her into his arms and carry her? Stop! She chastised herself. No overthinking, no planning, just let it happen. As much as she tried to contain herself, her legs trembled with nervousness.

Brad turned the car into the driveway of the Camden house. "You hop out," he said. "I'll put my car on the street. That way, if your folks come home early, I can sneak away, and they'll never even know I was here."

"Ah, good thinking," Cece said, feeling like a sneaky teenager.

She put her hand on the door and glanced at Brad over her shoulder. She gave him a come-hither smile. "Don't be long. You do not want to keep me waiting."

Brad grabbed her wrist. "Believe me, I won't." His kiss was fast, deep, reckless.

She jumped out of the car and hopped along the driveway in her bare feet, her shoes in one hand, her coat in the other.

"Cece?" A deep voice came out of nowhere. She froze at the foot of the steps. The moon behind him illuminated his silhouette as he rose slowly from a chair on the front porch.

Doug. Cece gripped the handrail. In the dim porch light, she could see that he'd grown a full beard. He looked thin, but his eyes were large and full of hope.

"Oh my God," Cece said. "What are you doing here?"

"I had to see you."

"How did you get here?" Cece asked, still immobile.

Doug took a hesitant step toward her. "I drove." He paused, pointing to his truck parked by the garage. "That's a great dress."

Cece tried to shake the fuzziness from her head. Her heart pounded. It must be a dream. She wanted to move or scream, run to him or run away, but she was paralyzed. Her limbs felt as if they had been disconnected from her body.

A small beam of light hit Doug in the face. "Hey," Brad said, pointing a keychain flashlight at him. "Who are you?"

Doug squinted, his hand over his eyes. "What?"

"You heard me, buddy. Who are you?"

"Who are you?" Doug asked.

"It's okay, Brad," Cece said. "I know him."

The two men eyed each other, and Cece could read Doug's expression as he put two and two together. His face went rigid. His weary shoulders straightened. His hands clenched. In slow motion, the scene began to unfold. Cece's head swam as if she were sinking into a pool of water. She was an elephant seal lying on the beach, and these two fierce, fiery males were about to fight to the death to win her. Boy, would Patty love this.

Brad nudged her. "So, who is he?"

"He's Doug."

Brad's eyes opened wide. "Doug? Your old boyfriend?"

Cece nodded. Tears threatened. She had trouble breathing.

"Well," Doug said, "I guess you've moved on." He sounded defeated.

Moved on? It sounded like an accusation, as if she'd done something sinister.

"Was I not supposed to, Doug?" Cece tried to stay calm, but shock and confusion made her heart pound. "You left the country. And now you show up here out of the blue? Expecting me to, what, welcome you back like you were on some mission to save the world?"

Doug dropped his head. "Just the rainforests." He glanced at Brad. "And while I was slogging through the jungle crying over you, you were out chasing this...this stud in a monkey suit?"

Brad shifted his position. "To be fair, I did most of the chasing."

"I don't even *know* what I'm doing." Cece climbed the steps. "Everything's changed, Doug. I don't have a plan anymore. You left, and that changed my life and everything in it!"

Doug grabbed her shoulders. He wrapped his long arms around her like a vice and kissed her mouth with such desperation and fury that it hurt.

The sound of Brad clearing his throat interrupted them. "Cece, could you...could I have a minute? Um, Doug, do you mind if I talk to her for a sec?"

Doug, still holding onto Cece, looked at Brad. "Will you give her back?" He sounded like a little boy who had been asked to share his toy truck.

Brad laughed. "If she wants me to." He held his hand out and motioned for Cece to come down the steps.

Cece walked toward Brad. He put his arm over her shoulder and led her away from the porch. They stood facing each other, Christmas decorations illuminating Brad's face. His dazzling green eyes met hers. "What do you want to do?"

Cece dragged her hand under nose. "I don't know. I'm confused."

"Well, I think I'll make it easier for you." Brad rubbed the stubble on his chin. "I'm gonna take off."

That was unexpected. Cece felt some relief, but also disappointment. Didn't he want to stay and fight? As if in answer to her question, Brad said, "I'm too old to fight over a girl."

"Maybe you think I'm not worth fighting over," Cece said, sounding sharper than she'd intended.

Brad toyed with the tips of her fingers. "I assure you, that is not the case."

Cece glanced at Doug, who was leaning against the railing with crossed arms. "I had no idea this was going to happen."

"It's okay, I can handle it." Brad stepped closer. "Listen, we haven't known each other all that long, but I understand you better than you think."

Cece suddenly felt young and naïve, embarrassed by her lack of experience with men. "What do you mean?"

"The decision you need to make has nothing to do with him or me." Brad took her face into his hands and kissed her on the lips, soft and lingering, as if to say *see what you're missing*. "It isn't about the guy you want. It's about the life you want." He kissed her again, differently this time. A kiss goodbye. "I hope you find it."

Cece felt him let go of her, slowly, regretfully. She watched him take a few steps down the driveway. Then he stopped. He turned. With a slight lift of his head, he flashed his irresistible smile. "Happy New Year, Gorgeous."

43

*D*oug was sitting on the steps waiting for her. His head snapped up as she approached.

Cece sat beside him, twelve inches away.

"He seems like a nice guy," Doug said.

"He is." Cece turned her head to the side and looked at him. "You grew a beard. And you look skinny."

"That's what men do in the jungle—grow beards and walk a lot."

Cece gave him half a smile. "Did you get me a monkey?"

He reached into his pocket. "I did."

She held out her hand, and Doug placed a tiny, porcelain monkey with a curly tail in it. It was adorable. "Thanks, but I wanted a real one."

"I thought about it, but they'd have thrown me in jail."

Cece closed her hand around the monkey and looked at Doug. He scooted closer to her. Without meaning to, Cece flinched.

"It's only been a month, Ceece. You couldn't have stopped loving me already." He grasped her hand. "Please. Say you still love me."

"I do," she whispered. "I still love you, but a lot has changed."

"I don't care. We still love each other, so we can figure out the rest."

"How?" Cece asked. "Just go back to the way it was before my birthday, before I said what I said that changed everything?"

Doug nodded. "That is what you want, isn't it?"

"It was," Cece said, "but not anymore. I can't go backwards."

"Then we'll find a way to go forward. We just need to be home, back in LA."

"I'm not going back." Cece shocked herself as much as Doug, but it felt right as soon as she said it.

Doug's face drained of color. "What?"

"I'm not going back to LA. I mean, I'll go back to get my stuff, but I'm moving. I'm moving home. Back to Clearwater."

"When did you decide that?"

"Just now. Just this very second." Cece could barely believe it herself, but it's what she wanted, what she needed to do. "I'm a ballerina, a dancer. I want to teach dance, here, in my hometown, where I started."

"But you hate it here."

Cece shook her head. "Actually, I don't."

"Wow," Doug said, his leg bouncing up and down. "It's because of him, isn't it?"

Cece thought for a moment. Every major decision she'd made in the past had been influenced by somebody else. She picked up Doug's hand. "It's not. It has nothing to do with him. For the first time in my life, I'm making a decision that has nothing to do with anyone except for me." The certainty she felt made her giddy, as if she'd been looking through cloudy water that suddenly cleared. She could see everything through it. A new plan came into view. "I've finally discovered what I was meant to be—what I was meant to do."

Doug stood and took a few steps down the driveway. He ran his hands through his wild hair. "You're really going to live in this small town? You're a city girl; you said so yourself."

"Turns out, I'm not." Cece shivered in the cold air, but it felt refreshing, freeing.

Doug looked disoriented. He paced in circles. Cece got up and took his hand. "Let's go inside. I'm freezing."

Doug followed her through the front door. They went into the kitchen. "Hungry?" Cece asked.

"Starving."

Cece pulled leftovers from the refrigerator, and they ate standing at the counter. Doug looked lost, and it tugged on Cece's heart. "Did you like the rainforest?"

His head snapped up, as if she'd awakened him. "It's the most beautiful place in the world."

Cece smiled, and a calm washed over her, as if things were falling into place. "You should go back."

Doug wiped his mouth with the back of his hand. His brown, puppy-dog eyes studied her. "Well," he said, a bittersweet smile forming, "I guess now, I might as well. They want me back. My photos were fabulous."

"They always are," Cece told him.

Doug and Cece covered the food with foil, put it away, and went upstairs. At the door to her bedroom, Cece stopped. "You can sleep in Ryan's room."

"Seriously? I drove all the way up here, and I don't even get to sleep with you?"

Cece pointed down the hall. "Bathroom on the right. Bedroom on the left."

"Can't we just—"

"No," Cece shook her head. "We've got to move forward, Doug, and that would only take us back."

Cece went into her bedroom. She slipped out of her perfect little black dress and hung it up, wondering if she'd ever wear it again. Standing in front of her dresser, Cece removed her earrings and placed them in a dish under the mirror. The photo of her young self with the beautiful ballerina caught her eye.

She stepped into the hallway and called out, "By the way, Doug, I want my ballerina painting back!"

EPILOGUE

𝒲hen word spread that the renowned Cecilia Rose would be her new assistant director, gossip about Natalie's demise silenced. The Lurensky Dance Studio was back on top, students clamored for spots, and enrollment skyrocketed.

At the end of January, and with great fanfare, Cece returned to the studio and started her new life in Clearwater. The dance moms adored her, the students worshipped her, and Natalie cherished her.

Best of all, Cece fell in love with ballet once again.

~

Two days after starting her new job, Cece asked Natalie where Dawn was. She had missed her lesson.

"She'll be back next week," Natalie said, sitting on a chair in the main studio with her laptop. "She's in New York with her dad."

Cece was taken aback by that news, but she and Brad had not spoken since New Year's Eve. There was no reason for her to know anything about where he was.

For the last month, Cece had been completely absorbed in dismantling her life in Los Angeles— breaking the lease on the house, helping Barbara prepare for the grand re-opening of The Art Stop, and convincing Patty she was more than welcome to move up to Clearwater. And while she thought about Brad often, she hadn't contacted him on purpose. Her decision to move home to Clearwater had nothing to do with him. Besides, he had her number too.

'Hey." Natalie looked up from her computer. "With everything going on, I totally forgot about your, um, what was it you called it? Holiday fling?"

Cece brushed it off. "Listen, that's all it was. Actually, not even. A few dinners out. It was nothing. Just a distraction."

"A distraction. Nothing better than that to help a girl move on." Natalie gave her a sympathetic smile. "We've hardly had a chance to talk about anything since you got here. What happened with Doug?"

Cece smiled. "We're definitely over, but we're good. I think we might even manage to be friends someday."

"Really?" Natalie looked surprised.

Cece nodded. "Really. He's gone back to the rainforest, living the dream. I'm happy for him." And she truly was. In fact, she had started painting Doug a picture to replace the one she'd taken back. It was of him in the rainforest with four little monkeys hanging from tree branches behind him.

The door to the studio burst open and a little pink ballerina rushed toward Cece.

"Olivia!" Cece said, holding her arms open wide. "I've missed you."

"Look, Miss Cece," Olivia said, opening her mouth. "I got my new front teeth. See?"

"You certainly did."

"Are you going to be our teacher now?" Olivia asked, grabbing Cece's hand and jumping up and down.

"Yes, sweetie, I am. And I will help you become the best ballerina you can be." Cece wrapped Olivia in her arms and spun around in circles.

~

Dawn returned to her lessons the following week. She was almost as excited about Cece's return as Olivia had been. "I'm so happy you're back, Cece!"

"Me, too," Cece said, meaning it. "How was New York?"

"Amazing! My dad took me to two shows and to Lincoln Center to see the ballet. It was so fabulous. It's the most incredible city. And my dad's apartment is right by…"

Apartment? Dawn rambled on about New York and shows and restaurants and Central Park. Cece reminded herself how little she actually knew about Brad. It didn't matter where he was though, because Cece hadn't moved back to Clearwater for him, but for her true love—the ballet.

~

The weeks flew by. Cece worked harder than she'd ever worked in her life. She took as much off of Natalie's plate as she could, so that Natalie could care for her mother.

When Patty decided to stay in Los Angeles, at least for the time being, Cece found a cozy, one-bedroom guesthouse for rent a few blocks from the lake and moved out of her childhood home once again. She set up her easel in a corner of the living room beside a glass door that opened onto a little porch that looked out toward the lake. It was the perfect place for painting. In her bedroom, the photograph of nine-year-old Cece standing beside the Sugar Plum Fairy was displayed on her dresser with her butterfly necklace hanging over the corner of the frame. Her painting hung on the wall above it. They were uplifting reminders that Cece had landed right where she belonged.

Every day, she made decisions to move her life forward. And while it was not the easiest transition, she never once questioned the choice to return to her hometown.

She received no more calls from an unknown number. *Unknown number* had been replaced by *Mom*. Taking tiny steps, Cece and Kathryn made progress toward having a relationship, and Cece began to forgive.

~

It was a warm Sunday morning in March, Cece's first day off in weeks. She lounged in bed until the sun streamed into her bedroom through filmy curtains. Cece got up and decided to take a walk along the lake.

The water was cool and crisp and sparkling clear. It made her feet tingle. She did a little turn, a hop, a spin. She jumped and splashed like a little girl, laughing. A man with a fishing pole walked down the pier. He untied the little boat, got in, and rowed away, waving to Cece as he left. "I'm gonna get myself a little boat," Cece said to herself.

She went home, showered, and got ready to spend the day painting. With a towel wrapped around her wet hair, she went to make coffee. "Oh crap," she said, remembering she had run out of beans. She threw on her sweats and sneakers and headed to Nutmeg's.

Only a few customers were there. Cece stepped up to the counter and smiled at Trevor, the barista who had served her at least a hundred cups of coffee during the holidays.

"Hey, Cece. Large black coffee coming up."

Cece laughed. Oh, how she loved this small town. "Thanks, Trevor. A pecan sticky bun too. Perfect Sunday breakfast, don't you think?"

"Absolutely," said Trevor.

Cece took her coffee and sat at a round table in the corner of the patio. She closed her eyes and inhaled the fresh smell of spring. It reminded her of her childhood.

She opened her eyes when Trevor delivered her sticky bun. He placed it on the table with a stack of napkins and silverware.

And that was when Brad Redmond passed by her table. Without seeing her, he opened the door and went into the bakery.

Cece's jaw dropped. Her hands shook. Her heart raced.

Trevor poured hot coffee into her mug. "Need anything else?"

Cece looked up. "What? Oh, no thanks. I'm good."

Trevor left. Cece peered through the window, hiding herself behind a potted plant. It was definitely him. Brad Redmond was inside ordering his coffee, and in a matter of seconds he'd be walking out the door and passing right by her.

"Shit," she said under her breath. She scooted her chair further back behind the plant.

Through the glass, she saw Brad pay for his coffee, chat with the barista, and stuff money into the tip jar. Cece held her breath, wishing the plant were larger.

Brad turned and moved toward the door. He pushed it open, stepped outside, and walked past her again. Cece had only two options: hide like a silly teenager...or don't.

Say hello, you idiot. Stop him.

By a stroke of luck and good timing, Brad's cell phone rang, giving her time to think. He put his coffee on a table, his back to Cece, and answered. "Hey there," he said. "I'm glad you called."

The sound of his voice sent a shiver up her back. She watched his position, trying to predict his next move. The call sounded friendly. More than friendly. What was wrong with her? What did she expect? Over two months had gone by since they had stopped dating, if she could even call it that.

"Right," said Brad, a smile in his voice. "That sounds

perfect. See you then." The call ended. He picked up his coffee, took two steps...

Cece jumped to her feet. "Brad, wait!"

He turned. He looked confused, but for only a moment. He gave her a curious smile and seemed to be pleased, or maybe puzzled. It was hard to tell.

Cece was breathless. She didn't know what to say. She giggled nervously. "Hi."

Brad seemed to be as tongue-tied as she was. "Hi."

"Um..." Cece had no idea how to start the conversation, so she just took a leap. "It's a good thing you're here," she said, showing him her sticky bun. "I can't possibly eat this all by myself."

The corners of his mouth turned upward, and his dimple appeared. "I don't have any silverware."

"No? I thought you always carried some in your pocket."

"Not today." Brad took a step toward her. "I'm afraid I'm unprepared."

Cece took a step toward him. "Not nearly as unprepared as I am."

They sat at Cece's table. She cut the sticky bun in half and handed him her fork. He took a large bite and chewed slowly.

Cece cleared her throat. "You didn't know I was in Clearwater, did you?"

"That would be correct." Brad handed back her fork.

Cece didn't know what to make of his answer. It seemed flippant. "I guess there was no reason for Dawn to tell you. After all, she never knew that we had..."

"I've been away," Brad said.

"Right." Cece ran a finger around the rim of her coffee cup. "I kind of thought you, I don't know, would've called me."

"Really?" Brad leaned back and crossed his arms. "If I remember correctly, the last time we were together, your boyfriend had come to claim you. So clearly, the ball was in your court."

Cece considered his response. "I guess it was."

"I assumed you two got back together." Brad picked up his coffee and sipped, his eyes never leaving Cece's.

"We didn't," Cece said, breaking from his stare. "Not even for a minute. I made him sleep in Ryan's room that night."

Brad laughed. "You're kidding."

"I'm not. I realized you were right. It wasn't about choosing him or you. It was about choosing a direction. And I chose to move forward."

Brad nodded. "Well, that is progress."

Cece twirled a curl beside her neck. "And when I got back here, I found out you'd moved to New York."

Brad's eyebrows went up. "I didn't move to New York."

"But Dawn visited you. She said you had an apartment and everything."

"I'm working on a case, so I stay for a few weeks at a time. I assure you, I did not move."

Again, Cece was reminded of how little she knew about him. She wasn't even sure what kind of lawyer he was. But the news that he hadn't moved away pleased her. "You still live in Clearwater then?"

"I do." Brad smiled. He took the fork out of Cece's hand and ate another bite of sticky bun. "Nothing's changed."

Cece knew what he meant. And she took the bait. "As I recall, last time I saw you we had some, what would you call it, unfinished business?"

Brad choked. "You have moved forward, haven't you?"

Cece licked her lips. "I'm just a girl who knows what she wants."

Brad leaned on his elbows. "And what would that be?"

Cece lightly touched the side of her neck with her fingertips. "Do I really have to spell it out for you?"

"It's the least you can do."

"Well," she said, "perhaps we should start again. You said something to me the first time we met."

"I said many things. Which one are you referring to?"

Cece tilted her head. "That our bumping into each other was somehow meant to be."

"I did say that, didn't I?"

"You did. And now, I think so too." Cece picked up her coffee, waiting for his response.

Brad crossed his legs, relaxed and sure of himself. "Would you like to have dinner with me tonight?"

"I'd love to," said Cece.

"And then afterwards," Brad said, "if you'd like to, we'll go to my place…"

"You're going to make me wait 'til tonight?"

Brad busted up. "Are you the same person I fell for three months ago?"

Fell for? Cece liked the sound of that. She licked her finger and picked up some crumbs off the plate. "In some ways, yes. In some ways, no." She ate the crumbs.

Brad's chest rose and fell. "Unfortunately, Dawn is at my house. She had a little slumber party last night."

"Plan B?"

"I'm not going to your dad's house. That didn't work out so well for me last time."

"There is a plan C."

"Yeah?" Brad's face brightened. "What's that?"

"I have my own place now."

His grin spread across his face, and the dimple dipped more deeply than ever before.

"My car is parked right over there." Cece pointed.

"I'll ride with you." Brad stood and held out his hand. Cece took it. He pulled her up, and she fell against him. His kiss was warm and wet and sweet.

They abandoned their coffees and half a sticky bun and jumped into her car. Cece drove fast.

"Slow down there," Brad said. "You don't want some small-town sheriff pulling you over."

Cece put a hand on his leg and squeezed. She slowed down, but only a little. When they pulled up in front of her little house, Brad rolled down his window.

"This is charming," he said. "It suits you perfectly."

"I think so," Cece said, trying to hide her anxiety and reject her old habit of overthinking every step. They got out of the car and walked to the door.

"Hold on." Brad stopped her. "I want to be sure you're sure. I mean, this is pretty impulsive, especially for you."

Cece's answer was to throw open the unlocked door and pull Brad in by his collar. She pushed him against the wall.

Brad tugged her sweatshirt off and over her head. "I guess you are sure, then."

"Oh yeah," Cece said.

Brad kissed her hard on the mouth, making her dizzy, then picked her up. She wrapped her legs around his waist and let him carry her into the bedroom.

He leaned over the bed, let her down, and rested himself on top of her, his face above hers. "You are so beautiful." His kiss was gentle, luxuriating.

Brad lifted himself on muscular arms. His green eyes studied her.

"What's wrong?" she asked.

Brad turned and sat on her bed. He ran a hand through his hair. "I might be a fool for interrupting the momentum, but I have to tell you something."

Cece sat up. She leaned against her pillows, knees pulled into her chest. She furrowed her brow. "Okay…"

"I've spent the last two months trying to get you out of my

head." He grinned. "Which frankly, surprised me. I'm usually more, I don't know, in control of things."

Cece held her breath. Where was he going with this?

"What I'm trying to say is, I'm not interested in a casual fling with you. I want more."

She didn't have to think twice. "I do too."

His face filled with happiness. "You do?"

Cece picked up his hand and pulled him toward her. "Absolutely."

His kiss was full of so much emotion it brought tears to Cece's eyes. She felt his longing, his need, his hunger, not only for passion but for…dare she even think it?

Brad pulled back. He searched her face. "I've fallen for you, Cecilia Rose. Hard."

Cece smiled. "I'm good with that." She put her hands on his cheeks, kissed him, and jumped into his lap.

She lifted his shirt and pulled it off quickly. When his head popped out, he said, "Wait."

Cece almost laughed. "Seriously?"

Brad licked his lips. "Let's not rush. This will be our first time. We want it to be special."

Did he really just say that? Her heart pounded. "Oh, it will be," Cece said.

And it was.

$\sim$

What happens next?

To find out about Book Two in the Clearwater Series, continue reading…

AFTERWORD

Dear Reader,

I hope you enjoyed your time in Clearwater. If you have a moment, please click on the link and write a quick review: Long Dance Home

Reviews and word-of-mouth recommendations are critical to a book's success. So if you liked *Long Dance Home*, please tell your friends about it. Thank you!

∽

Would you like to return to Clearwater?

Find out what happens with Cece and Brad, meet some new, quirky folks, and catch up with Patty who gets her turn as main character.

Road to Somewhere is available on Amazon and wherever books are sold.

View on Amazon

ROAD TO SOMEWHERE

When the going gets tough, Patty Sullivan runs.

The day her kitchen ceiling collapses on top of her, Patty's life unravels.

Whether a sign from above or plain bad luck, she has no idea. But her brush with death shakes her to her core.

With no boyfriend, no plans, and nowhere to stay, she leaves her condemned Venice Beach home and heads to California Wine Country to be near Cece, her best friend, confidante, and quintessential voice of reason.

A few days in the quiet small town of Clearwater should give her the comfort she needs to contemplate one of life's most enduring questions: "What now?"

But one day into her stay, Patty's troubles multiply—Cece suffers a crisis of her own; a gourmet shop owner ropes her into a demanding situation; and an enticing yet complicated man has her spinning toward romantic disaster.

However, it's the mysterious arrival of her younger sister that pushes Patty to the brink and forces her to question everything she thought she knew about her childhood and the family in which she felt she never belonged.

Now, faced with a monumental decision, Patty has no choice but to gamble on the one person she trusts the least —herself.

Grab a sneak peek on Amazon!
View on Amazon

ABOUT THE AUTHOR

Julie M. Brown is an author, playwright, and essayist. She lives in Palos Verdes, California with her family, her boxers, and hundreds of wild peacocks. When not writing, she's reading, baking, and attempting to grow organic vegetables.

View my website:
juliemayersonbrown.com

And while you're on my website, be sure to subscribe to my newsletter ~ it's a great way to get in touch with me and to learn about my new books and projects.

Let's connect on social media, too!

Made in the USA
Middletown, DE
11 September 2021